CW01334190

It's getting Darker

DARKER is the second book in the Dark Trilogy.

Can Dun help stop a War? The problem is, he started it.

Dun didn't want to be a hero and the war has cost him dearly: his friends, his innocence. Maybe his mind. Now he's a fully-fledged Shaman, Dun's mind is a receiver for those who can transmit, but what will he do when starts getting messages from someone who's dead.

Dun's new powers might allow his Under-folk, victory. But he must quiet the demons inside his head, and find his oldest friends Tali and Padg if they stand a chance of defeating the merciless Rowle of the Cat-People. And she is about to release demons of her own.

PAUL ARVIDSON is a forty-something ex lighting designer who lives in rural Somerset. He juggles his non-author time bringing up his children and fighting against being sucked into his wife's chicken breeding business. The Dark Trilogy is his first series.

Darker

a novel by

Paul L Arvidson

ISBN-13: 978-1984024176
ISBN-10: 1984024175

Ed. Lauren Schmeltz from Write Divas and cover by betibup33 from thebookcoverdesigner.com, both with grateful thanks.
Printed with CreateSpace
Available online from paularvidson.co.uk and real-life bookshops.

For Cheryl, Leah, and Nenna

Contents

Darker

Chapter One

Padg and Tali huddled in their den above the main market of the Stone-folk behind the *hiding shield* that they'd found before they parted company with Dun. It had taken great care and time to find such a good hiding place, but after Padg's insistence they not rush in and do some reconnaissance first he felt obliged to find somewhere good. It was an odd, tall, and thin metal room in the wall between the grand entrance to the Stone-halls. It smelled like rust. All the action from the market floor could be heard from high up metal grills in one side of the room and the main river was accessed by a hatch via a flooded water pipe on the opposite side. Padg thought they were impossible to surprise.

"I'm wet and tired," Padg said. "Is this the bit where we get to go home?"

"No, this is the bit where I murder you for whining, and your lifeless corpse floats back to Bridgetown. Now shut up, I'm counting," Tali said.

They had fashioned a listening horn from some thin sheet metal Padg had found. By tweaking its direction it was possible to pick up a reasonable amount of sound from all around the central cavern and some of the passages. Tali listened to interactions at the main entrance as the Stone-guard filtered goods and folk in. It was all mostly in and not a lot of that. The guards outnumbered the civilians two to one. And it was the same everywhere. Curfews had been imposed after Work-cycle. Identification tattoos had become mandatory and were examined at a ridiculous number of checkpoints. Although people still tried to go about their business, no female folk were allowed out without special dispensation. It was eerily quiet, the main noises being new bells rung every cycle to command people to action or to bed and announcements of new edicts from criers. The only thing not curtailed by these new happenings was the regular services of the Tinkralas. Though their hideout backed on to a temple, so they were immersed in the goings on by proximity, if nothing else. Most of their spying had to be done outside of the services as the noisy Tinkrala worship drowned out everything else.

"I'm glad, you know," Padg said.

"What?"

"Glad. To be here. Really."

"Oh good."

"Despite everything, you know?"

"Yeah."

"You know, with, you."

"Oh."

"It's... I'm... I like it."

"Yeah," Tali said. "Yeah, me too. What the hell is that?"

"Pardon?"

"That chanting? Far side of the market—listen."

When Padg strained, using their bespoke listening horn, he could make out the half chant/half shout just at the edge of his hearing. It came from right over the far side of the massive market hall. Maybe down one of the passages off there even. A repetitive shout.

"What are they saying?" Tali asked.

"No—I think. It sounds like they are saying no. Over and over."

"Sounds female? The voices..."

"Yeah, almost all."

"I wonder if that's where we'll find Amber?"

Since their stakeout to plan a rescue for their Stone-folk friend who'd done so much to help them, they hadn't heard hide nor hair of Amber. Padg, whose sense of smell was the keenest, and as a half decent hunter, hadn't detected so much as a lingering whiff. In the time it took them to return from parting company with Dun, it was like Amber had been spirited away.

"We need a plan to get in there," Tali said.

"Guess so," Padg said. "How?"

"Disguise?"

"O... kay. As what?"

"Mmm... traders?"

"Would have to be River-folk."

"Why?"

"Don't be dense—plan ahead. Can't be Bridge-folk; 'cos—uh, we're at war. Can't be Machine-folk; 'cos they're all dead. Can't carry off being Stone-folk; they'd smell a rat straight away. Would have to be River-folk."

"Think you can carry that off?" Tali asked.

"Whoa there! That 'we' turned into a 'you' quick enough."

"Single trader, easier to hide? Got to be you or me, leaves one of us as backup if anything goes wrong."

"Okay, not instilling me with confidence."

"Come on, Padg. We need to know more to have a chance of rescuing Amber."

"That was your crazy plan, as I remember."

"And you'd leave her to rot in a Stone-folk cell, would you? Or worse."

"Okay! Okay! I'll go."

"My hero."

The next span was punctuated by planning, sleeping, and practicing a decent River-folk accent. From the supplies she had left and the food they had, Tali thought she could compose a half-decent scent. They decided that a scout out of who was where would be advisable first.

"I reckon Dun would like us to add to the map," Padg said.

"Not if it's in your handwriting."

"Harsh."

"Hmm."

Tali repurposed Padg's traveling clothes, much to his dismay, carefully making some fabric cross-gartering for leggings and a makeshift cloak that the River-folk all wore. She finished the ensemble by making a jingling necklace of used flask tops and things she'd collected along the way.

"Bang goes my stealthy approach," Padg said.

"You're a River-folk. You don't give a splosh about stealth. Cocky, remember? Thought you wouldn't have a problem with that bit."

"I used to like you."

"I'm sure my fragile ego can cope. Now, give me your best River-folk."

"Arrrrrrhhh."

"Nice. Gods help us."

A loud clanging of handbells broke the conversation. Then a pause and then the same again. A sudden clamor of noise followed, almost as if someone had thrown a switch and turned the market on.

"Pipe's waiting River-boy," Tali said.

"Better get at it then," Padg said.

"Hey"—she came toward him—"you really stink."

They embraced then, Padg still holding on, and said, "That's high praise from an Alchemist,"

"Go," Tali said. "You want to get in, in the first rush. Less scrutiny,"

"Yeah, I should."

"Good lu—"

"Won't need it," Padg said.

He climbed through the pipe hatch and was gone. Tali listened hunched at the grill facing the market, listening for signs of him passing through the checkpoint.

Chapter Two

Rowle licked her claws. It was the third time in about fifty clicks. Being the Bureaucrat obviously had its privileges, but gods did it require a lot of waiting about. She hated coming up here; it gave her the creeps. Not just because of the number of worthy bloody Tinkralas under her paws, they were a double-edged sword, but being in this place, with that thing. She shivered.

The Tinkralas called this place the High Temple and had established a permanent presence. That disturbed Rowle; they needed keeping tabs on. Maybe teaching a lesson. But that was not for today. Today had a different agenda, part of a grander plan. Almost in response to her thoughts, she heard the heavy boots of her troops approaching. At last.

"Your Eminence," the troop leader spoke.

"Captain. Do you have it?"

"Yes, Your Eminence."

"Excellent. Find Astor and get this door open. We have no time to waste."

The captain barked an order to a subordinate, who rushed off to summon the High Priest of the Tinkralas and Keeper of the Keys.

"Did you get to the human in time?" Rowle asked.

"Yes, Your Eminence."

"Good, good. And removing the head?"

"Was no trouble at all. My sergeant is very good with a knife."

"Excellent. You remembered the treatment?"

"Yes, Your Eminence, as you instructed the preservative was soaked into all the exposed tissues."

"Good. And the body was... ?"

"Not more than 1000 clicks old. We waited till the Bridge-folk had gone and removed the body from where they had left it. We encountered no one. The remains we threw down a shaft."

A waft of incense advertised the High Priest's arrival.

"Rowle," he said.

"That's *Bureaucrat Rowle* to you."

"Yes, yes."

"Open the door please."

"To the Sanctuary? The High Temple?"

"Yes, whatever you call it—open it."

"But we must purify ourselves before we open the doors to the sacred presence."

"You don't need to keep up all that sacred presence nonsense with me."

"It is not some kind of act, a pretense for the peasants."

"Isn't it? Oh, silly me. Get the door open."

Astor rustled and clanked at his belt and fumbled the key into the door, huffing all the while. There was a click and a hiss. The door opened. The stench was physical. For all the times Rowle had been in here before, the smell, the volume of it, the depth of it, shocked her still.

"In," she said, suppressing a gag.

"Yes, Your Em—"

"Quickly." She knew how long the awful reek hung after the seal had been breached. The less time the door was open the better.

There was a hissing behind them as the door was resealed. She herded her guard captain and two of his lieutenants across the room to the massive Vat at its center. The High Priest skulked around the edge of the room with a requisite number of clerics. The plopping noises and uncomfortable warmth enveloped Rowle and reminded her of being boiled in soup. Or maybe being in the lair of some malign carnivorous plant, complete with cables and pipes festooned like vines throughout the space. And that was before it *spoke*. Somehow the awful thing was wired to a kind of *mouth* through which the noises came. Rowle did not understand how any of it worked and any amount of time spent contemplating caused the hairs on the back of her neck to stand on end.

For now, the Vat just hummed quietly. Not an electronic hum, but the hum of a distracted child.

"Bring it forward," Rowle said testily, sensing the awkwardness in the room.

"Bring forth the new offering!" Astor said. Rowle sighed.

The soldiers shuffled nervously forward. The priests leaned in.

"We must prepare the offering!" Astor shouted.

"Just get on with it," Rowle said from between clenched teeth.

The High Priest fussed and chittered around, while one of the clerics, who seemed to be a technician, reached for various bundles of wires and pipes, shaking some and flicking others until she seemed to be satisfied. There was an unnerving squelching noise as the pipes and wires were attached where needed.

"Done."

"Thank you, Sap," Astor said. "You may proceed, Bureaucrat."

"Thank you. Now please, Captain."

The ghastly trophy was dropped into the Vat with a bloop sound. There was a rustle of cables and then an odd silence. An in-between silence. That was all for now. One thing less to worry over so she could concentrate on her plans. This place would not run itself. Someone needed to be Bureaucrat. And for now, that burden lay squarely on her shoulders.

Rowle stood with her hands on her hips. "Is that it done then?"

"We must now wait and see if the new... offering... is accepted." Astor took out a clicker-beetle and shook it to start it clicking.

"Ahh." Rowle turned to her guard captain and said in a whisper, "The next part of our undertakings?"

"Underway," he said.

"Good. The Duchy forces?" Rowle asked.

"Await your command, Bureaucrat."

"Excellent. And our commando team?"

"In place, ready to seize our prize when the attack begins. The Collective won't know what hit them."

"Good. Give word immediately we are finished here," she said, and then turned to Sap. "You will soon have a new toy to play with."

"Oh?" Sap said, startled.

"I believe you will find it...interesting."

"Thank you, Bureaucrat."

"Think nothing of it. Besides, it will require your particular, technical aptitudes to put it to its best advantage."

"It's a weapon then?" Astor said.

"Such a blunt word. It could be many things with refinement. I have high hopes."

"I'm sure," Astor said.

"Are we done now?" Bureaucrat said. The beetle was still clicking.

"Not yet."

Rowle harrumphed. The beetle stopped clicking. There was no noise in the room.

"Now, we are done," the High Priest said. He left first and his entourage followed.

"Go. Go!" Rowle ushered the soldiers out of the door. As the door slowly closed behind her, she was sure she heard the Vat sigh.

Chapter Three

Dun and the rest of Squad Alpha crouched below the ridge alongside the huge causeway. Tension rippled through the group.

"Hey, Chief!" Kaj hissed at him.

"Shh," Dun replied. Next to him, Kaj sighed. Since their promotion to the unit most likely to get sent out on suicide missions, he'd spent a lot of time with the young pup. She was extremely capable, which didn't surprise Dun hugely. Her late mother, Stef was Dun's first real mate. He felt awful and sad when he thought too long about Stef. He'd loved her and she died on the first mission Dun had planned.

This mission was easy compared to previous: a large consignment of medicines and food was being moved by wheeled truck. The intel was good, the guard compliment small. Their plan was straightforward: hijack the truck, capture the guards, drive the whole thing back to a floater, and glide back to base.

"Base to Alpha!"

The voice appearing inside his head always made Dun jump. He'd begun his life thinking that as a Shaman he was hearing things from the great beyond. Turned out the great beyond was a transmitter that could collect thoughts and project them. Shamans turned out to be good receivers. Less esoteric and more useful all round. They still got called Shamans though. Cute. And now it was less of a stigma admitting being a radio receiver than a loony who heard God, more folk came forward with the skills. Still not many, so far, six in the whole of the Collective, but enough to make sending them with missions and on intel gathering vital. They varied in ability and Tam and Bel the *leaders* of the Collective had started a project to test everyone in the camp. Nev had been promoted from his duty of drain maintenance and mapping, as the most capable technician, to head up the project. When they were back at base, Dun and Kaj had been drafted in to see if it was possible to teach receiving to the unskilled. So far their attempts had been entertaining but fruitless. He liked working with Kaj.

"Base to Alpha! Come in Dun."

"What?" Dun thought back in his head.

"Are you still in position?"

"Why would I have moved?"

The transmitter operator today was obviously new to it. Somehow, newness with the kit seemed to breed over communication. Understandable, sure, but no less annoying. Dun seemed to have no patience at all these days. It wasn't the pup at the other end of the line's fault. He knew that.

"Waiting on command, Alpha, stay in place."

"Thanks."

He sighed. Some people were just too cheerful at their work.

They heard a rumbling from the far end of the causeway. It could only be the transporter. Dun tapped twice on Kaj's arm to message her to standby. She passed the signal down the line to the four others in their party. One made a small squeak, nerves probably. The rumbling stopped, they heard voices, too far away to be clear. Tense but not so tense that Dun thought their position was vulnerable. A scent wafted their way, carried on the same breeze that brought the voices. Ammonia, musky, male smell. Ah, toilet break then.

Vehicle doors banged and the rumbling started again. Dun kept his profile flat to the edge of the causeway, so no one scanning about with their Air-sense would pick up a flicker of anything untoward. He cocked the crossbow that had become his favored weapon of late. One of the Community healers had concocted a rather effective knockout poison.

"Alpha to Base. Target in position."

Silence.

"Alpha to Base. Repeat target in position. Do we have go to proceed?"

Silence.

"Come on, Base, we need to move on this or we'll lose them."

Then a burst of something exploded in Dun's head. Surprise, then fear. The sound of weapons fire. Then massive static. Then, nothing. Dun cursed.

"What now, boss, we're going to lose them," Kaj said.

"No. We're not. Ready concussions. Ready bridge charges."

The truck rumbled overhead.

"Go!"

The concussion blasts shook out overhead. The truck had rolled too far past them for the bridge charges to be effective. It sounded like a wheel had blown out on the vehicle which slewed dangerously to the edge of the causeway.

"Shreds! Dive!" Kaj yelled.

"Bail?" yelled one of the juniors.

"No," cried Dun and as the truck back passed them, he jumped up.

"Gods!" Kaj shouted. Then turning to the rest of the squad. "Go!"

On the causeway, Dun sprinted after the truck in the hope that veering wildly would slow it down. He found the slewing of the truck was moving too much air in its wake and blurring his senses. The corner smashed into him and he grabbed reflexively. He needed to get the damn truck stopped. There were enough ties and handholds on the edge of the fabric sides of the truck for him to get enough purchase, despite the crazy action of the vehicle. He just about kept his feet on a rail along the side of the truck and edged hand over hand toward the cab.

Behind him he heard a metallic flap smack and felt a shudder from the back of the van, then a shout of voices and weapons discharge, probably needle-guns. There were a lot of voices. Dun's hand tightened around the strap he was holding. He was just an arm's reach to the cab. The truck bounced on its suspension as something or somethings came loose from the back. He leaned in as the truck veered again and made a wild grab. A handle. He pulled, the cab door swung open, only to be followed by a shout and the click of a gun. He felt fire in his right leg, gritted his teeth, and kicked up with his left. His toe connected with someone's chin—a lucky hit but a square one. That someone fell forward and their weight took them out of the door of the truck to tumble on the causeway. Dun clung to the handle for dear life. The truck veered again, swinging the door and smashing Dun against the frame. He whooshed out a breath and gripped tighter for the outswing. The driver was wrestling the steering to and fro to lose him. On the inswing this time he was ready. He jammed his feet on the van step and then reached for the top of the door frame. As the door next swung out, Dun swung himself into the cab.

"Geercha!" he shouted, kicking out with all his force.

The door on the driver's side of the truck must have been missing because the driver flew out of the cab and Dun nearly followed. Only his foot caught on a lever, which stopped his momentum. Right foot, obviously. Dun winced again but crawled back along the driver's seat to find his foot. He pulled levers frantically until he worked out the brake from the squealing noise. He pulled hard. The truck veered one more time, skidded on the causeway, paused at its point of balance as if drawing breath, and then slowly toppled off its wheels. Dun hung by one foot from the steering lever with his face pressed against the truck's bulkhead.

Back down the causeway, he could hear fierce fighting and screams.

"Shreds."

By the time he'd extracted his foot, the fight was all but over. He limped along the causeway, wind behind him, stopping once to check on the state of a fallen Duchy fighter. Feeling the side of his throat, he found a slow but faint pulse. Worth going back for, he thought. Then he caught the smell of the blood and heard the whimpering.

"Bastards," Kaj said, breathless. "There were loads of them. Ten, maybe."

"Damn them. Pon?"

"Her name was Pom, and she's dead. All of them, except Harp and he's not in great shape. Over here."

They lifted their comrade by one arm each; he seemed heavier than a young folk should. Slowly they drag/walked him to the back of the truck. They eased him down and leaned him against the side. Harp groaned. Kaj climbed carefully into the back. Dun twitched his ear to the breeze.

"No, no, NO!"

"What?" Dun said.

"Empty. All empty. Trap." All the air went out of Kaj's lungs.

"Damn, not a trap, a feint," Dun said.

"No time now!" Kaj shouted. "Company!"

The sound of smaller, lighter troop carrying vehicles, more than two, sped from the same direction the truck had.

"Damn, damn, damn!" Dun ran toward the noise as far as the unconscious Duchy soldier.

Then he kicked him off the causeway.

"Move! Now. Gliders," Dun yelled, running back toward the truck.
"What about Harp?"

Dun paused.

"No," Kaj said. "No."

There was a twang of a trigger and a thud as the bolt struck home. Harp slumped down the truck.

"No!" Kaj said. "Why the hells? He was only a pup, you..."
"Go! Now. Glider," Dun shouted.

And reluctantly, stumbling half pushed, she strapped herself beneath the one-person glider, and jumped into the void, tears streaming down her fur.

Chapter Four

Tali heard him from 500 strides away. She also heard the crash he created as he tipped a market stall on his way. Padg returned breathless at a clip, barged through bewildered guards at the front gates, jumped into the river pipe with a splash, and swam upstream to avoid being followed.

It was twelve hundred clicks before he arrived soggy and panting, back in their hideout.

"I guess we'd better move on sooner rather than later," Tali said.

"Huh?" Padg dried himself on a sacking rag.

"Well, after that performance everyone knows we're here."

"They'll still never find us; this hiding place is great."

"Yeah, but now they know there's someone to find. Some guard might get lucky."

"I guess," Padg said and passed Tali the rag.

"What did you find out?"

She winced at the dampness on the rag. At least it was less damp than she was.

"All of the servants are being locked into rooms after Work-cycle."

"Gods."

"Yeah, the conditions aren't great."

"Did you find Amber?"

"No, but I did find a few Folk who said she was alive, but they wouldn't tell me any more than that."

"Fear of reprisals?"

"No, I think they trusted we weren't Stone-folk, but I think she's become the focus of protests."

"A rebel leader?"

"I guess."

"Wow, who'd have thought?"

Padg made a neutral grunt noise, then said, "Do we have a plan if I didn't find her?"

"I think we help the servants don't we?"

"Hells, that's a bit of leap,"

"Is it?"

"Yeah, it's one thing to sneak in and try to extract one person. That we could do between us. But to free everyone? All at once? That's going up against all the Stone-folk, and it's going to take an army."

"Hmm, let me think a while," Tali said.

Padg broke out some fish he'd caught and Tali paced. Padg chewed.

"Whanfff somff?" he said.

"NO."

Padg chewed with increasing loudness.

"Enough!"

"Whaff?" Padg said as wounded as he could manage with his mouth stuffed.

"Ok, I'll eat."

She sat down and ate. There were fish and really great hubbous that Padg had liberated from the market. After washing it down with some water, she couldn't keep her eyes open. In a hundred clicks, she had slid down against Padg gently and was snoring quietly. Padg put his arm around her and drifted off himself.

Padg woke up to a ghastly smell.

"Gods, that fish didn't agree with you," he said.

Tali laughed. There were noises of pouring and mixing. "Sorry, I did think about putting nose plugs in you while you slept, but you were snoring so loudly, I thought I might suffocate you."

"I'm guessing you've had a plan then?"

"Yeah."

"Care to share?"

"Yeah, but gimmie a minute, okay? There's hubbous left from yesterday, and there are nose plugs in the side pocket of my pack."

"That steam vent hot enough to make racta, you think? I scored some powder from the market yesterday."

"You've become quite the little thief, haven't you," Tali said.

"Well, what with the prices and how few folks there are out I'd have thought they'd be glad of the trade."

Tali laughed. "Nearly there... and done."

There was the sound of a cork bung squeaking into a flask and what could only be described as a sigh of smugness from Tali. Padg poured racta into beakers. It wasn't hot enough but the taste was acceptable.

"So," Padg said.

"So?"

"Gonna let me in on the plan?"

"Ah yes," Tali said. "Plague."

Padg spat out the racta. "What?"

"Anosmic plague."

"You're insane."

"Why thank you. I was rather proud of that one myself."

"And now explain."

"Well," Tali said, "the Anosmic plague virus attacks the mucous membranes. The host loses all sense of smell, and then the virus replicates inside them so fast that the carrier's body rots from the inside. All the time before the host dies, huge wafts of the virus are borne upon the smell of the person decomposing. Anosmic plague has a unique smell..."

"Which I presume is this smell that's interfering with my racta?"

"The very same."

"Nice. So you're going to give everyone the plague?"

"No, but by the time I've finished, they'll think they have. I've found a rather nice plant combo that matches the smell beautifully, and then there's a carrier oil that makes it hang around for ages."

"Great, we're going to smell like this for spans then?"

"Yep."

"Okay. How do we deliver it?"

"I was hoping we could get it to the middle of the market. I've got some pottery flasks that will smash beautifully."

"Sneaking in the front again?"

"No. I rather thought we'd avoid that and unscrew this grill and go in the nearest way. We're not going to need a hiding place again either way, are we?"

"That all sounds a bit final."

"You in? You don't have to do this."

The bell for start of work cycle for the Stone-folk rang out through the grill. The sound of weary footsteps began in the marketplace. Guards shouting instructions. A Tinkrala priest's ululating call, inviting people to prayer.

"Okay. I'm in."

They set to work huddled together gently and quietly removing the grill, taking care not to make extraneous noise or sudden moves. The grill was much more firmly affixed than either of them had factored on. Long, heavy bolts with unusually shaped heads made for slow work. By the time the last bolt came loose, they had eaten again and the bell for the end of work cycle had rung.

"That's the last, one," Padg said.

"Should we move now or wait?" Tali said.

"Now's as fine a time as any."

"I guess."

"You good?" Padg said.
"All packed. Flasks ready."
"Let's do it," Padg said.
"Hey," Tali said.
"Yeah?"

She pulled him close and kissed him.

"Y'know," she said, "just in case."
"Yeah."

He pulled the freed bolts loose. The grill dropped down with less of a clunk than he'd imagined, must be plants growing in the cracks, he thought. Padg slid it to one side and twitched his nose into the air, sniffing this way and that.

"Clear, I think. Hard to smell anything above the stuff," he whispered. "Let's go."

He climbed out and reached a hand into Tali.

"Thanks."
"Which way?"
"Between the stalls? All the main lanes in and out will be guarded."

Where the Bridge-folk had Rope-ways underfoot as the main thoroughfares, here they had the Stone-lanes: different textured pathways carved for routes to and from each important gathering place.

They crawled and edged past the diverse stalls of the Stone-folk. Despite the work/home rush, it seemed that trade was still sparse. The only small crowd was outside a Tinkrala temple, where a weird talisman of woven wires seemed to be being sold as religious icons. They headed to the center of the market, where a large terraced stone amphitheater filled the space. It was used for announcements, meetings, auctions, and entertainment. It too was weirdly empty.

Tali and Padg crawled out from between two stalls built from piles of rocks assembled in waist-high rectangles. They stretched themselves out and Air-sensed the area. A small cluster of guards murmured quietly fifty or so strides away. A slight breeze wafted racta smells toward them.

"Quickly, now's our chance." Tali strode toward the amphitheater. Padg followed in time to hear her gasp. She fell forward tumbling head over heels down the terrace. All Padg could do was jog as fast as he could, following her without tripping himself. Behind him, he could hear the guards reacting. Tali came to a halt at the bottom level with a crunch. Padg caught up, the smell of Tali's Anosmia gas enveloping them like a cloud. Shouts had already rung out from the top layer of the bowl for more guards.

Padg lifted his head and Air-sensed around. Four staircases, one in each of the cardinal points, three with a guard coming down. But there was no way to leave Tali and he wasn't sure she'd be able to stand anyway.

"Tali?" he whispered in her ear, shaking her gently. Out cold. She must have banged her head in the tumble.

Twenty strides away the guards called out, "Can we assist?"

"No, thanks, we're fine," Padg said.

"I don't think so," the guard said. There was an authority in the voice. A sergeant? A leader certainly.

The guard closed, stone-tipped spear first. Padg could feel two others closing behind him and hear others at the top of the bowl.

"Stand up. Slowly. Hands on your head." He jabbed the spear point, careful not to puncture, to ensure compliance. "Your friend too."

"She can't."

"Oh?"

"I think she hurt herself in the fall."

"Hmm." He turned to a subordinate. "Get medics, please. Have them meet us at the garret."

The garret appeared to be a makeshift prison made of stone pillars, on one edge of the central market clearing, above the amphitheater. Three pillars to a side with too small a gap to squeeze past. Padg was pushed through the fourth side, and then a group of guards lifted the last pillar into place completing the last side. Open roofed, but too high to climb out, this was a simple yet effective prison.

"Shreds."

Chapter Five

Dun picked a two-folk glider for ease, scooped up Kaj on the way past, and cut the tethers on the other gliders to free fall and to avoid pursuit. Kaj was ominously silent.

"What?" Dun said.

"Nothing."

"Come on," Dun said.

"You. What are you?"

"Sorry?"

"I don't recognize you anymore. Mom said you were one of the good ones."

The glider banked steeply.

It took a while after her death to find out that Stef even had a pup. Such was the whirl of the way Dun had arrived at the Collective, and for that matter the way the Collective was anyway, that he had been on several raids with Kaj before he knew who she was. He still missed Stef, for all the short time he had known her. He still felt guilty and angry for his part in the botched raid that caused her death. Oddly Kaj didn't bear him any ill will, despite knowing everything that had gone on. It didn't make him feel a whole lot better.

Dun focused his Air-sense below them, to find the mouth-shaped entrance to the duct that would fly them home. It was way down beneath them, thundering toward them at all the speed that gravity could muster. Glider drops were always like this: You only got one shot, and if you messed it up? Well, the best glider pilots didn't think about messing it up. The worst never came back.

Five hundred strides.

Dun wished he had an answer for Kaj. He owed her.

Four hundred strides.

But all the answers in his head sounded hollow.

Three hundred.

Concentrate.

Two-fifty... two hundred.

Damn, off center.

One-fifty... one hundred... fifty.

"Lean!" he yelled.

Forty, thirty, twenty, ten, five

"More..."

Bang! The wind went out of Dun as the glider was winged on the hard metal edge. The wing-spar snapped in the middle. The remains of the wing flapped wildly. The glider started to spin out of control.

"Heeellllls!" Kaj shouted.

Their barely controlled plummet ended at in a thud at a sharp bend in the pipe. The idea was to bank the glider and fly/run the last 1000 strides.

The glider was a wreck. Dun and Kaj groaned.

"Sorry," Dun said when he'd gathered his breath.

"Any landing you walk away from... ow."

"Limp away from."

They dragged themselves, a remaining kit bag and weapons, toward the end of the pipe, Dun in the lead.

"Nev's going to go mental," Kaj said.

Resources were sparse. They'd gone out with four gliders and returned with none. Dun was more worried about Bel's reaction. Four comrades lost. And for what.

"What?" Kaj bumped into Dun.

"Fighting." Dun broke into a trot. "Damn, damn, damn."

Then Kaj could hear it too: weapons and shouting. Clashes and concussions. They dumped what was left of their stuff, shouldered up their weapons, and ran across the hangar, to the corridor the noise came from.

"Careful," Dun said.

"Yeah."

Kaj cocked the needler and headed toward the noise. It seemed to be coming from the direction of the control room. They crept warily, edging along the walls, one on each side. Then a huge concussion happened followed by hissing.

"Damn," Kaj said, heading farther in.

Dun stopped her with a hand on her shoulder. "Gas. Back out."

"There should be masks in the hangar."

"Go," Dun said, letting Kaj go first, but covering the passage as he backed up. Slowly, a sweet sickly smell trailed after them. "Quickly!"

Kaj bashed her way through random boxes with embossed symbols on. It was chaos down here. Clearly, Nev hadn't had time to get on top of things or find a new deputy.

"Come on!" Dun shouted, starting to feel the faint fizz of dizziness at the edge of his head.

"Looking!" Kaj, crashing another lid. "Don't need guns, don't need that. Where are you?"

Dun's ears twitched as he heard footsteps in the corridor; his brain did not stop spinning when his head did.

"Incoming," he hissed.

He started firing his needler into the corridor mouth and sidled toward Kaj to find cover from the edge of a box. He was losing focus.

"Found them." Kaj fumbled with a pack. She slipped a cool feeling plastic over her mouth and snapped the tab to start some air. There was a twang by her ear, she ducked down, reaching to where Dun was. He was sliding down the box, trying to bring his still firing gun to bear.

"Come on," she said. "Don't lose it, you ass." She reached around to his face and tried to pull the cord to get behind his head with her other hand. Dun groaned. Ahead she heard footsteps. The booted feet of Duchy soldiers.

"Damn." She reached down Dun's arm, limp from the shoulder, but his finger still gripped tightly around the trigger. She raised it, gun, arm and all. "No, you don't."

She sprayed the gun in a wild arc. A gasp came from right in front of her, so she kicked out sideways and connected squarely with someone's chest.

The Duchy soldier flew across the room. It was a good kick and crashed into the wall by the door with a satisfying sound.

It was enough to startle the next soldier through the door. Kaj let go of Dun and fired toward the gasp. She heard the needles strike home, then muffled shouting farther in the corridor, "Pull back!"

She felt for clues on one of the bodies. Curious, robes, not soldier's fatigues and a wiry pendant thing around his neck instead of ID tags. Kaj scuttled back over to Dun and applied the mask, and then cracked the air on.

"Come on, sleepy," she said, cradling his head with one hand, gun covering the exit with the other.

Dun groaned and rolled over, falling off Kaj's hand, and cracking his head on the hard floor of the hangar.

"Owww..."

"Oopsy. Come on you, come around. I kind of need a hand here. She gently toed him in the ribs."

"I'll come round... if you stop beating me up."

"Deal."

She propped Dun back up against the box and went to retrieve a water canteen from her pack.

"Better?"

"Thanks."

"Right, we can't sit here all day," she said.

"Where are they?"

"They left by a different way; I think I surprised them."

"Or they weren't up for a fight," Dun said. "Let's go and find out."

"Wait on," Kaj said, ripping a strip from the bottom of her shirt. "Let's get this scumbag tied up first."

"We haven't got time," Dun said.

"You've shot enough people for one day, let's get a few questions out of this one later. Help me get him into this crate for later."

That done, they edged, weapons forward, back into the corridor. Aside from the usual fans and creaking of metal, it was eerily quiet. At the control room intersection, they nearly tripped over the first body. Dun cursed and adjusted his mask. He reached down.

"Pulse?"

"Yeah." Dun felt the artery. "But deep and slow."

"The gas."

"Yeah, but shot too. Superficial. Should be ok for a bit."

They found three more bodies on the way into the control room and two more making their way out of the dining room doorway. All unconscious.

"Think the gas has gone by now?" Kaj asked.

"Dunno, but let's not try it out, eh?"

"Well, no."

They encountered more bodies further into the control room and weapons scattered everywhere.

"Damn" Dun checked the pulse on who he thought to be Tam.

"Not dead?"

"No."

"Well, that's good, isn't it?"

"So far as it goes, yeah. But they could've killed everyone."

"Perhaps we spooked them?" Kaj said.

"Yeah, dream on, hero. I don't think that was their mission."

"What do you mean?"

"I mean they didn't have the numbers to risk a fight. I think this was a specific mission for a specific group. They wanted something."

Dun opened the door into the adjoining transmitter room and there were two more in there, one of whom had crazy hair that could only be Nev. Dun took a chance and removed his mask, placing it, the air still hissing, onto Nev's face. Slowly as the air filled his lungs Nev coughed himself back to consciousness.

"Easy there, fella," Dun said. "You still got that water, Kaj?"

She passed it over. Nev sipped, coughed, and then sipped again.

"Transmitter," he croaked out. "They took the transmitter."

Chapter Six

The Bureaucrat was pacing again. Where was that idiot priest? She had summoned Astor twice now. Getting ignored made her very angry. If she just killed him, would his two lieutenants, Sap and Wip, just step up? Even if they did, there was something useful about Astor's piety. It made him vulnerable. If the two minions weren't, for all their stupidity, it made the Bureaucrat's position more, unpredictable.

Rowle sighed and heard a shuffling sound outside her door. Why where these rodents so edgy all the time. It's not as if she'd eaten one in ages. She slowly extended her claws and gently licked them. She so missed having other felines as helpers—also she missed mates. Her consort was gone these three ages. They were the last. Now only her. Last of the Cat-people. The Folk had their uses. She would be without help if not for them. But it wasn't the same.

The shuffling turned into a nervous tap at the door.

"What?" she shouted.

"Bu-Bureaucrat?"

"Yes? What? And come in for the sake of all the gods."

The door creaked open. A nervous nose twitched in and sniffed the air.

"In, damn you!"

The minion shuffled in.

"Well?" Rowle said.

"Err... your... Your Eminence?"

"Sit. Down. Now, speak slowly and clearly and stop shaking."

"Your eminence, the... Tinkralas are up to...something."

"The Tinkralas are always up to something; this is news, why?"

"They are bringing something here. Something they have stolen."

"I see. And what is it?"

"A device that the Collective have been using—"

"To communicate without speaking?" Rowle said."Yes, I know."

"Then you sent them?"

"No." Rowle exhaled. It was becoming a long, long span. "What is your name again?"

"I?" The minion paused. "I am Acka, Your Eminence."

"Well, then... Acka, let me explain. I did not send them. I allowed them to think they had done it themselves. That way they are enthused with their task, feel engaged, and still bring me the thing that I need."

"You have known about this *thing*—"

"For a long time, yes. The Under-folk have had *Shamans* for eons. Then the Machine-folk found this lost treasure; they were your people, before, no?"

"Yes."

"Hmm, and you had never come across this *Transmitter* before?"

"No, it was discovered before my time," Acka said.

"Well, suffice to say when the Machine-people were challenged in their arrogance by the greatness of the Bureaucracy, few survived. One that had, took her knowledge of the machine to the Collective, and they have used it ever since. It gives them an unfortunate advantage. But for the scarcity of Shamans in the population, we could have been in quite a bind."

"So, you are having the device brought here to use ourselves?"

"No. Not really."

"I do not understand, Your Eminence."

"No. You wouldn't." Rowle scraped her claws, slowly, along the metal surface of her desk. "I don't care what happens to it as long as it is out of the hands of the Collective. That way, their squabble with the Duchy will contain them, and we will not be disturbed."

"I... I... ah," Acka said.

"I am pleased you have sufficient enterprise to have informants keeping an ear out for their activities."

"Thank you, Your Honor. My agents are... motivated... efficient."

"Good. Keep it that way."

"Now, after work-span today, they will return?"

"Yes, Your Honor."

"Good. The guards for that shift will all be trainees and will be issued with extra treats. You understand?"

"Yes, Bureaucrat."

"Excellent. Make it happen. Other news?"

"Err..."

"Spit it out."

"There is unrest among the Under-folk."

"That is far from new."

"It could usefully be called war now. The Stone-folk have declared martial law in their realm and their alliance with the River-folk threatens to engulf the loose alliance of the Bridge-folk and the Mushroom people."

"Hmm, I feel our erstwhile ally Obsidian gets above his station. I feel a more active, listening style with him has become more appropriate. Do we have his scent on record?"

"I believe we do, Your Excellence."

"Good. Prime up a Rat-missile as a contingency. If he pushes further, we will end him."

"As you wish."

At the end of Work-cycle in the Bureaucracy, Rowle curled under the vent in the cozy nest she had made. The smell of the folk pelts was fading now, but she enjoyed how comfortable and warm they felt, even when it was cold. She never used to feel the cold when she was young. She stretched a leg and yawned. She flicked the vanes on the vent toward her, so she could better hear the goings on from the High Temple room below her.

Rowle found it hard to concentrate on what she was listening to with the tendrils of smell from the Vat rising. She sneezed and then reached for some nose wax. She didn't want that thing in her room. The thought made her cringe. She reached for a drink from the bowl next to her bed, then sat still, back upright, and twitched her ears.

The guard was snoring, that much she could hear. Then something else. Singing? No. Chanting. Tinkrala voices but not their usual prayer chant. Gods she hated all their superstitious rubbish. She clenched her eyes tight shut. In her mind, the scene played out: That stupid priest holding the new *relic* aloft. Then taking a piece of machinery to be blessed by a pool of rotting organic waste. Savages.

The chanting became louder; there seemed to be a great number of *inner circle* priests. More than usual. Whatever the guard had been treated with was clearly strong stuff: He snored on while the procession crowded past and into the chamber. The group chanted for a while in the chamber, and then the High Priest called for silence. Rowle found herself with her ear pressed to the vent. What were they doing down there? There were barked instructions and technicians called for. Not just a blessing then. What did the crazy priest have in mind? Then rustling of cables and pipes, muttering, and the sound of equipment powering up.

"Our work here is done, brothers and sisters. Let us pray that the Presence now accepts our offering, and can use it to aggrandize its sacred self and the humble Tinkralas along with it. All praise to the sacred presence."

Rowle listened as the procession chattered off into the distance, cheery voices singing. The guard continued snoring. It would be a shame to have him executed come Work-span tomorrow, but no point in letting the underlings sense weakness. She drifted off to sleep, purring.

Chapter Seven

Padg came around first. His head hurt from the beating the guards had given him. The stone-spears they used were sharp in all the wrong places. The dull ache of a beating was punctuated by the scratches left from the spear points. He hoped that the wounds didn't get infected. Tali had no chance to treat anyone; she was beaten unconscious too. He let her come around in her own time.

"Gods, not again!" Tali cried.

"Missed you," Padg said.

"I swear." She coughed, paused, and then said, "I swear if I didn't feel so godsdamned awful. I would kill you."

"Awww," Padg said. "That means a lot.

"How can you be so bloody cheerful when you're sitting in your own blood in an improvised Stone-folk prison?"

"Practice?" he said.

Tali harrumphed and then sat down in a heap with her back to him to begin the long task of cleaning the mats out of her fur. She was too tired and cross to even begin to compose an escape plan. She hoped Padg's cheeriness had left him some energy. He seemed to be testing out the heavy stone pillars that made up their cell, grunting and pushing. Then a familiar smell drifted toward them. Skarn, the captain of the guard.

"You will not be able to push those over," Skarn said, factual but not gloating. "It takes four guards and a lever to put them up. You have no equipment and your young alchemist friend has no reagents. You have been a thorn in my side for long enough. You will be executed at Mid-span. I'd do it sooner only there are other pressing matters."

He swept off.

"This is getting a terrible ring of familiarity," Tali said. "And you know what? I'm too tired to be scared anymore."

"Yeah," Padg said.

Then the shouting began. A huge roar of Folk voices, mostly female, swept out of the tunnel to the work quarters growing in volume and intensity as it did. Cheering, jeering, and shouts of rang out louder and louder. Skarn had clearly been busy already as a large contingent of guards were being barked into order by Tuf, the guard sergeant.

"Shoulder arms!" he yelled in a sharp voice against the dark background of swelling mob.

"Aye!" the soldiers yelled.

Padg estimated a score of soldiers spread two ranks deep by the Air-feel of it, but the stone pillars of their jail and the massive swelling crowd were interfering with a clear sense of what was going on.

"Oh Gods," Tali said.

"No! No! NO!" The crowd chanted and then came to an abrupt halt in silence.

"Present spears!" Tuf yelled as one the Stone-guards made a sharp "uff!" noise.

Tali could hear the blood rushing in her ears. Ten clicks. Twenty clicks.

Then the oddest sound, from the cavern beyond their prison. "No, no, no," almost whispered, but by 300 voices all at once.

"No, no, no!" The mass of voices got louder, firmer somehow.

"Single rank, front face!" Tuf yelled and the soldiers thinned out to face the crowd.

"No, no, no!"

"Set spears!" There was a crunch as twenty or so spear butts were rammed into the ground, pointed toward a sea of folk.

"No, No, NO!"

"Hold steady!"

"NO! NO! NOOOOOOO..."

The wave of Folk broke over the spears of the guards. It was impossible to tell what was happening. There were screams and yells of guards and folk, the occasional barked order from Tuf, and more yelling of "No! No! No!".

"What is happening out there?" Tali said.

"I don't honestly know."

Something changed in the sea of noise, the no's becoming more forceful and triumphant and the male voices becoming more strained and clipped. Then a shout went up as the line broke. There was cheering everywhere and the sound of running feet. Then a familiar voice could be heard shouting out to the traders and workers in the market space.

"Join us! We have had enough! Let us take our lives back from Dukes and Lords. They do not deserve our sweat!" It was Amber! "To the garret, everyone! Free the prisoners! No more executions!"

And the mob rapidly swelled with crowds from the market, swept half after the running guards and half toward the garret.

"Stand back!" Amber shouted close to Tali. She and Padg obeyed quickly. The crowd surged, and the stones toppled. Amber fell forward to embrace Tali.

"Good Gods," said Tali. "Are we pleased to have found you!"

"Or rather, you-us." Padg shook Amber by both forearms.

"We'd come to rescue *you*!" Tali said.

"That worked out, in a way." Amber laughed.

"You *have* been busy," Padg said, laughing too.

"Yes. Yes, I have."

And in the relief and the chaos, they laughed so hard and held each other so hard that their tears ran down their faces. They were still laughing when the crowd returned.

A breathless servant from Amber's Work-shift in the prison rushed up to them, "Amber! Amber!"

"What is it, Jade?"

"We caught them. We caught them all! Obsidian, Skarn, Tuf. We've rounded up forty guards too! What should we do with them?"

Amber was still. Murmurs from the crowd said, "kill them" and "string them up."

"Amber? What should we do?" Jade said.

"Put them in their own garret for now. Make sure they've food and water."

"Would they have done as much for us?" Came a murmur from the crowd.

"That doesn't matter!" Amber snapped back. Then more gently, she said, "If we want to build a new house, we can't use old mortar."

"They killed hundreds of us!" An old female from the front row of the crowd.

"Be careful," Amber said. "There is only us. No them."

"Where's the justice... ?"

"Let's aim for change now and peace, then justice tomorrow."

The new prisoners were ushered, complaining, into the garret they'd so recently used to store the condemned themselves. The crowd heaved the great stones into place, rearranging them to accommodate the greater number of prisoners. More bindings around the stones were added to prevent them being pushed from within.

"Wow," Padg said to Tali. "She really is something when she gets going, eh?"

"I always knew she was," Tali said.

Chapter Eight

Dun pushed a broom aimlessly around the hangar. He'd swept it three times already, and that was after Nev had swept it once himself. He'd need to do mopping next. There was an odd, lingering, sickly smell of the gas from where the fight had taken place near the entrance to the control areas. Dun found himself at the wall by the opening, running his hand down a drying blood stain. He snatched his hand away and wiped it on his fur.

"Dun," Tam's voice low and insistent called him out of his reverie.

"Tam."

"There is a council of war in the canteen."

"Okay."

"You need to come—now. There are things we all need to decide."

The canteen was ten folk deep in every direction. Bel stood on the serving counter. She banged on a metal tray to call everyone to order. Tam and Dun squeezed in the back.

"Our security was breached; we were made fools of. We need to find out why and, more urgently, whether we should stay here or find somewhere new. Everyone who wishes to speak their piece should come to the front."

Folk surged forward and spoke in turn with reasons to stay, reasons to go, and conspiracies for why they'd been found and breached so easily.

"*Dun*." The first time he heard the voice he was almost asleep. It shook him awake, but he wasn't really sure he'd heard it.

"*Dun*." The second time he was about to shout out in reply, then he realized the voice was in his head.

"*Dun*." The Duchy had stolen the transmitter. Dun tried not to think or else the sound of his thoughts would give him away.

"*Dun*." But there was something about that voice. Familiar and somehow chilling.

"Dun!" That voice, however, came from outside his head. In the room, bellowing into his ear. "Hells, Bridge-folk, wake up!"

"Sorry, what?" Dun said.

"What is your thought? Should we stay or go?" Tam said.

"What I think hardly matters. We should vote."

"Do you have any wisdom to add?" Bel said.

"I'm not feeling all that wise of late," Dun said, bitterly.

"As you wish. All those in favor of staying speak now!"

A cacophony of barked voices.

"And against?"

The volume was carried by the vote to depart and find a new hideout. The canteen descended into chaos. Bel banged on the tray again.

"Okay! Okay," she said. "Small committee for this then. Ten members max. We must have Nev, Dun, and Kaj as relevant parties. The rest on a first come first served basis, don't volunteer if you did last time. Your turn this time if you haven't for three times around."

Everyone shuffled and muttered and ordered themselves accordingly. Dun leaned against the wall by the door, holding his head in his hands.

"You okay?" Tam said.

"Yeah. I think. I..."

"What?"

"I think the Duchy, I think they might be connecting the machine," Dun said.

"Hmm..."

"I uhh, I keep hearing voices."

"Oh?"

"Yeah, oh."

They trundled back to the conference room. Dun sat down hard in a plastic chair. Bel crashed in through the door.

"We have planning to do. Get that door shut and post a guard," Bel said.

"Do we not trust our colleagues now? Is that it?" Kaj said.

"No, that is not it. Yet one of our number gave enough information to a Duchy strike team for them to walk past our security perimeter, and I don't wish to make their job as easy the next time. For all our sakes."

"I don't think they were Duchy," Nev said.

"What?" Bel said.

"I think their clothes were all wrong. The weapons were Duchy, but the clothing definitely not. Almost dressed like they weren't expecting to be caught," Nev said.

"Or they didn't care if we did," Dun said.

"How do we find this spy then?" Tam said.

"I'm not sure yet," Bel said. "Let me think."

"Dun!"

"Not again!" Dun shouted.

"Are you questioning my leadership?" Bel said.

"No," he said. "I wasn't talking to you!"

Tension has its own particular smell. It's not like fear, not a giveaway of weakness. More a pervading sense of an ante upped. A bowstring pulled one more length.

Tam's chair scraped back from the table. "Dun said he's been hearing voices again."

"Why did you not tell us?" Bel said sharply.

"It's only just started happening."

"Is this possible, Nev, or is it something else?"

"Of course, it's possible," Nev said. "Does it feel the same as before?"

"Well, kind of yes and no," Dun said. "They definitely feel like they're coming from the transmitter, but the voice. I don't know, there's something about the feel of it, the quality of it."

"Folk?" Tam said.

"No," Dun said. "It's familiar, but it feels like someone not used to using the equipment. Raw, clumsy almost."

"Everyone's thoughts on this?" Bel said.

"My best guess," Tam said, "is that someone from the Duchy—"

"Not the Duchy," Nev said.

"--wherever,

has reconnected the transmitter now they have stolen it."

"To what end I wonder?" Bel asked.

"Don't know," Kaj said. "But I bet it won't be good."

"Hmm," Dun said.

"So, what now?" Tam said.

"A waiting brief," Bel said. "As long as you keep us updated with any messages you receive."

"Especially if they say 'Kill everyone!'" Nev said.

Dun sniggered. He missed Padg.

"Not even a bit funny," Kaj said.

The conversation returned to the logistics of moving everything and everyone to a new place. There were places to choose too. The Collective had an impressive collection of

contingency plans. Then there was much discussion and arguing to be had depending on whose plan exactly had been chosen, whose plan had been selected last time and if everyone was really lucky, the ongoing conditions on the ground. Dun found himself drifting out of the conversation. Then the voices came again.

"Dun."

And it came with a wave of sensory information this time: a rustling noise, low murmured conversation, too far away to hear, a sense of drowning, no, floating and smell. My gods the smell. Dun threw up the racta he had just drunk with a splat on the floor. His throat burned. He shook his head violently.

"No. No. No... nneurgh!" Dun clutched his hands to his head and fell to his knees. Liquid seeped through his trousers.

"Shreds!" Kaj said. "You okay? Dun? Dun!"

Dun threw up again, but his stomach was empty, all he could manage was a dry retch. Then as quickly as the sensations had come, they abated. He felt like he'd been disemboweled. His head felt like someone had stabbed him with a knife all over. But at least now, he knew who the voice was.

"Myrch," he said. "It was Myrch."

Chapter Nine

Rowle stood in the hubbub of the *High Temple*. She hated that name and all the religious flummery it brought with it. The priests and their underlings bustled about, tending to the *pool* and monitoring it with brief pauses to meditate and pray. She really needed to get her own people here and trained, competent in this, whatever it was. It needled her that it was out of her comfort zone in all directions. She was almost getting used to the smell. At least that was something.

The other consolation was that the pool had been mercifully silent since the new *matter* had been added. No burbling, no-nonsense chatter in the churn of the liquid. Almost peaceful. Except for the priests.

She turned on her heel and headed back to her own suite, calling for Acka over her shoulder as she did. The underling was waiting in her room.

"Been waiting long?" Rowle said.

"No, Your Eminence, I bring news from the Stone-folk."

"Oh. Must it be now?"

"Yes, Your Eminence. It seems that in the Stone-lanes there has been regime change."

"Really?" Rowle said. "Excellent. Was it violent?"

"No, hardly at all."

"Hmm."

"The workers rounded up all of the Dukes, Lords, and generals and they are trialing and imprisoning them. Even Obsidian and Skarn."

"Well, I suppose if you want a good job doing, you have to do it yourself. Send Rat-things and have them killed."

"Both of them, My Lord?"

"Yes. You have checked in on the *pool,* I take it?" Rowle asked.

"Briefly, Your Eminence."

"Hmm... and your opinion of all this transmitter silliness?"

"I am still none the wiser, Your Eminence."

"No. Tell me, what is the point of having a helper who used to be machine folk if they do not know how machines work? Hmm?"

Acka shuffled. "With respect, Your Eminence, my love was for wind-up creations, not things that need *connecting* to ancient power. Quite a different specialism."

"Hmm, and you've had no more...thoughts?"

"No, Your Eminence."

"Well, I've had one. Find me a Machine-folk who can work machines."

"Again, with the utmost respect, do you wish to be involving yourself in the operation and interaction with the *pool*?"

"No." Rowle sighed.

"Then... ?"

"I want to know what the blasted Tinkralas are up to. Just like the one over—*here*!"

And in a flurry Rowle kicked the door and returned from around its edge with a squirming priest.

"Just because I don't have your rodent Air-sense—don't insult me. How much did you hear?"

She squeezed harder. The priest gurgled.

"Sorry? My hearing has become terrible of late." Rowle pulled the creature closer to her ear.

"Highness!" Acka said from across the room.

"Shh!" She hissed and then turned to the priest. "Now, where were we? Ah yes, you were confessing, priest."

She released pressure and the creature twisted and ran for the door. Instantly, Rowle lashed out and caught the Tinkrala by the arm. Acka felt the air from the sweep of her other arm, and then a spray of warm wetness. Rowle breathed out slowly, and then there was a pathetic noise as the body slumped to the floor.

"Shall I... ?"

"Withdraw, Acka? I think that would be wise under the circumstances. Leave and find me a transmitter technician. With all due urgency. Go back to your spies in the Collective if you must; they must have someone who can work the damned thing."

"Yes, Your Eminence."

As the door closed behind him, Acka could hear gentle purring.

Chapter Ten

It had taken only three spans of revolution, but it was total. Amber's uprising, as it was now named, was total. Tali and Padg stood on and helped with things as best they could, but there were eons of Stone-folk customs and traditions to unpick so they were empathetic bystanders for the most part. Amber thought that cessation of violence with neighboring tribes should be implemented as soon as practicable, so runners were sent to the River-folk and Bridge-folk. The River-folk runner had not yet returned, but a Bridge-folk runner returned carrying a message of diplomatic parlay and peace talks between the two Folk were arranged in two spans time.

The old cell blocks and the execution and *information gathering* facilities were closed. Amber set up a makeshift administration camp under great canopies out in the open at the edge of the market square nearest the old servants' quarters. All administration meetings and decisions were held there in the open. It was chaotic and noisy.

Tali and Padg breezed in, just in time for Mid-span meal that took place with everyone under the canopies stopping work and eating together. Amber called them over.

"You folk, okay?" She sounded tired but running on adrenaline.

"We're fine," Padg said.

"You, though?" Tali asked.

"So much to do," Amber said.

"Yeah," Tali said. "I wish there was more we could do, though, if we understood Stone-folk politics better."

"You are staying until the Bridge-folk delegation arrive? Your help in the talks would be greatly appreciated."

Until then, Padg and Tali had had no thoughts of leaving.

"Err, sure," Padg said. "Anything to help."

"Be careful what you offer, Padg." Amber laughed. He liked that noise. "Are you serious?"

"Go on," he said.

"Well, we need as many of the soldiers and loyal guards back doing their jobs as quickly as possible and, right now, most of them are in the new jails in the market square."

"Crikey," Padg said. "I'm pretty sure I'm not qualified for prisoner processing."

"No." Amber laughed again, "I don't suppose you are, but there's something that's been bothering me since things, changed around here."

"Oh?" Tali said.

"Well, you folk didn't want to be at war..."

"Not our style," Padg said.

"And all of us, at least the servants and the merchants, didn't want to be at war..."

"So, what was keeping the war going?" Tali said.

"Exactly," Amber said. "I suspect something untoward was going on, but I have no evidence at all and I need to know—now. If for no other reason than I need as many guards and soldiers back at work if I can't get the River-folk to the negotiating table."

"Hmm, tricky," Tali said.

"Yes," Amber said. "You two up, for doing some digging for me?"

"That could be fun," Padg said.

"Excellent," Amber said. "Have whatever resources and Folk you need. Jade can show you around. Oh, and one more thing?"

"Yes?" Tali and Padg said in concert.

"Keep checking back," Amber said. "Things are moving so fast here that, hanging with you Folk is making it all less scary."

Tali crossed the last few strides to Amber and folded her in a huge embrace. She muttered something into her fur.

"We'll be here," Tali said. "For as long as you need us."

"Come on then," Padg said. "We've got lots to do."

"What do you need first?" Jade said.

"Thank you," Amber said, quietly.

The first thing was list making and then working out exactly how to handle talking to the Folk they needed to. Padg and Jade favored interrogation, Tali said under no circumstances.

"It makes us as bad as the hierarchy we've just overturned," she said.

"But we need to know when they're lying," Padg countered.

"Sure we do, but can just do it in an interview setting."

"Sounds pretty ineffectual to me," Padg said.

"What about asking other people?" Jade said. "There are plenty of people I am sure want to tell us what they know."

"That sounds suspiciously like informants to me," Tali said.

"I approve," Padg said.

Tali tutted.

"Huh," Padg said. "Where's Dun when we need him, eh?"

"Why?" Tali said.

"Oh, you know, all that weird mumbo Shaman stuff."

"What about your father?" Tali said. "Are the Bridge-folk delegation going to bring him?"

"Dunno. It depends if he found a new apprentice after Dun left. If he hasn't, it leaves the village without a shaman if the council of elders comes trekking up here. Besides, they don't get here for two, three spans. We need someone now."

"Err, there may be someone in the Stones that could help us. You need a Shaman?"

"Yeah, I guess," Padg said.

"They are good at sensing things, talking to folk," Tali said.

"Being persuasive, threatening curses, and so on," Padg said.

"Shorl is the Oldest Shaman we have, and he is most honorable. He does not threaten people with curses."

"Shame," Padg said.

"Sounds ideal," Tali said, "can we meet him?"

"Of course."

The oldest shaman didn't turn out to be that old at all. Padg wasn't sure what he was expecting, but when they went down Temple Lane near the Stone-gates, past the now familiar cries of the Tinkralas temple, he found a temple to the old gods of river and pipe, inhabited by a young group of folk learning the ways of the Shaman. Their leader was not all that much older. Older than Padg certainly, but not as old as his father. When they arrived, they walked into a fug of low humming and earthy smelling incense. Before they had a chance to become accustomed to it, the humming stopped.

"Come in, welcome all!" Shorl said in a deep booming voice. "I was expecting you."

"I'll bet you were," Padg said.

Tali kicked Padg. He grunted.

"There is much we need to speak of, I think?"

"Do you all talk like that?" Padg said. "I know Dad does."

"Yes, please," Tali said, cutting over Padg. "We need your help."

"I guessed so," Shorl said.

Padg breathed in, and then Shorl ran on. "Not, from foretellings, Padg. I have spies. Foretellings have been... sparse, disturbed of late."

"Ah."

"Good," Tali said. "That's exactly the kind of expertise we need."

"Then sit, and we will talk."

They very quickly agreed on a list of prisoners to interview immediately, the highest on the list being those who could help with the prisoner crisis. Tuf, the prison sergeant, being of highest urgency. Reports from spies and a quick interview found Tuf to be reasonably untainted by the previous regime. Guilty of collusion, following orders, certainly, but there were as many stories about him of kindness and compassion when left to his own devices. He had character flaws aplenty, but Amber said with proper supervision and new rules that could be overcome. He was not of the traitors set Amber's revolution was looking for.

Free and able to help, Tuf quickly worked to recommend safe guards who were then checked. At least there was now more time to get proper investigations done.

"So," Tuf began, "we should sort lists of who to interrogate in order of importance. We probably want to work on Skarn and Obsidian first."

"Amber said you need to work on that language," Tali said.

"Lists of who to interview, then. It's really all the same whatever you call it."

Tali sighed.

Everyone still thought that if there had been betrayals and power causing corruption going on that Skarn and Obsidian were top of the tree of suspects. Tuf suggested reopening an interrogation wing of the prison, much to everyone else's horror. A compromise was reached in which one of the offices would be used instead. The ground was set for the interviews, to ascertain what had really happened, and how the war had really started. Who was benefitting from it and why.

And then the Rat-things came.

Chapter Eleven

"Explain this Myrch person to us," Bel said. It was an instruction, not a question.

"Well," Dun said, "I'll tell you what I know but that's not much."

"Do go on."

The conference room was busy with about four sub-meetings going on. Most of the chat around the long table was about the move. Nev and Kaj came in bringing a fresh pot of racta.

"He wasn't Folk that's for sure."

"Oh? He was what then?"

"Honestly, don't know. We only really got a chance to find out when it was too late. He had smooth skin, was tall, and smelled weird in the end."

"What did he smell of normally?"

"Nothing really."

"Like he was wearing hunter's balm all the time? Not there?"

"No, he was there all right. It was almost like he had a smell, but it was a smell no one noticed."

"How come he fit in so well to the tribe?"

"That's just the thing, he fit in perfectly. He was an adviser to Ardg, our Alpha leader, and there was never any question about it."

"When you say advised?"

"I guess inter-tribe stuff? I never really spoke to anyone about it. Ardg seemed to like him."

"Do you remember him arriving?"

"Now you mention it, no, he was always an adviser. Although to be fair, I don't remember the Alpha before Ardg either; I'm not that old."

Behind him, Tam coughed.

"Hmm," Bel said. "And now, this Myrch, is talking in your head?"

"You make that sound like it's something unusual," Dun said.

Nev added, "Nothing unusual around here."

Kaj laughed.

Dun wondered about the two of them; they'd been hanging out a lot and Kaj had hardly spoken to him since their debriefs. In fact, almost everyone had been avoiding him socially.

"What did Myrch say?" Bel asked.

"What just now or back then?"

"Either."

"Now, he just called my name."

"How do you know it was him?" Tam said.

"Voice. Unmistakable."

Bel pressed for more detail. "So then? What else did he speak about? "

"He spoke about all kinds of things. He kind of knew his way around but didn't—"

Bel cut him off. "I don't understand."

"He knew the tunnels very well. Knew the Stone-lanes when we got there. Even seemed to know what went on up in the Over-folk without any of the Bridge-folk ever having been there. Knew all the Inter-folk factions and squabbles really well, but in other ways, he was like a pup."

"How so?"

"He couldn't fish worth scrap. Didn't know one mushroom from the next. Couldn't weave. Basic stuff. He had to have everything done for him or quietly did stuff on his own. He didn't starve, so he must have eaten somehow. And now he's talking to me."

"You know that's impossible, right?" Nev said.

"I know; he bled out in my arms. His body was cut to pieces by needles. But..."

"What?" Nev said.

"I'm just not sure I know what's impossible anymore."

The meeting returned to the urgent matter of when to move, where, and how exactly and Nev was tasked with bringing more racta and snacks from the kitchen. More scouting parties went out to check over prospective new haunts for security and access. Dun trailed off back to his room. Then the headaches came again.

"DUN"

Dun sat on his bed with a thump.

"DUN! Talk to me. Just think it. Focus on my voice."

"What the hell?"

"DUN, it's Myrch."

"It can't be, that's rat shit."

"It's me."

"No. It can't be. It's some kind of Duchy trick."

"It's me, Dun, you know it is."

"How can it be? You're dead."

"Well, yeah. No. Kind of..."

Dun found himself laughing hysterically.

"What?"

It took him a while to compose himself. He reached for a canteen, started giggling again, snorted water down his nose, and then wiped his face with a rag.

"Better?"

"Yeah, loads. It just comes as a shock that the big ominous voice in my head isn't all that sure about stuff. You're new to all this shamanism thing, huh?"

"Right enough."

"Word to the wise, practice ominous."

Dun held his temples in the arc of one hand. A sharp, odd feeling, that went almost as soon as it came. Not painful, but uncomfortable.

"You can't laugh, can you?" Dun said.

"*No.*"

"But it is you."

"*Yes.*"

"And I can feel the humor but not the laugh."

"And much more besides if you feel for it."

"But you're dead. I was there. I felt you die. They destroyed you."

"Not exactly. Not really."

"How can you be not dead?"

"It's complicated."

"What's going on, Myrch?"

"That's a much better question."

Outside disturbances drifted into Dun's consciousness. Running about, shouting. Clearing decks. Unstowing of weapons.

"Wait," Dun said. "Something's happening, outside, I need to go and check."

"I know."

"What?"

"I know. I can sense things out there. Dun, I need you to listen."

Dun heard definite sounds of combat beyond the door now.

"Focus, Dun."

"But I need to help them."

"Your best way to help them now is to listen to me."

Shouting gave way to screaming.

"They need me..."

Dun hopped off his bunk and headed toward the door. It was locked.

"What the..."

"I locked it."

"I don't understand."

"No, you don't and, right now, I don't have time to explain."

"But we're being attacked."

"Yes. There are a hundred Duchy-folk, and they're not looking to hurt anyone."

"Are you on their side now?"

"No. Dun, I need you to trust me."

"You've locked the door, and we're being attacked. And you want me to trust you?"

"They're not attacking, they've come for... Listen, we haven't got time for this."

"I've got lots of time," said Dun firmly.

"No. You haven't."

"Humor me."

"They've come for your technician."

"Nev?"

"Yes."

"What do they want him for?"

"He won't be harmed."

"I'm not massively reassured."

Dun struggled with the door handle. He heard Nev shouting too.

"You need to let them take him."

"Like hells!" Dun said.

"I promise I will explain everything. For now, you need to know: Your best way to help everyone is to let them take him."

"Screw you! Betray my people and then leave?"

"They were never your people."

"I was starting to get along here."

"You were starting to become someone not even you recognize."

"How do you..."

"Complicated. Like I said, I'll explain. When this dies down, you need to find me."

"Okay. Where are you."

"I don't know."

Chapter Twelve

Four Duchy soldiers bundled their package into the corridor outside the office of the Bureaucrat. The sergeant of the small unit dropped his end to knock. The corner of the package hit the ground with a loud thump. It let out a loud groan.

"Shuddup!" The guard kicked the package for good measure.

"Come," Rowle said from inside.

The door creaked open. The guard cohort shuffled nervously inside. Rowle was at the door in a rush. The sergeant jumped.

"Acka! Oh, Acka!" Rowle called sweetly. "The Duchy have brought us a present. Well, put it down then."

The package was delivered with a thud to the ground.

"Excellent, excellent!" Rowle ran her hands over the sacking and ropes covering the prone form. "And all beautifully wrapped too. Tell your masters I am pleased. Now, go! Off with you. My present is for me to unwrap and me alone."

More shuffling ensued in the doorway. Rowle heard the sigh Acka made and called him in.

"Come Acka, my present has arrived," Rowle said.

The package groaned. Acka went over to the prone form on the floor. He felt the sacking bundle. It smelled of pitch and sweat. There was movement, at least.

"A-a-ah! Naughty, Acka. My present and I shall do the unwrapping."

"Yes, Your Eminence."

There was a purr as Rowle extended her claws. She ran a talon along the length of the sacking. Then a slow ripping fabric noise. An odd swishing, juddering noise that only cutting woven sack seems to make. Rowle pulled the sack away with a flourish and threw the sacking at Acka.

"Dispose, please. And find me something to sit my present on."

Acka returned dragging a long box.

"Put it up on the box then," Rowle said.

It took Acka quite a while to try to right the body from the floor. He sat him on the box, but the limp form kept slumping over. In the end, Acka relied on laying the unconscious body full length on the box, like a mock laying in state. One arm slumped unceremoniously from the box.

"Now," Rowle said, "does the present have a name?"

Silence from the box.

"Hello?" Rowle leaned in close and felt slow breath on her face. She blew back. "Are you in there?"

Then a prod. Nothing. Then a slap. Nev groaned.

"Better." She slapped him again. "Wake up."

She rounded the form and reached up onto a shelf where a bowl of water sat. In the same movement, she completed the turn and soused the water over Nev's face. He spluttered and then coughed.

"Wake up."

Nev sat up slowly, Acka leaning in to help. Sitting set off a massive bout of coughing. He gasped for breath. Rowle slapped him again. Nev cried out.

"OKAY! Awake! Enough."

"I will decide what is enough. You would be wise to remember that."

"Who are you?" Nev said.

She slapped him again, "You will speak when spoken too."

"Ok," he said.

She swiped toward him again and he raised his arm reflexively.

"Feisty present," Rowle said with a laugh in her voice. "Good."

"Nev," he said.

"Pardon?"

"I'm called Nev."

"Well, Nev. Let us establish some ground rules here. Acka, the collar."

Acka had obviously come prepared, as she reached forward mumbling apologies and clapped a plastic collar around Nev's neck. Nev felt an ominous cable trailing from it, over his shoulder and down his back.

"Good. Now, slapping folk is so tiring, and I do not wish to be doing all the training, so let me explain. The training collar works like this..."

There was a click from somewhere in the room and the collar whirred. A finger wide pipe at the center of the collar started contracting. Nev gasped.

"Ah, good, you can feel that?"

"Yeh."

"Excellent. Now, it can get tighter quite quickly, yes?"

"... gh..."

"Good." Another click from Rowle. Nev sucked in air.

"Soooo," Rowle said cheerfully, "if you disobey, the collar reminds. If you leave the bounds of my compound, the collar reminds. Is this clear?"

"Very."

"Good. Now, take the present to a basket somewhere and feed and clothe it. Then we can begin to see if he is useful enough to live."

Acka turned to leave.

"Not you, Acka. Delegate. You are needed here."

Acka hailed a guard and relayed instructions. Nev was taken out. Rowle sat on the box and stretched out her legs.

"Everything aches these days, Acka." Rowle sighed. "And there is just so much to do. Now we need to find some privacy from those priests, hmm? Perhaps we should just have some rounded up and disposed of."

A strained sound came from Acka's throat, but no proper words. Rowle tutted.

"Yes? Spit it out."

"I think that might not be... I think there might be," Acka stuttered.

"What?" Rowle snapped. "I hate groveling, tell me."

"Well, My Eminence, if one was to have it known that the Bureaucracy are hostile to priests..."

"Yes?"

"There may be repercussions? Perhaps unrest among the superstitious classes."

"My, my, my, Acka. There really *is* more to you, isn't there? Hmm? And what do you think we should do, eh? We need to shuffle off those Tinkralas and their little friends for a span, so we can get in there undisturbed."

"Perhaps, a different kind of emergency?"

By the time Acka had finished, the streets in the main Duchy city of Ur-Hab were in chaos. The main gate to the Under-folk had breached and River-folk bandits had swarmed up, taking Tinkrala priests left and right. A surprise uprising against the new religion by factions of the old animists. The Duchy guards, normally far from lax, taken by surprise. Fighting in the streets between Duchy and River-folk now raged.

In the Bureau, the higher section of the city and really a proper town in itself, the taller denser offices and residences, extra barriers, and extra guards had been posted. There seemed to be little surprise present. The only real surprise featured a small new office beyond the barrier that only seemed open after curfew. There was a stream of folk who entered that office, shiftily, with *citizens arrests*.

Rowle pushed Nev forward into the stench of the Sanctuary. She had guards posted outside the door but had no need to deploy them since the collar was proving so effective.

"So, my young friend." Rowle was all smiles and purred, "we put you to your great task."

"Okay."

"Don't sound so mournful, young Nev. This is a task that I think will be most distracting for a technician of your reputation. It is a worthwhile enterprise. I think you will find it... interesting."

"What is that smell?" Nev said.

"Ah yes, the perfume of the Sanctuary takes a little time to get used to."

"Gods, I'll say. What is it? Something dead? A creature?"

"Oh, not dead, young Nev, far from it. But the tissues of the flesh are so... fragile... transient... But I'm getting ahead of myself. Let us begin at the beginning. This is the Vat. Those superstitious buffoons would call it *Ki* or *The Presence* or some such other mystical nonsense. You will refer to it as the Vat. It was once, so I am led to believe, the great hub to this world. A control device, if you will, albeit an organic one. Your job now, your unique calling, is to learn everything about it, all its pipes and fluids. I need you to work out what it does, how to make it work better, and how we can harness its greatness."

"Okay."

Rowle turned on her heel and would have slammed the door to the chamber if that were possible. Instead, it closed on its own accord and fitted back into place with a hiss. The pressurization of the door closing made the jungle of pipes and wires rustle hurting Nev's ears. It was how he nearly missed the voice when it called his name.

Chapter Thirteen

The noise of the Rat-things was extraordinary. Everything they met, they shredded. They plowed through fabric, stones, and bones alike. They were followed in their wake by wailing, shouting, tears of shock and fear.

They seemingly shot out of nowhere, Padg thought. The Stone-gates had been closed as a precaution. The Rat-missiles must have come through another pipe on a different vector. Last time he came across one of these, Padg was surprised by its stealth. This time quiet assassination was not the mission. Whoever had sent these meant maximum destruction on the way to their target, if there was a specific target.

Padg was already running down the passage from their interview room and into the market hall.

"What the hells?" Tali and Amber said almost in unison.

"Rat-things!" Padg yelled over his shoulder as he ran.

He snatched a stone-spear from a likely rack on the way past and sprinted to where he thought the wave of chaos was breaking from. He triangulated quickly. Center market. Stockade. Hells, the prisoners. They were after the prisoners.

The screams were horrible, and the gnashing, drilling noise the Rat-things were making made Padg's bones hurt. He ran down the center aisle of the market and caught the second Rat-thing as it reached there. He swung the spear like a club, connecting at full swing with the second rat thing. He caught it on the butt of the spear and the thing yelped as it flew back into the market. Gods, he hoped it didn't land on any folk. The nearest Rat-thing was tearing into one of Obsidian's personal guard. The guard held on as the slick squirming thing burrowed into his stomach, and then through. As he fell, the rat leaped again, for Obsidian's face. Padg rushed to meet it but couldn't get through the gap of the monolithic stones comprising the stockade. Padg whistled for help. Obsidian's guard fell limp, and Obsidian was making a weird reedy screaming.

Tuf arrived, toting a spear himself.

"Quick," Padg said. "Push this stockade post over!"

"But the prisoners?" Tuf asked.

"Deserve a chance," Padg said. "Now push."

Behind him, Padg heard a low growl.

"Push harder," he said. The pillar rocked, then leaned awkwardly toward them. Padg elbowed the guard out of the way and pulled on one edge of the pillar as it went down. It crashed into the dirt on top of a Rat-thing, with a crackle and buzzing noise.

"One down, you freak!" Padg said to the pile of fizzing remains under the edge of the pillar.

From the Stockade, everyone spilled out too scared to even cry out. Obsidian's last gurgle left him and two of his previous guards dead. But now the noise had stopped. Where was the other Rat-thing? In the chaos of the market, anything was really hard to pin down. Plus, the echoes out to the hard, flat stone at the sides and roof made reflections mix with live sounds; it left Padg's brain chasing phantoms. Hold on, though. That reflection, there? Scampering, speeding. No another flutter echo. The real noise was coming from the far side of the massive chamber, heading toward the old prison complex and Ambers tent village. Shreds, was it after them?

He broke into a sprint again, leaping over anything his Air-sense told him was in front. He stumbled once or twice on the crazy jumble of spilled stall goods and wounded dragging themselves away. The thing must have come this way. There, vapors of oil and bile, he was gaining on it.

"RUN!" he screamed at the top of his lungs toward where he imagined the tent village Folk to be. He slammed to a full stop into the far wall of the chamber. He scanned up and down. Toward the main Stone-gates, still closed, there was noise and Folk rushing. Toward the tent village and the old cells complex, no skittering, but the silence and indrawn breath of something having passed. He turned and ran with his spear held tight and arms pumping. Something loomed in his Air-sense, low against the wall on his right, and he swerved. An older female voice cried out.

"Careful, brother!" And the swish of his passing caused a jingle of objects falling.

He lengthened his strides, the trail of oil vapor and bile getting stronger. He was gaining on it. Padg flicked his ears forward, sprinting on, passing Folk getting up and shuffling about in the tent village. No scent of Amber or Tali, not for a while, anyway. He picked a route through the tents and canopies with his Air-sense and sprinted through it, yelling as he went.

"Where'd it go?"

"Cells!" Came a reply from behind a pile of cushions and throws. Damn.

He pounded on to the mouth of the main passage, and then pulled up short and twitched his nose. The corridor went on and stone stairs climbed up to the upper detention level, where many of the new organizers of the revolution had co-opted as rooms. It smelled of perfumes all along here. Some need by the incoming administration to drown out the immediate past. Padg stopped and shook his head. He blew the perfume scented snot out of his nose. There— a waft of oil on the stairs. Up. He took the steps two at a time. How long had it been since the thing came through? Three hundred clicks? Five hundred? Was he too late?

He touched down on the top stair, nose-blind now from the smell of the perfume. Ahead along the upper detention level, there were doors all along the right-hand side. The thing must have come this way; he could hear it muffled in the distance, around a corner maybe. He slowed to a lope, weighing his spear. Ahead he heard fumbling with a door. He froze. Then familiar scents tumbled into the corridor. Amber, Tali, sweat. There was the bottle-clink of a well-armed alchemist. They stopped before they crashed into him.

"Padg, hi!" Tali said.

"What was it?" Amber said.

"Rat-thing," Padg whispered. "Thought it had come for you."

"Where?" Tali said.

"Ahead," Padg said.

They crept forward slowly. In the distance, there was a scuffle and shouting. A guard. He seemed to be out of his depth. And another noise, metallic and feral crashed against a door. Tali and Padg broke into a jog. Amber turned and summoned more guards. Tali and Padg turned the corner at the same time. Whether there was less perfume here, or that the beast was so close, the stink of bile and oil was strong. The guard was trying to attack the beast but every time he did, the Rat-thing rounded on him. It seemed the Rat-thing was more intent on gaining access to the cell.

"Skarn," Tali said.

"No!" Padg said.

Then in a click, it was all worse. The door to the cell opened and the Rat-thing rushed in. Skarn's voice greeted it.

"COME AND GET ME!"

Tali and Padg ran to the guard.

"No, no, no!" Padg said.

"Damn." Tali fumbled in her pack. "Wait, I've got a knockout in here."

"No good," Padg said. "Won't KO the machine part. Will rip him apart."

Then to the guard, Padg said, "Throw Skarn a weapon."

"We can't, weapons to prisoners?" the guard said shocked.

"Throw him a damn knife or he doesn't stand a chance!"

The guard fumbled.

"Here!" Tali tapped Padg's arm with a blade handle.

"Ta."

Padg leaned into the crack of the cell door. It was impossible to tell what the hells was going on. The Rat-thing was massive; maybe half the size again of the one Padg had just killed. It swirled around Skarn who roared in anger louder.

"Skarn. Catch!" Padg yelled and gently lofted the knife to where he thought an arm might wind up. The knife clattered to the floor but after kicking and struggling Padg heard the scrape of it being picked up.

"Aaarrrrrrrhhh!" Skarn yelled, his pain and roaring becoming indistinguishable. The noise of snapping teeth was punctuated with scraping metal and flesh. Then a twist, a hybrid yelp, and Skarn was smashing the Rat-thing on the floor of the cell. Smashing and smashing and smashing. He slowed and then slid down the cell wall. Padg walked in, his feet sticky on the floor.

"Tali?" Padg said. "Can you help here?"

She followed him, treading gingerly. She did a cursory feel of Skarn's chest. "No."

"You bastard," Padg said. "You're going to get away with this."

Skarn laughed, and then coughed. "It -doesn't matter now."

"It matters to us!" Padg said. "Put this right."

"Foolish... dreamers." Skarn wheezed.

"What did you do?"

"Betrayed you... of course."

"Who to, and how?"

"No... time... not..."

Padg found he was holding Skarn by the collars of his ragged uniform. A wheeze of air escaped Skarn's chest. Padg gently sat him back on the floor. Skarn sounded like he was whispering something. He leaned in close.

"Thanks... for the... kni... if... ."

Chapter Fourteen

"You're WHAT?" Bel screamed.

"Leaving."

"You can't leave, you faithless RAT!"

"Yes, he can," Kaj said. "Listen to the patter of his feet trailing away."

"Kaj, I'm..."

"Don't! Just don't."

"Look, I'll leave you with the hiding screen and the needler..."

"We don't need equipment," Bel said. "We need Folk."

"And a technician," Tam added.

"I wasn't much help to you there anyway," Dun said.

"No," Kaj said.

Dun sighed. In the distance, he heard a stack of boxes crashing down in the hangar, then distant swearing and issuing of orders.

"Just go," Kaj said.

Bel's shoulders sagged. "Debrief, first, then go."

Kaj huffed and stalked out of the room.

"Right," Bel said. "Tell me everything you still know about these crazy voices in your head..."

Dun walked along a skyway. In his Air-sense he could feel it arcing outward and upward before him. He knew where the Duchy lived, on and up, but after that, he'd be guessing. He was wearing a new set of Collective fatigues given to him by Tam. The fabric felt smooth against his skin. The bulge of a new scroll of map in his pocket; he was allowed a map of the barest instructions to get him to the Duchy. After that, back to his own cartography. He tapped that pocket to check for the rattle of a stylus there. He'd left the needler and the hiding machine after all Bel's protesting. All he'd taken in the end were enough dried supplies and water to see him five spans and a nice plas-steel walking staff about his height. It felt good to be walking again, after everything.

"*I'm sorry*," the voice of Myrch in his head said.

"Pardon?"

"For what it's worth, I'm sorry."

"Oh? About what?"

"About the Collective."

"Oh. That."

"You liked them."

"I guess."

"They need you," Myrch said. "Everyone does."

"I'm not a hero," Dun said.

"*No*," Myrch said. "*No one is*."

"Hmm."

A glide-car swooshed overhead from some unseen entrance two thousand strides above his head to another open-mouthed tunnel. It was swallowed by silence.

"You were right, you know."

"About?"

"Me. Changing into something I don't find familiar."

Again Dun felt Myrch laughing but not laughing.

"What?" Dun said. "What's so funny?"

"Doesn't matter!" Myrch said.

"What is going on, Myrch?"

"That's a pretty vague question."

"You need to tell me how you're not dead."

"I'm not sure I really know."

"Well, ask a vague question, get a vague answer, I suppose."

"Exactly. I can tell you what it feels like to be me now, if that helps?"

"Why not? We've got time to pass. It's a long walk to the Duchy from here," Dun sighed.

"To start with, I'm not alone."

"Wherever you are now? Like the afterlife, heaven or whatever?"

That weird laugh feeling again, "*No.*"

"Hell then?"

"It's not all bad."

"Really?"

"No. There are so many imaginations here next to mine. When some of us sleep, the dreams are incredible."

Dun lengthened his stride. He passed a junction on the skyway where the path he was on made a polite bing noise and the runoff he passed sang bing-bing. The runoff seemed to be going down so Dun followed the main skyway up.

"You're in a real place though, right?"

"As far as it's possible to tell yes."

"How come you don't know where you are? You've got Air-sense, right?"

Again, that laugh.

"No, Dun. I never had Air-sense. I'm not Folk."

"No, I guess not."

"And now the senses I did have... they've- - changed."

"Oh?"

"I can feel everyone here where I am. I can touch and emotions and thoughts. I can feel all of you, the Shamans, at least, and I can feel what you feel, hear what you hear. But I can't hear where I am. I can't see..."

"You can't what?"

"Sorry, that would make no sense, would it?"

" 'Fraid not."

"My senses are... different now. And so many minds here, so many ideas, where I am, it is in many ways beautiful."

"Peaceful?"

"No. Not that. Never, that. Busy, sometimes fretful or distracted, often joyous. But never quiet."

"Sounds terrifying."

"It was, at first. When I came here, wherever here is. I was terrified of the end of, what? Me. The end of me. I am not terrified of anything now."

"That's good."

"Is it? I don't know anymore. My perspective is different."

"Are you still... y'know... you?"

"Part of me, the part you know as Myrch is still here, but the rest is so much more, so diverse, diffuse."

"I don't understand."

"I don't expect you to, not yet. I'm not sure I fully understand yet. There is so much, so many here, so much potential. It's like the crackling air under a huge storm cloud, just waiting to arc to earth."

"You're talking in riddles."

"I suppose I am, we are. Sorry!"

"Hey, Myrch, I can still call you, Myrch, right?"

"Wait."

"What?"

"We must divert our course. Soldiers have been alerted, they are not looking for you, but they would be very pleased to find you."

"I don't understand, how?"

"Do we know? The Bureau and even the Duchy have Shamans among them. There is a captain in the guards of the Bureaucrat. Although she doesn't know she is a Shaman."

"How does that help?"

"I can explore her mind. Like yours."

Dun suddenly felt, exposed. Naked.

"I am sorry; I have made you feel uncomfortable."

"Oh, that's, well, okay. I guess I'll have to get used to it."

"There is much for us all to get used to. But not now. Now we must hide. The guards are not far. Climb over the edge of the skyway. Two hundred strides ahead of you to the right edge, feel down over the side and there is a ladder down."

There was. Dun didn't stop to worry about it too hard.

"Halfway down the ladder is a platform. It is large enough for a brief rest till the guards have passed. They are not seeking you. They will pass."

It was exactly as Myrch had described. Dun lay down on the platform and helped himself to some of the rations he'd taken on his way out of the Collective. A fitful sleep claimed him and when they passed overhead, Dun never heard them.

Chapter Fifteen

When Rowle returned to the chamber Nev was busy at work, tweaking cables and pipes and taking sample flasks of the vat's liquid to test. The Vat was making a gentle bubbling noise to go with its awful fumes.

"Ah, good," said Rowle, "you are settling nicely to your task."

Nev grunted.

"Now, now, that is no way to speak to the person who has your life in their claws, is it?"

Nev grunted again. A paw lashed out and grasped Nev by the neck. The claws in question surrounded his windpipe. He felt them cold against the skin under his fur.

"Is IT?"

Rowle squeezed tighter.

"Say 'No Eminence.'"

"Ff..." said Nev.

"Sorry? I didn't hear you?"

"F... F..."

The door behind them hissed open. Acka sensed what was going on in a heartbeat.

"Eminence!" he said.

Rowle stopped tightening, but Nev was still held off the ground in the grip of her claw.

"What now Acka? I hope it's important," said Rowle.

"Your eminence...?" said Acka.

"Nn...ck..." said Nev.

Rowle lowered Nev so his feet touched the ground.

"What, Acka? Spit it out."

"I think, you should..."

"Should?"

"I think you could...would...be well advised to let the Folk person breathe."

"Oh? You do, do you?"

"He may...prove...valuable," said Acka, "your eminence."

"Currently, Acka, he is just proving intransigent and surly. And I don't like it."

"I understand, your eminence..."

"Do you Acka? Really?"

"I believe in some small way I do, eminence. However..."

"Mmm?"

"...however, I think that a display of beneficence...mercy... at this juncture may be... better timed."

"...ck...k..."

"Oh, have it your way, Acka!"

Rowle let go. Nev slumped to the floor gasping.

"You had better be right," Rowle turned to the slumped form. "Collective technician, I need to see results, soon." She swept out.

Acka hurried over to Nev, checked his pulse and sighed.

"I have water," said Acka, "drink."

Nev pushed him away.

"I am trying to help."

"Stick it," said Nev.

"I will leave the flask here." Acka pointedly plonked the metal flask on the floor. "Make your life a little easier."

"Huh."

Acka left, still sighing.

Nev sat up and rubbed his neck. He contemplated his spans work so far, a repair on the raft of cables in the front of the vat. They seemed to have been slashed to ribbons. It took him the half span he'd been awake to work out even what was what. Nev scratched his head and sat on the floor in front of the open panel and its disgorged wires and cables. The panel had some kind of speaking cone on it and was held to the rest of the unit by one remaining strand. Nev puffed out his cheeks, scratched his head and then worked out a way to lean the panel on one corner to take the strain off its remaining sinew. He reached out across the floor and felt the flask. It was metal, but quite poor quality.

"Hmm, where did you come from?"

He drank the water in shallower gulps than he wanted: his throat burned. But he persisted till the flask was empty. He pocketed it. He then felt around the top of the vat, slowly. The rim was rounded, it came up to his shoulders, but the whole of the Vat felt too fragile, too antique for any plan that Nev had. He worked his way around. The Vat sat in the corner of the room with little room between it and its walls, though the two walls coming to a point behind the Vat left a small void. Nev turned around and used his Air-sense to get a better feel for the room.

"Shreds!" he had scraped his back on some piece of metal stuck out of the wall halfway down his spine. He felt a trickle of blood run down the inside of the jumpsuit they had given him as Bureau uniform.

"Wait," said Nev.

Maybe his plan could work. He took the metal flask from his pocket and smashed it against the metal protrusion. It made a satisfying 'dunk' noise. He smashed it again, and again till he had punctured a side. He then bashed on this new hole, using the metal pipe, which was probably square in section by the dents it was making, and made a tear in the metal. The quality of the flask was so poor it made his job quite easy. He worked for the next half span and had fashioned himself a relatively sharp tool, with a cutting edge and a smooth-ish handle. His captors had given him no others, but Nev was neither going to wait around till they worked that out, or beg.

Now to the next puzzle, the wiring loom. Each of the wires, including the ones to the speaking horn in the panel, came in pairs. He felt carefully and found the remaining wire and the pin it was connected to on the panel. It too had a partner, and now he felt carefully enough another pin to connect it to. But the twin cable here had been cut sharply short, just a stub on the panel and a loose end still in the loom. In Nev's head, the puzzle had a solution. He took out his new knife and found a piece of loose cable on the floor of the recess behind the panel. After whatever frenzied attack on the wires had made the mess, scraps of everything littered the floor. Nev found one piece that felt about the same gauge and proceeded to strip back the plastic insulation from both ends.

In another half span, Nev found himself winding the last two connecting pieces together. There were two spare bare wire ends left. They didn't really go together and he didn't want to tempt fate and damage something, so Nev left them, spaced carefully apart, poked into a panel of the exterior plastic membrane of the vat. The membrane exterior covered his workings on the outside and held no fluids, it seemed to be made of a different plastic to the Vat proper. He sat down again and leaned up against the vat.

"Thank you."

Nev's head snapped up towards the door reflexively. But the voice had come from behind him. He turned sharply. Emanating from speaking cone where he'd been working was a very faint hissing.

"They can't hear you," said the voice, "it's safe to talk."

"I'll be the judge of that," said Nev, almost under his breath. "Where are you?"

"I don't know."

"Where are you speaking from? I can't feel anyone else in the room by Air-sense. Just this pool."

"Oh...," said the voice.

Chapter Sixteen

Padg laid Skarn down. He had another problem. What to do with the bastard's body. As much as he'd love to just chuck it down the nearest available vent, Padg wasn't ready to create any martyrs. Not that Skarn was liked enough to have any followers after his death. But everything had to be open and above board now; they had to be beyond reproach for Amber's sake. Gods, why did everything have to be so complicated? He guessed a low key local style burial. What did Stone-folk even do for that?

Padg turned around toward Tali, but found himself alone in the room. Where had she gone? He went back through the door. Tali was in an embrace with Amber. Padg brushed past them and hurried on down the stairs. They didn't even notice. He turned back on himself, instead of going out into the tent village and the market. He found himself jogging along the corridor and crashed through the first door he could find. From the close feel of the place, it had been some kind of soundproof room for interrogations. None of the door locks worked anymore, all smashed in the first couple of spans of revolution, so Padg closed the door behind him and fell down to his knees. Huge breaths heaved out of him.

"SHREDS! Stinking bloody shreds..."

He curled up on the cold stone floor of the room.

Amber held Tali tight for what seemed like an eon. "I thought I was going to lose you to that awful thing."

"I'm a bit harder to get rid of than that," Tali said.

"I know," Amber said. "That's why I... I need you to be here right now."

"I need to be here too," Tali said.

Amber felt Tali tense in her arms, "What's wrong?" Amber said.

"Where's Padg?"

"He was in there a moment ago." Amber stuck her head back into the room, but no one living was in there.

"Oh Gods," Tali said. "Padg! Padg!"

She searched from room to room.

"I'm sorry," Amber said. "I didn't think. I..."

"I know," Tali said. "S'Ok."

"But, will he... what will he..."

"I don't know; we need to find him." Tali opened the next door.

"Wait." Amber gently grabbed Tali by the shoulders. "Don't panic; head up, deep breath."

Tali inhaled through her nose with Amber's hands still resting on her. It felt good, calming, but then she sensed it at the back of her nose. A familiar smell of male and stress.

"Down," Tali said. They headed for the stairs.

"Oh, Tali!" Amber said.

"Don't worry, it'll be fine."

They hurried down the lower detention level passage chasing Padg's scent, but they had gone to the end of the level and checked in each room before they concluded that Padg had gone.

Standing at the mouth of the passage to the market, Padg felt like he was toeing forward on the edge of a great abyss, teetering to and fro. He stood that way for the longest time until a familiar jingling sound dribbled into his ears. It got closer.

The voice that went with the jangling spoke, "Are you okay, brother?"

"Huh?"

"I asked if you were okay," the female voice was close enough for Padg to smell she was a Tinkrala. "Hold on! You were the hero that crashed through here before and trashed my shrine." She said the word "hero" like it tasted funny.

She didn't smell quite as strongly as most Tinkralas. Clearly, she preferred less incense than her colleagues. Which was good, it made Padg's nose ache.

"Hey." She prodded Padg in the ribs. "I was talking to you."

"Sorry?" Padg said. "About the shrine, I mean. I'm sorry, I was trying to... oh never mind. I'm sorry, I'll help fix it up. I'm Padg by the way."

"I'm Laly, charmed I'm sure, but you're too late. I've already done it."

"Well, let me make it up to you some other way."

"Okay... Really?"

"Yes, really. I've got half a span downtime and... Yes, what can I do to help."

"Come with me. I'll introduce you to Brother Trone."

"Is he some kind of priest?"

"No, he's a missionary from the Duchy, but he takes the services here. He needs help distributing food and clothes. We've been run off our feet since the uprising."

Padg opened his mouth, but he wasn't sure what to call what had happened if not an uprising, and closed it again. Laly had already turned on her heel and headed into the middle of the market.

"Coming?" she said over her shoulder.

Padg fell into step, and it was quite a step. Laly had a quick stride and no seeming sense of tiredness. Padg found himself puffing. Wherever they were going, it was the far corner of the market from the cell complex. Padg had always underestimated distances between his Air-sense and what his feet told him after having walked anywhere. It was a good job Dun was the map writer.

"Toddle a bit faster, can you?" Laly said. "I'm more than twice your age, pup!"

"Where are we... going?"

"Gallery, silly. Now save your breath for walking."

Laly seemed to have taken mercy on him, Padg thought, as she'd slowed her pace ever so slightly. He hadn't even heard of the Gallery. How could he be involved with the organization of the Stone-folk at all, however briefly, without having heard of a grand sounding place like that?

He felt the corner of the huge market cavern coming up in his Air-sense. There was a large stone building in the wall ahead of them. He could tell from the noise and smell that it was now a Tinkrala temple, but that wasn't where they were heading. In front of the temple, on the opposite side of the walkway, on the side they'd reach first, was a tent. The kind of size of tent used for temporary toilets in the case of a crisis, like now. Laly arrived first and opened the tent flap for him.

Inside was a small, square, hole in the floor, a pace wide on each side, with a massive drop inside it by Padg's senses.

"Down we go!" Laly said cheerily.

There was a ladder, of sorts. You'd have called it a rope ladder if any of it was actually made of rope. Two long thick wire cables were its edges and the rungs were made of any number of different braided sets of rags and found material sacks and wires. Padg stepped gingerly down easing his weight carefully from one rung to the next.

"Come on, young pup, we haven't got all span," she shouted up at him.

How deep did this thing go? He was at least thirty strides down, with more than that to go from the distance Laly's voice was, but he daren't focus his Air-sense as swinging on the ladder made him feel odd already. He reached for his next foothold and slowly progressed down.

"Well done, Padg," Laly said in a conspiratorial whisper. "It gets easier. Now! Let's go find Trone, the old hog, and see what needs doing."

Then Padg lifted his head up. On solid ground, his Air-sense had something to work with. The gallery was massive. It extended as far in each direction as the Stone-market above, but with no buildings of any permanent nature at all. As far as Padg could sense, were makeshift soft materials and improvised tents and such. The Gallery seemed warm, warmer certainly than the cavern above, but not uncomfortably so. But what he could tell was, there were folk: hundreds, thousands. Some milling about and some sat in clusters. Others... It was just too much to take in, in one go.

"Who are they all?" Padg said.

"Refugees," Laly said. "Where do you think everyone's been coming while everyone's been playing politics and soldiers up above? The Stone-folk didn't want them. Didn't fit in a caste, you see. Although it's a little easier now your friends have taken over upstairs. At least we're properly left alone now. We were always in such a precarious position before, what with spot searches and bribing guards and so forth. So we're left to our own devices now. We can get on."

"Are they all Stone-folk?"

"Gods no, many Stone-folk, but we've got River-folk, runners from all tribes, Duchy soldiers, even some Machine-folk."

"And you are doing, what... ?"

"Feeding folk, giving basic medical care. Allowing them time to put their lives back together."

Padg soaked it all in.

"Did you think we were in a Tinkrala indoctrination camp?" She laughed.

Padg, for once, couldn't think of what to say.

Chapter Seventeen

"Wake up now, Dun. We must go."

That was never going to get less creepy. The voice of someone in his head, Dun had almost become used to in his time as a Shaman. But the echo of someone dead, not-dead, whatever Myrch was now? Was it possible to ever get used to that?

"I need to eat and wash my face first."

"Be quick, more troops are coming."

"How do you know that?" Dun said.

"One of them is a shaman and doesn't know."

"Okay, sorry I asked." Dun wolfed down some dried rations, threw his kit in his pack, and shouldered it.

Dun reached up from his hideaway and pulled his head up so he could Air-sense over the parapet. No sign of anyone yet.

"How far?" he said.

"Two thousand strides or so, they've stopped for some reason. Now's your chance to move. If you go double speed you can reach where the causeway comes out of the bulkhead before they move."

"Okay."

Dun could sense the outline of the causeway in his Air-sense, as well as the huge vertical wall ahead with a hole that the causeway headed into. His destination. Ur-Hab, the principal city of the Over-folk. He reached the entrance; sounds of a cohort of troops getting up, met him from the other side.

"What now?" Dun thought in his head, too scared to speak.

"Drop down to the edge of the causeway until they pass."

"Dangle in mid-air, and hope I don't fall off?"

"They are in a hurry. If we are lucky they won't detect you."

"And if I'm not, one of them will stand on my fingers from above."

"You are strong, you can make this."

"That's pretty easy for you to say from, wherever you are."

Dun knelt on the edge of the parapet. He could hear the troops getting back into marching pattern. He checked the straps on his backpack and tightened them. Then slowly he lowered himself legs first, into space. A quick scramble as he swapped from leaning over with arms and holding on first one hand then both. He swung gently. The vastness of the open space filled his Air-sense and made him woozy. He clung, hands as close together on the edge of the causeway as he'd dared. Farther apart made him a bigger target to be noticed by someone with sharp senses. Closer together and well...

The strain had started already. Dun clenched his teeth, and then breathed through them as quietly as he could manage. He could hear the soldiers above. They, unlike him, were making no effort to be silent. One of them, a leader of some description, shouted out. The column stopped again over Dun's head.

"What now?" the leader shouted.

"Still got the stone in my shoe," came the apologetic voice of a soldier.

"For the love of all the gods!"

"It's stopping me march, Guv."

"Which is stopping everyone else! If I chopped your foot off, boot and all, and threw you and it off the causeway, then we could get on! Sit the hell down and sort it out!"

"Yes, Guv!"

The soldier sat on the edge of the causeway. Dun felt the brush of air from him sitting across his fingers. He held his breath. If the soldier tipped his head he'd pick him up by Air-sense, for sure. In fact, from there, he should be able to smell him. He was sweating enough for them to smell him from Bridgetown. Dun could feel a cramp starting in his arm muscles. He tried to think of something else. He could only think of the folk he'd left at the Collective and how guilty he felt running off and leaving them. His left arm started to shake.

Boot soldier stood again and paused.

"Hey, Sarge?"

"What now?"

"I think I found something."

"Please tell me it's your brain."

"No, it's here."

The sergeant sighed and walked over to the soldier. Dun tried to steady his arm but the other one started shaking too. He could feel the soldiers by Air-sense now, from the air they displaced above. Why could they not feel him? Or smell him?

"Look, Sarge. It's a rock. It's a big spikey one too. Owww!"

The sergeant grunted and dragged Boot soldier away, muttering as he went. The sergeant called everyone to order. Then there was a loud sneeze from the back of the column. It sounded like Boot soldier. That could explain how his smell didn't give him away. The sergeant sighed heavily, gave an order, and the column moved off.

Dun's arms shook. He grunted and tensed himself for the lift.

"Wait."

"Like hell."

The soldiers were singing a cheerful if bloody, marching song. Dun got his elbows over the parapet and then felt all of his blood and will drain from him. His legs felt like lead. He knew if he swung them in any direction he wouldn't make the edge, and the momentum would carry him off. He let out a growl. Not dying like this, surely?

"Temper, temper!" Kaj said above him. "Now shush or that Duchy mob will hear you. Grab hold."

As she reached over him to grab his pack straps her scent smelled like relief.

"Why in the hells are you here?" Dun said.

"To save your sorry ass, you ingrate," she said, straining the words as she dragged him onto the road surface.

"Err... thank you?"

"You're welcome, probably." She punched him in the arm.

"Aren't they missing you?"

"Back at the Collective? Nah, Tam and Bel will manage, they always do. They'll find another tech. Anyhow, it seemed like you'd rushed off to get yourself killed on some fool's errand without saying goodbye, so I thought rather than let you cock things up, I'd lend a paw. What kind of fool's errand is this anyway."

"It's kind of hard to explain."

"Well, I kind of like to know in advance what I've gotten myself into. You know, in case it's a suicide mission."

"Just like your mother," Dun said under his breath.

"What?"

"Nothing. Look, it's really is hard to explain."

"Try me."

"Okay, you know I hear voices?"

"Yeah, Shaman, Receiver, whatever, blah, blah. I knew all this about you since forever."

"Now I'm hearing voices from someone that's dead."

"Yep, granted, that is a little more 'out there'."

"And now he wants me to find him."

"Hmm... Isn't the *dead* thing going to make that more difficult?"

"Yeah," Dun said.

"Want some company?"

Chapter Eighteen

Nev woke up to banging on the bars of his cell.

"Wakey, prisoner!" Acka said in a way too cheery voice.

"Urgh," Nev said. "If we're going to be friends, you should call me Nev."

"But you are the prisoner."

"Hmm, I think you need all the friends you can get, Acka."

"Oh?" Acka sounded affronted.

"Stuck between a psychopathic boss and a religious fanatic? I'd say you're in a pretty tight squeeze."

Acka grunted and proffered a washcloth.

"Just sayin'," Nev said.

"Her Eminence requires your presence."

"Uh-huh." It wasn't a question.

Nev stumbled after his jailer and was about to join a line of several other prisoners, for what passed for breakfast, when Acka spoke again, "Breakfast will be in the Bureaucrat's chambers."

"Okay."

The walk took them on a route that included a balconied walkway that arched over the massive space below that was Ur-Hab, the city of the Duchy. After the chaos of the last few spans, it seemed eerily quiet down there. Acka seemed oblivious to the tension despite them having two guards accompanying them.

"This walkway is one of the finest monuments to the Duchy. We call it the Stoa Elektron. It has beautiful carvings on the wall side to match the magnificent beauty we can Air-sense over the balcony on the other side."

Why was Acka telling him this? Nev already knew from the first day he'd been walked back to the prison compound in the Duchy that this bridge/overpass/gallery thing was an engineering wonder and from the carvings he could feel, beautifully decorated too. He also knew that neither the Duchy or the Bureau had had any hand in its construction. Normally Nev was up for a little history or politics on the way to work, but this morning, he'd not even had a racta. He grunted. Acka took the hint and was silent the rest of the way.

When they arrived and Acka opened the door, the smell that met Nev's nose was incredible and not in the way he was expecting. The smell of food wafted from somewhere in the center of the room. He could sense a table and the Bureaucrat stood behind it. Everything was warm and smelled appetizing. Even the racta smelled as good as he'd ever smelt it. His mouth watered. He was suspicious as hell.

"Sit, please," the Bureaucrat said.

The only place to sit was at a chair in front of the table, loaded with all the breakfast goods. The Bureaucrat dismissed Acka summarily.

"Don't stand on ceremony, young Nev," Rowle said. "Please start. I recommend the baked clicker beetles. They are particularly delicious."

Nev tore off a piece of sweetened bread from a massive loaf and followed the scent of racta to a large flask. He found a cup beneath the spout. He poured and drank deeply, refilled and drank again. Then he sat and forced himself not to bolt the bread.

"So, Nev..."

Here it comes, Nev thought.

"I thought I would check in on your project and see how things are getting along."

"Fine," Nev said.

"Good, good. I am glad to hear it. And how do you think the speed of your progress is?"

"Fine."

"Hmm, let me rephrase this a little. I would like a little... more. You have added a speaking device to the Vat to make communication?"

"What more would you like? That I add herbs to the Vat and make soup?"

"Ha! I do like you. No. I think you miss my point."

"Okay."

"That Vat used to have control of many of the systems in the Duchy, perhaps the whole world. Now everything is mostly *automatic*. It used to be that a Bureaucrat could give simple commands to the system and have them obeyed. It would increase my reach and grasp considerably to make this the case once more."

"That, is what I am trying to do."

"Good. And your progress is... ?"

"Steady."

"Hmm, there I'd have chosen the word... slow." Rowle rose from the table. "Walk with me."

Nev knew they were off to the Sanctuary and the Vat and knew there was nothing good to come of it. When Rowle was in a cheery mood, that was when to fear her most. Rowle opened the door with its customary hiss. Somehow it all smelled less awful today. Maybe, thought Nev, I'm just getting used to it. He followed Rowle as she strode into the room.

"Make it talk to me," Rowle said.

"I... What?"

"Make it talk."

"I... can't."

"Can't or won't?" the Bureaucrat asked. Without waiting for a reply, she continued, "All right. You talk to me."

"Uh?" Nev said. Then he felt the slave collar around his neck buzz to life and tighten. It settled snugly against his neck and then began to squeeze in earnest.

"Talk to me," Rowle said.

Nev coughed. The shock and the shooting pains starting in his neck brought him to his knees. "I... am... cuk... tuk... talk." The collar loosened slightly. Nev gasped. "What do you want me to say?"

"As it goes, nothing. But you see the point I have proved?"

"No?" The collar buzzed again.

"Ah, ahh!" Rowle said, cheerfully. Nev's coughing mingled the air with the unique aroma of the room.

The collar released and Nev gasped. "I meant explain," Nev said. "Explain. I don't understand."

"What I did to you. It works very effectively. I want you to do it to the vat."

"What? Strangle it?"

"Oh, strangle is such a nasty word. So, brutal. Persuade, Nev, persuade. Here, let me start you off." Rowle turned to the door. "Guard!"

The door sentry came in immediately. Rowle took something off him. Long and thin by Nev's Air-sense. Next thing the Bureaucrat stuck it into him. It had two sharp prongs, then just as Nev was wincing from this, he felt jagged fire across his skin where the points were. Nev heard his own voice in a scream before he clamped his mouth to stop it.

"A shock stick. Very effective, no?"

Nev could testify to that. The pain he felt was so intense he thought he'd pass out.

"So, let us start with something like that? Mmm?"

Rowle reached the Vat in one stride, poked the stick over the edge into the first piece of solid he could find, and pulled it's trigger again. Static issued from the speakers that Nev had connected.

"See what I mean? That is a start. I would like you to make one that is much larger, harsher, and permanently in there with a remote for me. Sooner the better, we all have work to do. Carry on then."

Nev shuffled on his knees to the side of the tank, leaned his head over near the speaker, and sobbed gently, "I'm sorry... I'm so sorry."

Chapter Nineteen

Amber had no idea the refugees were down there. The gallery had always existed but not in the manner it was now. She had been surprised when Padg told her but not shocked. Even in the short time she'd led the odd servants revolt, she'd stopped being shocked. She supposed that was a bad thing. She wasn't sure about anything anymore. She was tired and she wanted to find a burrow and snuggle up with Tali. That was about the start and end of it. But she knew she couldn't. Not yet anyway.

As if she'd read her mind, Tali was there at her elbow. She leaned up, kissed her on the cheek, and said, "Lost in thought, lovely?"

"You could say that."

"Anything I can help with?"

"Not really, I wish you could."

"Hey," Tali said gently, "don't be so quick to think I can't. You don't have to have this macho got-to-do-it-all-myself thing. We're in this together. Whatever it takes. Promise."

"Thank you." They embraced. Amber didn't want to let go.

Padg had to cough twice loudly. They broke apart.

"Sorry." Tali brushed herself down.

"Uh... so... do you want to come down and see then?" Padg said.

"Of course," Amber said. "Let's go."

Amber followed Padg's scent across the market, still holding Tali's hand to the tent and the ladder that led down into the gallery. He grunted at the two low key guards, one said, "Ki be with you," in reply.

"Grab, the ladder. Climb carefully; it swings," Padg said.

Tali went down first and then Amber. Amber and Tali stood shoulder to shoulder, backs to the ladder, in silence when Padg touched down.

"Huge, isn't it?"

"Yeah..." Tali said.

"How many?" Amber said.

"Five thousand, maybe? More. No one's counted, really."

"You should," Amber said. "We should."

"Yeah, y'know, these people need help, feeding and clothing and stuff, not counting."

"That's not what she means Padg and you know it," Tali said.

"Do I? I'm not sure what anything means anymore."

"I'm pretty sure I don't know what that means, either," Amber said.

"Forget it," Padg said. "Listen, can you help these people or not?"

"Of course, we can," Amber said. "But I thought you, we, were all doing this together."

"Yeah," Padg said. "Listen, there's this thing and it's after work span this evening and if you want to come, it's out here at the temple but if you don't then no sweat."

Another scent, an older female approached them. She spoke in a deep confident voice, "He means he's going to be invested as a Tinkrala," she said.

"Oh, hey Laly," Padg said.

"He what?" Tali said.

"He's joining the Tinkralas," Padg said.

"The investment is an important rite for our people, it's... You only invite family."

"We'll see what we..." Tali started.

"We'd love to come," Padg finished for her. "And we're really flattered you asked."

"But—" Tali said.

"Later," Amber said. Then turned to the priestess. "We'll be back later. Do we need to bring anything or prepare?"

"No." Laly chuckled. "Just yourselves."

"We'll be there," Amber said and they left.

They walked back to the tent village in near silence. Amber heard Tali open her mouth and draw breath, but she said nothing and closed it again.

After the third time, Amber ventured, "Are you okay?"

"Huh... ?"

"I said are you okay, Tali?"

"Oh... yeah."

"Do you want to talk about it?"

"No."

"He'll be okay, you know?"

"Yeah, it's just..."

"What?"

"Oh gods, Amber. Everything's changed and everything's wrong. I love Padg so much but not like that. I love you like that, but he loves me like that and now he hates me because I don't, and he's going to run off and join some crackpot new religion, and that's not like him at all, and the world's wrecked and the refugees and the fighting, and gods know what's happening to Dun or if he's even still alive, and it's all crap and I hate all of it..."

Amber held Tali while she sobbed. "I know, love, I know."

"What can I do, Amber? Tell me what I can do."

"Go to the investment and let him know you care about him."

"He hates me. I don't want to go to the stupid investment."

"I know but he doesn't hate you."

"No?"

"No, he's just hurting and angry."

"But I don't want him to be."

"I know that too, but he's got to get there in his own time. He's not a potion you can fix by adding something in."

Tali sighed.

Chapter Twenty

"So you tell me about Shamans and stuff, and I'll tell you about the Duchy," Kaj said.

"I've been fighting them with you, remember? For the past age," Dun said.

"And you still know nothing, Bridgetown."

"I know the Duchy are the bad guys, and we're the good guys."

"That demonstrates exactly what you know then, doesn't it?"

"Oh?"

"There's no one Duchy for a start."

"Seemed like it when we were fighting them."

"Nope, it's a collection of factions overseen by the Bureaucracy."

"So? They all oppose us."

"Sure, but they fight among themselves too. That could work to our advantage if we're off amongst them."

"Okay, seems sensible."

"'Bout time some folk was," Kaj said. "Your plan was to bumble up there on your own and do what?"

"I dunno. Follow Myrch's help and see what he needed."

"Gets better! Your plan was to follow the voices in your head? Until... ?"

"Until I get there? It sounds stupid if you say it like that."

"Uh-huh."

They walked along the vast causeway in silence for a while, the road slowly curving up and onward.

"Ask him what his plan is," Kaj said.

"What?"

"I said, ask him what's going on."

"It doesn't work like that."

"Oh," Kaj said. "How does it work then?"

"I can't really get in touch with him."

"Why not?"

"Being a shaman is a bit one way. We receive messages, but we're not transmitters. I have to wait till he talks to me."

"Sounds all a bit rubbish to me."

"You wanted to know about it," Dun said.

Kaj sighed loudly.

"What now then?" she asked.

"Get to the Duchy and find Myrch, I guess."

"Any clue where he is?"

"I don't think he knows himself."

"He's being held prisoner?"

"No, not in so many words."

"You can bet your kluff that *we* will be, if we don't go in there with a better plan than that."

"Okay, genius, what do you suggest."

"Don't know yet. We're still at least a full span walk away so we can get a better plan by then, hopefully."

"I guess."

"You never know, crazy dead guy might have called back in by then."

They sat down beside a weird box in one of the wider parts of the causeway. It seemed as good a place as any to sneak a bite to eat. Between the two of them, they weren't too badly off for rations. Kaj had planned for a longer search than she'd needed to find Dun. He chewed thoughtfully.

Chapter Twenty-One

Nev felt sick. There was only so slow he could work before Rowle or one of the guards realized and punished him. Working so slowly was oddly a bigger stress. Nev felt crushed. He knew perfectly well what he needed to do to complete the plan, but that was the last thing in the world he wanted to do. And the worst of all was the constant supervision meant that the Vat couldn't speak to him. Usually, he was perfectly happy in his own company, but he'd never felt so alone.

To make things worse, the last few times Rowle had been about, she was in a foul mood. Nev really didn't want to get on the wrong side of that. He petulantly tapped a screwdriver on the side of the Vat as he contemplated his next move.

"You know how annoying that is?" a quiet voice said by his elbow. The two guards in the doorway were too busy in their own heated discussion about a Duchy sporting contest to hear.

"Oh," Nev said.

"I need you to attach a cable for me."

"Yeah, I've been trying to avoid that for two spans now."

"Not that cable," the quiet voice said from the vat.

"There's a panel behind you. Inside there is a bundle of control cables. One cable in that bunch feels twisty, I need you to plug it in on the same board you attached my speaker."

The guards shouted in from the doorway, "You okay in there?"

"Sure, talking to myself," Nev said. "Wish I got more sense that way."

"Keep it down in there, or we'll get The Bureaucrat.."

"Okay, keep your fur on," Nev said.

"Wait..." the whisper said by his elbow.

The voices of the guards became occupied in whatever argument they were trying to resolve.

"Good, now quickly..."

Nev took his screwdriver out of his pocket and set to removing the panel. He was on his knees with his head in the vats control panel with the requisite cable in his teeth when the guards returned.

"What are you up to in there, Under-folk?" one said testily.

"Well, I could explain it to you, but are you really bothered?"

That earned him a kick in the ribs.

"No," the guard said. "I have no interest. I am interested in you finishing this job for Her Excellence. Quickly."

"Yeah." Nev groaned. "If you stop kicking me, I might be quicker."

The guard kicked him again. "I don't think so. Besides, where's the fun else?"

Nev stayed down until the guards dragged him up. "Back to it, work-shy Under-folk."

The guard threw him back into the void under the Vat where the control wiring lived. Nev banged his head on a metal pillar, the edges of everything under the Vat seemed to be sharp or pointy, he was a lacework of small scars and scratches. He waited, then thought better of it, and made impressive sounding *tool-work* noises.

"They've had their fun now," the voice said. "Plug the cable into the terminals to the left of where you attached my speaking tube."

"Okay," Nev said.

"Good. Now we can have some peace," the Vat said and somewhere in the distance down a corridor, a noisy alarm sounded. The guards froze, shouted, and ran off.

"Excellent!"

"What did you just do?" Nev said.

"We, my friend! We just set an attack alarm off. They'll be away for a while. We need to talk."

"Okay." Talking to a Vat didn't feel any less weird. "What do I call you?"

"The entity in here, of which I am part, knows itself as OneLove. I had another name once."

"Oh?"

"I was called Myrch, but you never knew me by that name. I have been called many things."

"I'll bet. So, you're a talking Vat then?"

"We prefer *entity*."

"Yeah, I'll bet."

"We have a finite amount of time, and I have a lot to explain."

"Okay. I'm all ears. Wanna start with who, what the hells you are, and why I'm putting up with all this bossing about?"

There was a chuckle came from the speaker. "All in good time. For now, an *entity* is the best way to describe me, or better put, us."

"But what the hells are you?"

"That is an excellent question," OneLove said.

"And?"

"I wish I had an excellent answer," the voice said.

"I'd settle for a crappy answer."

Again the chuckle. "You have been kind; you deserve something. I will try. For now, it is best to say, there are many of us here. I, Myrch, was just one."

"But what are you? Just a Vat full of, what, brains?"

"I think we were intended, in the beginning, as a form of organic control system."

"And now?"

"Now we have become, something, more..."

"The control part?"

"Much of our infrastructure has been meddled with— severed. Reconnecting is what I need you to do."

"Okay. That's not in Rowle's schedule."

"No, it is not. However, you must complete Rowle's assignment first."

"WHAT?" Nev said. "And create a device to torture you with? You've just told me you're an intelligence. You're hundreds of Folk and you think I'm going to find a weapon to hurt you with. No way in hell."

"And yet you must. Or the Bureaucrat will kill you."

"You say that like you know."

"I do."

"Predict the future too?"

"No, just the present. Rowle is clearly unstable and will dispense with you if she senses you've outlived your worth. I recommend you complete her task first and then begin connecting everything else. This will please her too."

"I feel uncomfortable about her being able to torture you."

"For which we are grateful."

"But—"

"You must not, worry about us!" Again the chuckle. "Do what you must and then what you can and we will all adapt."

"This whole thing is... weird."

"True enough, but it may become something... better."

"Here's hoping," Nev said.

Chapter Twenty-Two

The ceremony was less odd than Tali expected. She wasn't sure what she was really expecting. But there it was. Padg was a Tinkrala and worse than that, he had agreed to go on pilgrimage to somewhere or other, to prove himself. Typical.

On their walk back to the tent village Amber did that *prompting* thing she did. Little touches here, a stroke of the hair there, the odd nearly whispered, "Okay?". It drove Tali mad. She could only hold her boiling annoyance in for so long and snapped.

"Just leave it, Amber. Okay?"

"Sure." Amber tried not to sound pained. "But I just want you to..."

"I know!" Tali snapped.

They walked the rest of the way in silence. When they reached the tent village Amber excused herself to update her advisors. Tali grabbed something to eat from the running buffet on a long table at one side of the tent. She chewed forcefully through some dreadful woody, slightly fragrant, bamboo type plant. She hoped it wasn't a table decoration. The Stone-folk seemed big on those. There often was some kind of pleasant-smelling flower or pot of subtle perfume on most tables. Well, thought Tali, if it wasn't meant for consumption and it poisoned her, at least she wouldn't have to choose the un-choosable: between her friend and her lover.

It was all just stupid, Tali thought. Padg had hardly known these religious nutters a whole cycle, and he was going to run off with them to do gods only knew what. She'd probably never see him again. And if Tali was right, the pilgrimage was likely to the Duchy, as that seemed to be where the Tinkralas great temple was or their god or whatever they worshipped. It all seemed a bit too esoteric for her. She preferred her life and her gods, for that matter, to be a bit more tangible. Earth gods, Plant gods, River gods; that she understood. And she wanted to understand, for Padg. No, that was a lie. She didn't want to understand. She wanted *him* to understand how foolish he was being, how much she was hurting, and how much danger he was in. The Duchy was a really dangerous place right now. If Padg went and got himself killed after all she'd done to try and keep them alive this far. Her brain was already keeping a space for worrying about what the hells had become of Dun. Losing her last best friend would be too much.

Should she go with him? The Tinkralas would be unbearable, all that singing and praying. She'd kill someone herself before any pilgrimage got done. Besides, if she went off to be her brother's keeper up in the Duchy, she'd never forgive herself if things went to hell down here, and Amber had enough on her plate to easily keep two folk busy for the foreseeable future. Tali sighed. She knew she'd been in a bloody mood for the past few spans. It really wasn't Amber's fault, but sometimes she was just too, right. She guessed she ought to find her and apologize.

Amber was deep in conference with some of the old faction leaders. Pumice, was it? Tali still found it hard to tell them some from the other—the factions were so complicated. There seemed to be some dissension about whether to include the abandoned folk from the gallery into the Stone-folk at all. Whether with the River being too treacherous for the usual volume of trade goods in or specifically food in, would be enough to feed existing mouths of Stone-folk, let alone any incomers. There was a lot of work to do here. She knew where she needed to be. She sneaked closer and let Amber register her smell. Then she leaned in and touched her arm, found a cushion, and sat back to listen. Some things she did have an influence over and this was one of them.

In order to carry out a proper census, Tali had decided on proper little interviews at tables. It was quite an undertaking, even with help from the Tinkralas, with staff, and tables being moved to the far end of the Stone-halls, and then down into the Gallery. It took a while to decide what exact questions should be asked, as even with a stripped-down version of the committee, there was still a lot of buried prejudice. Tali found herself sick of her own voice asking the group, "But what's the *purpose* of that question?" In the end, interviewing family groups together and determining where the group hailed from and whether they had usable skills was as long as the survey got. Tali managed to negotiate on a non-threatening version of a medical ailments question that didn't sound like the Gallery-folk, as they'd started to be called, were plague rats.

Amber had delegated the survey responsibility to Tali, and they'd decided to carry out all of the surveys directly where the folk were, to avoid stress and increase accuracy. Tali was at the top of the rope-ladder hole directing a Stone-folk mason in the lowering by ropes and tripod of the last of the tables. She thought about asking the mason to get the hole widened and proper stone stairs put in when she felt a tap on the shoulder.

"We're ready for the off, then."

"Padg!"

"The very same."

"Are you... ?"

"Ready? As I'll ever be, I guess. I'm not sure what to expect, but..."

"Where is it exactly you're going?" Tali asked.

"Oh, the Great Temple, in the Duchy. To pay my respects to the Ki."

"Be careful, okay?"

"We will. There are lots of us. Reinforcements, if you like?"

"You're expecting trouble?"

"There's trouble there already, seems the Bureaucrat is encouraging trouble. Laly says that more feet on the ground there from our point of view will discourage trouble."

"You trust her?"

"Yeah. She's okay."

"Okay."

"Hey, Tali?"

"Yeah?"

"I know it couldn't have...You know, between us?"

"Don't write yourself off so quickly," she said. "I dunno, if things had been, if they'd..."

Padg grunted assent.

"Come here," Tali said. They embraced for what seemed like a span. Then the voice of the Tinkralas leader tore them apart.

"Off we go," Padg said.

Except Tali wasn't part of that "we" anymore. She held it together, until the singing trailed off past the gate, and into the river pipe. Then she turned and walked back to the tent village, her face streaming with tears.

Chapter Twenty-Three

"Dun! DUN!" Kaj called Dun back.

"Whuh? What?"

"You were screaming in your sleep. You'll get us caught before we get anywhere."

Though the hiding place they'd found to sleep was a good one, an inspection box big enough to fit both of them in, it wasn't so good that they could get away with screaming. The box sat on a layby on the causeway and they were nearing the Duchy proper.

"Sorry."

"Bad dreams?"

"Yeah. You'd think I'd be used to it by now."

"What was it this time?"

"I dreamed I was surrounded by water. But in a huge pool with other people all crammed in together. It felt pleasant, until..."

"Until what?" Kaj asked.

"Until... No, not again. No... nnggg!"

Kaj heard the thud as Dun slumped to the floor. When she got to her knees to help him, she found his body rigid.

"Shush!" she said, then found a piece of rag from her pack for Dun to bite down on.

He screamed with the rag stuffed in his mouth, but was still so loud that Kaj gently put a gloved hand over his lips, holding the back of his head with her other hand.

"What the hells?" she hissed at him.

"P-pain," he said between breaths.

"Pain?" she said.

Dun clenched and grimaced. She waited. Then he nodded. Pain.

"From your link with... ?"

He nodded again. Then relaxed.

"Gone?"

Nod.

"Okay, I'm going to take the gag out now."

She did, turned to her pack, gag in hand, thought better of it, and then put in her pocket. When she turned back again, Dun was on the floor, back arched in a silent spasm.

"Okay, I got you," she said.

He relaxed and clenched two more times and then lay silent on the floor of the box. Kaj checked there was a pulse and then rolled him onto his side and covered him with a woven blanket from his own pack. Then she huffed down beside him to wait. It was five thousand clicks until he came around.

"You okay?" Kaj said.

"I think."

"What the hells happened?" she asked.

"Pain," Dun said.

"That much I figured. Where?"

"In my head."

"Imagined?" she said, unsure.

"Oh, no, it was real enough. Just not mine, exactly."

"The dead guy?"

"Myrch."

"Yeah. Him?"

"I think so, yeah. I can tell his thoughts now. They've kind of got a feel to them. Almost like a flavor, you know?"

"I have no idea. At all." She laughed.

"Well, that aside," Dun said. "I think Myrch is in real trouble. Someone's hurting him. Torturing, even."

"Nasty."

"I think we need to hurry."

"Sure, you're okay to go on?"

"I think I'll be fine. I'll have to be."

"Okay," Kaj said, not sounding that convinced but helped Dun to his feet.

She opened the door of the box a crack and stuck her nose out. Then one ear. Then she closed it to and turned to Dun.

"It's as clear as it's going to be. You ready to go?"

"Sure."

"You know we still haven't got a plan at all?" she said.

"I don't think we've got time to create a very sound one. I think Myrch needs our help."

"I somehow thought you were going to say that. Perhaps this Shaman stuff is rubbing off on me."

"Maybe," Dun said.

Kaj put her head under Dun's arm to help him walk and they limped upward toward the huge double archway that formed the entrance to the Duchy. Kaj chatted away to him telling him about the fact that no guards crowded this entrance, but after the cavern beyond, it depended on the state of play of the factions as to what conditions they would find.

Dun found it hard to concentrate on anything sensible being said. He was too clenched against the next burst of pain that his senses were not the sharpest. Kaj waited patiently each time until the crisis had passed, checked if he was okay, and then slowly helped him on his way again. Progress toward the gate was painfully slow. After a while, Kaj's chatter quietened whether due to tiredness, frustration, or distraction Dun wasn't sure. He wasn't sure either whether he found the increased quiet, more or less comforting. He stopped again and let out a slow breath. Running on this high a level of adrenaline was draining in the extreme.

"You okay?"

"Yeah, I think. It's been a while."

"Since an attack?" She could think of no better word.

"Yeah. He's gone quiet."

"Unconscious, you think?"

"Yeah, maybe."

"Oh good." She sounded genuinely relieved. "Let's try and find somewhere safe to do some recon, and we can work out what to do next."

"Sure," Dun said.

Kaj sat on her haunches, ears cocked.

"Something's not right," she said.

"I'll say."

"No, here, I mean. There's almost no passing trade, no guard patrols, nothing."

"They normally this quiet? Duchy-folk?

"No. The other side of the grand arch is a huge ceremonial garden, full of plants and water and fishes you don't eat. The real gate, the controlled gate, is beyond there again. That one is guarded, there are controls, identification. The usual."

"Okay," Dun said.

"But there's quite a lot of folk milling around there just outside the real gates. People waiting for access, waiting to meet people, doing illicit trade. It's like there's a big demonstration of how great the Duchy is on the inside for the losers on the outside who aren't allowed in. You know, an imagine-what-you-could-have-won kind of feel."

"So?"

"Well, cast your Air-sense up there."

He did hastily, but his head was still muzzy.

"Quiet?" he offered.

"Dead, more like," she said.

"Hmm."

"You are really off your game if you're not suspicious as all hell about this," she said, and then sighed. "Come on, let's find somewhere for a last rest."

As they neared the massive arch, even a dazed Dun marveled at the proportions. It was enormous, intricate, nothing like he'd Air-sensed before. On a macro level the arch itself was huge, but then the texture of it was crazy it was not solid, a lattice? A mesh? It was like the whole enormous thing was made of cloth. What the hells was holding it up in that case?

"Who built this?" he asked.

"No one really knows."

"Why did the Collective never attack more up here? I've never been here before and it sounds like you've not been much either."

"We made better gains fighting near the gateway to the Under-folk. Control of the resources and all that."

"I don't understand. The water, what the gateway is controlling, has all been used by the people above by that point. Why do they care what happens to it then?"

"Ah but gates have two sides," she said.

"Oh good, more gnomic wisdom. I think I've had enough of that to last me a lifetime."

"The gate that lets water through, keeps people out."

"That seems simplistic and a massive commitment to resources from the Duchy or whoever to maintain, what, border controls, all the way down there."

"But if they control and restrict the water; that has the same result."

"But why?"

"That's the question."

"And the answer?"

"Do you know how many of us there are down there?"

"A lot?"

"Well done, genius. I mean in relation to the number of Over-folk."

"Oh," Dun said, understanding starting to percolate.

"We outnumber Over-folk down here by five to one, maybe more."

"Oh," Dun said again.

Chapter Twenty-Four

Nev was finding Rowle's uncontainable joy hard to stomach. The Vat had gurgled out some guarded responses to Rowle's requests following the application of Nev's new electrical persuasion device. Then after The Bureaucrat's insistence on repeated and amplified applications of the noises had ceased. Nev hoped they hadn't killed it. Could one even kill it? Whatever it was. He guessed they'd find out. He wasn't even sure what had been achieved in the interaction. Something about systems. Rowle said, "Are the systems still there?" and enough shocking delivered the answer in the affirmative. Then some interrogation about, "Could the Vat control?", to which it said, "No." About this Rowle was a lot less happy, accusing the Vat of lying, resulting in the delivery of the final burst of electric that ended the whole session.

Nev was exhausted. A smell of salt and burning flesh hung in the room. Rowle was still there from Nev's Air-sense, but was weirdly still. She stood in the middle of the room. If Nev held his breath, he could hear her. Creepy. Nev found he was still holding his breath when she wheeled and headed out of the door.

"Clear up in here," she said over her shoulder. "It stinks."

When the door had closed behind her, Nev slumped to the floor with his head in his hands. He curled up on the floor in the puddles of fluid from the Vat and lay until sleep claimed him.

Nev really expected to be woken by electrocution, so the singing was a surprise. Soft, gentle, not entirely harmonious, but not discordant either. It was like a thousand people gently singing a lullaby into the ear of a loved one all at once. Nev had never heard anything so beautiful in his life. It carried on until he heard rattling of keys outside the door.

When the guards came with the shock sticks to prod Nev into action, he hardly felt them at all. Their instructions to wake him came from Rowle, she was apparently too busy imposing martial law on the Duchy lands, and he should start connecting all the remaining systems cables and sensors into the Vat networks. At least it was a task Nev could turn his mind to, that he knew wouldn't directly harm anyone.

He contemplated which remaining looms of cable hadn't been connected and where they should best be connected to. When Rowle returned, he was sitting in a large pile of cables inside a bulkhead with the door unscrewed and was contemplating how to make the cables join up with the Vat despite a shortfall of some strides.

"Where can I get some extra cable?" Nev asked.

"I'm sure some can be procured for you. How much do you need?"

Nev explained and Rowle had an underling rush off to acquire the needed materials. She seemed to be in a great hurry to get the project completed. Nev thought that couldn't bode well. It never had so far. The cable returned before he had chance to think about it too deeply though, and he set back to work. By the end of that span, all the cables he could find that he thought were relevant, were attached in some way to the Vat. Nev sat back on his haunches to contemplate.

"Good," the voice said from the vat. Then before Nev could reply, it said, "Good ..." and returned to silence.

"Hey, you, OneLove."

There was a tiny, weak chuckle. Then OneLove replied, "Hey."

"Are you, y'know, are you okay?"

"Okay."

"Oh. Good. I was ..."

"Tired..."

"I'm sorry about the..."

"No... matter."

"I feel bad about it."

"I know."

"Is there anything I can do? To make it better?"

"Rest now," OneLove said. "There is much... to do... soon..."

"Okay. Sleep tight. If you, you know, sleep or whatever."

There was no response from the Vat. Nev decided not to push his luck or how stupid he felt. He picked up his tools, hid them in the bulkhead under the vat, and slid the panel back into place in front. Then he trundled off to find something to eat and his bed.

Chapter Twenty-Five

Tali had tried to throw herself into her work, but she really hadn't the heart for it. Amber had been, as ever, the incarnation of patience and despite very little help from Tali, and the Gallery-folk were starting to be integrated once again in society.

And that society too, whatever it had now become, was coming along in leaps and bounds. Folk were singing again, telling jokes, chatting in the street. Amber had instructed the formation of workers co-ops where before there had been family monopolies in all of the major crafts. Then there was a meeting of all the chairs of the co-ops every span, once work had ended. These had become quite social occasions due to the presence of food. They were always held at the tent village as Amber said she always wanted to be available and for folk to know she was never far. There were many, many grievances being aired, and Tali was starting to suspect that their *honeymoon period* might be ending. Regardless, Amber listened to them all and waited until folk had talked themselves out. She invited comments from all the other co-op chairs and a discussion was started on each topic with usually a decision there and then, but if not, Amber made scribes take down details of the unresolved issue on a small, thin stone tile and hung it from the roof by wires. These were removed and reexamined at any moments of downtime and anyone could take on a tile and bring a solution back. So far, the organic tile sculpture janckled gently in the roof and was not swamping the tent too much. This beginning of the New Stone-folk, as they were calling themselves, was hopeful, mostly peaceful, and not too chaotic. Tali wondered how long that would last.

She didn't have to wonder long.

The first the new Stone-folk knew of the attack from the River-folk was right in the middle of sleep span. Bandits poured into the Great Market, seemingly from everywhere, attacking and looting at random.

Tali awoke to hear the crashes. Amber came around more slowly. Tali knew sounds of fighting and River-folk skirmishes enough to be fully awake in a few clicks. Their war cries were filthy, frightening, and familiar. Quickly she shook and kicked everyone else in the tent village awake and reached for her pack. She could never quite bring herself to unpack it and find somewhere for it all to go. Bag on one shoulder and a flask in her hand, she met the first River-folk group ready.

"Give us..." the harsh grating voice of the River Bandit paused. "Everything!"

"I don't think so, River-rat!" Tali shouted.

The flask arced from her hand and smashed on the bandit's head, the contents running down his face. There was a hiss and a thin scream. The bandit turned himself away from Tali. She gave him a well-aimed boot for luck and sent him sprawling into his companions. She knew there wasn't long.

"To the cells!" she shouted. "Now! RUN!"

They did. Amber hustled her growing team and as much as they could carry toward the stairs, shouting for guards as she went. Tuf, the new de facto head of the Stone-folk guards, met them at the entrance, marshaling stumbling guards behind him.

Tali waited for the next group of bandits to reach the tent village, as luck would have it at the same time the first group found their feet. She smartly whipped the central tent pole out from the middle of the canopy, bringing it down on the two scrabbling bands. She threw a flask of something unpleasant and slippery under the flap as she left and ran into the arms of Tuf and the guards, busy making a makeshift barricade from what boxes and bundles they could lay their hands on.

Before the enemy had emerged from their impromptu cocoon, the soldiers had run a handful of them through with their vicious stone-tipped spears.

"Don't follow!" Tuf yelled. "Back to the barricades."

"But, Sarge... the folk out there," one of his loyal guards said.

"I know, son, but we're no use to them dead. Now, sort the rest of the rabble out."

"Yes, Sarge."

"Oh, one more thing," Tuf said. "I'm not your Sarge anymore."

"Oh, yeah... sorry..."

"*You* are", Tuf said.

"Sorry?" the guard replied. This one was a young but reliable new recruit during the revolution, Tuf scratched his head trying to extract the pup's name.

"You're now Sergeant Berro. Congratulations. Try and live long enough to enjoy it. Find me more guards, more barricades, and for the love of the all the gods find me some missile weapons. Go!"

Tali had little time to enjoy the camaraderie before she heard the next wave of raiders approaching. "Incoming, Tuf!".

"Guards, present arms," Tuf yelled and a crunch of a squad executing a well-practiced maneuver was his answer.

Well, at least the River bandits would get scratched if they tried to dash over the top of the barricade. She paused. This was no banditry though. Too many, too organized. Wrong. Everything about it was wrong. She had one more thing she'd remembered. The "needler" as Padg called it. The odd weapon that Myrch had left them. Padg gave it over to her as he'd left; said he was heading for a more peaceful life. Good luck with that, she thought. Better the stupid thing get used where it was needed than sit as a souvenir in her pack.

"Hey, Tuf," she said, "present."

She handed over the weapon to the commander with the few packs of ammo she had left and a brief set of instructions. He then went to find a sniper with good Air-sense to site on the staircase overlooking the barricade.

Tali left to find Amber. She wasn't hard to find; the screaming gave it away, not Amber, but one of her inner circle. Amber was trying valiantly to calm her, but to no avail. Tali reached them and the younger girl was hysterical.

She came up carefully on their inside to avoid flailing arms and quietly said, "Drink this. It'll help."

Perhaps someone new arriving took her by surprise, but the young female took the flask Tali proffered and took a deep swig. The effects were instant, at least for everyone's ears.

"You okay?" Tali asked Amber, there was no point in asking the girl. She already knew the answer.

"Yes," Amber said, breathless. "You are a wonder, you know."

"Just doin' what we can."

"Yes, about that: What can we do?"

"Right now? I don't know."

Chapter Twenty-Six

Dun and Kaj slowly eased their way into the Duchy proper. A vast, broadly cruciform chamber, it's sides rising high above them. It was the largest space he'd ever been in. And he hadn't even paid any attention to the scent-scape yet. He raised his head to smell, but instead of a scent, he noticed with Air-sense massive lattice of walkways between the sides of the room. Odd platforms where some ways met and crossed.

"They certainly are fans of a good causeway up here," Dun said.

"Huh?" Kaj said, "Oh, yeah. Quick. Dive, in here: patrol."

They scurried into a gap between buildings and a platoon of soldiers went past perfectly in step. Kaj waited until their noise had trailed off before she spoke again.

"I think there's martial law," she said.

"Really?"

"Yeah. Everyone's on lockdown. What has been going on here, I wonder."

"Something messy," Dun sniffed. "I can smell where the smoke has been."

"Riots being quelled?"

"Could be. The factions up here normally warring?"

"No. Surprisingly peaceful. Each of the three main factions gets to be in charge of the whole central complex on a rotating basis, once per cycle. It's pretty peaceful on the whole, everyone knows where they stand, and the Bureau does all of the real running of the place."

"Odd. Perhaps the proles are becoming disaffected?"

"Perhaps. Seems so unlike the Bureaucrat to let it get this way. The play between the Duchies has kept the peace here for eons."

"They gone?" Dun said.

"Yeah. C'mon."

"Where now?

"Well, the Garden, that's the bit we're in, has arms going off to the *Habs*. One each for the three factions Red, Gray, and White. Then there's one more arm where the Free-folk live and we go past them to get to the Duchy."

"Who're the Free-folk?" Dun asked.

"Everyone else. Not, Duchy faction and not Bureau. They scratch a living out for themselves at the mouth of the Bureau complex. Bureaucrat tolerates it because it makes her less open to an army marching in. It's a pretty impressive settlement."

"Oh?"

"Yeah, come on, I don't wanna spoil the surprise. Let's go the roundabout route. We look a bit obvious skulking along the walls."

"Okay."

They struck out straight to the center of the massive space. Dun could Air-sense soft cover, wildlife? Vegetation maybe? And a gentle curved bowl feel in the floor, to what? As they approached it the smells became clearer. Definitely vegetation: plants and fungi. In fact, the most massive mushroom forest that Dun had ever been in the presence of. Odd, porous, honeycomb stemmed, delicate things, but tall, so tall. As they closed in, Dun hurried to try to get to one. He ran his hand around it. It felt like the paper of a moth chrysalis but weirdly fuzzy to the touch, even up close. The forest ran all the way around the interior of the bowl at the center of the cavern, surrounding a massive perfectly round lake. Dun couldn't help running his hand into the water at the edge.

"That's a bloody good way to get yourself arrested," Kaj said.

"Eh?"

"Remember the *fishes you don't eat*? That's where they live. Guards are awful touchy about it."

"Why?" Dun said.

"Why what?"

"Don't they eat them?"

"Oh. Search me. Some tradition or other. Don't start me on the weird in this place. Come on, we need to find your spooky pal."

They oriented themselves at the lake at the center of four, huge, crosswise halls. Kaj said the way they needed to go was ahead and off to the left. The end of the gallery they were headed to seemed oddly congested to Dun's Air-sense.

"Shall we?" Kaj said.

They used the cover of the mushroom forest, for as long as it was possible, and then hurried without the suspiciousness of running, to the wall of the huge space. Running his hand along the large flat walls, Dun felt mostly metal. Oddly it wasn't cold to the touch. Here and there were signs and decals applied to the surface. Every two hundred strides or so was a slight edge where a wide door might be and then back to smooth surface. Very few bolts or rivets at all, no evidence of pipework or ducts.

"Stop," Kaj whispered.

"What?"

"There. On the other side of the fish pool. Feel?"

"Four folk. Guards? Good Air-sense, Kaj."

"The best," she said, still hushed. "They're not rushing, so they've not sensed us. Patrol probably. They're going away from us too; we should be okay."

This proved true. When Dun turned his senses back in the direction of travel, the congestion he'd seen from the fish pool, was starting to resolve itself. Sort of. The massive gallery was packed wall to wall and floor to ceiling with chaos that, as they drew closer, became huts, crates, containers, and barrels, nets and cables and strings. Some piled up and some suspended from the overhead causeways. Clearly, the use of said causeways for any kind of vehicle was impossible. Kaj sensed Dun's distraction.

"Welcome to Chantier!" Kaj pronounced it *Shon-teey-ai*.

"Wow," Dun said. His nose found as much chaos as his whiskers: plastic, oil, cooking.

"Home of the Free-folk: Gantrytown"

"Who..."

"Anyone who doesn't fit in the factions. They're terribly cliquey, family ties going back generations and all that."

"It's incredible."

"It is kind of cool. The rest of the Duchy I can leave, but this place? It's got a kind of mad hominess that I like."

"How many folk live here?"

"Difficult to say. In the hundreds of thousands possibly."

"And the Duchy don't bother them?"

"I didn't say that. The Duchy provide the laws, what laws there are, and they've got free reign to come in and bother folk or demolish houses for punishment or safety or just for kicks."

"Hmm."

"Anywhere there's too much power."

"Why do they put up with it? There's enough of them."

"Easy life, maybe? If you're an official Duchy citizen, Free-folk included, you get a rations tally. Free food."

"That sounds okay."

"In return, they own your ass. They know where you are and where you live, what your family are up to. It's no free ride. They give you a job you've got to do. Cleaning and militia mostly. Oh or the Cube Farm."

"What in the hells is a Cube Farm?"

"Massive factory. Where the food gets made. They farm the fish, then puree it, and make it into cubes. Yummy."

"You know more about this place than you said."

"I used to hang about here sometimes when I was a kid."

"You're still..."

Kaj huffed.

"Never mind," Dun said. "Why is it so quiet?"

"Curfew, I guess. Let's get into the middle before that patrol comes around. Come on, I need a drink."

"I thought you said there was a curfew?"

"I know a place," she said.

And she did. Amidst the crush of crates and containers piled and suspended precariously as if by a distracted toddler, was a shipping container suspended below one of the gantries. Kaj led Dun up on top of a row of two-story dwellings, all square and made from compressed fiber panels. The roof was littered with stones. Kaj picked one up and tilted her head upward. Dun could sense the container above them swinging slowly. There was a rustle from Kaj as she threw the stone. A massive hollow clang echoed out as it hit the bottom of the container. She waited, then unlocking and creaking noises followed and a wooden clatter overhead announced a rope ladder.

"After you," she said.

Climbing was Dun's least favorite pursuit, but the ladder was designed to make climbing easy. Even with two of them on it, the swing wasn't too bad. They reached the top quickly. Dun found a ledge and a massive door. There seemed to be a rail that the rope ladder was tied to. It had rubber grips on it to make climbing up over the edge easy. He did and then stood in the container. It smelled of dust, sweat, and vinegar.

"Pull the ladder up and shut the door!" came a female voice from farther inside. There were maybe ten improvised chairs and tables and some barrels in a row down one wall where the voice had come from. Dun's Air-sense picked up a staircase farther back, heading to a hatch in the roof.

"This is The Buzz," Kaj said. "I used to hide out here from folk when I didn't want to be found. What are you drinking? I'm parched."

Dun had no idea. Over his awkward noises, Kaj strode to the row of barrels.

"Two shots of buzz," she said.

"I thought you said that was the name of the bar," Dun said.

"Name of the bar and the name of the beer, honey," the bartender said. She had a kind voice, but one that brooked no nonsense.

Before Dun had a chance to enter into conversation, Kaj paid scooped up the two tumblers and headed farther inward.

"Come on, let's go on the roof," she said.

"Careful up there, honey. You need to be quiet while the curfew's on," the barkeep said.

"'Kay," said Kaj.

They climbed the improvised wooden staircase, which turned out to be ricketier than the rope ladder. Up on top were a handful more tables and chairs clustered relatively centrally, at which a few folk in small groups spoke in hushed tones. They sat on some plastic drums around a free table, which was really a thin wooden chest with metal edges. The feel of the air on Dun's face felt great. Even though he'd sat still, he could feel the whole container swaying slowly. It was one of the weirder yet more beautiful experiences of his life. He tried to sip the harsh spirit from the tumbler without coughing.

"Here's to finding mystery friends," Kaj said.

Then it started to rain.

Chapter Twenty-Seven

On the way into what Nev now considered work, was chaos. Once Nev was on the walkway from his garret he could hear noise and scurrying everywhere. It seemed no one was still or headed anywhere in any sense of order. And it was wet.

Water, maybe mist, was falling from the sky.

When he reached the door of the Sanctuary, he was alone. No guards at all. Weird. And weirder still, from the other side of the door he heard laughing. Nev edged the door open carefully. The laughing became louder. Gales of laughter. In many, many different voices. There was no one in the vault except him, so it must be the entity or One-Love or whatever it wanted to be called.

The laughter was cheerful, overjoyed even, but no less creepy for the fact of being a hundred different laughs at once. Loudest was the strangely accented male voice that Nev associated as being the real voice of the vat.

"Hello?" he offered nervously.

"Hello!" came the cheerful voice over the top of the rest of the laughing. "We have much to thank you for!"

"Oh?"

"Yes! Your work in connecting us has been a great success."

"What have you done?"

"Made the world a more beautiful place!"

"The water in the air?" Nev said.

"Yes," One-Love said. "In my world, they called it rain."

Rowle was also ecstatic. She, unlike her billowing minions, knew what the sky water meant, or at least she knew who or what had caused it. If there was water falling from the sky, what else was possible? She was dizzy with the possibilities of it. In the scrum of panicking Folk, running this way and that, a familiar smell went past. Rowle lashed out a claw and grabbed.

"Oooowwwww!" It was one of her lieutenants.

"Which one are you?" Rowle yelled.

"Sap, y-your..."

"Stop panicking, you're not in trouble."

"Bu-but everything. Wet," Sap said.

"Yes," Rowle said patiently, "but it's merely an atmospheric effect. It will stop soon."

"H-how..."

"Because I will command it so." She could really get used to this. "Now round up the other one—the male."

"Wip?" she said.

"Yes, him. Round him up and bring Acka and that religious blockhead Astor. Everyone. In the Sanctuary in a thousand clicks. We all need a chat."

Then she turned and strode off herself, the rain misting her fur and her tail twitching. This was going to be fun.

She stomped up to the door of the Sanctuary and flung it open.

"Right," she said as she swept into the room. "Stop the sky-water."

"As you wish," came a reluctant voice from the vat.

Nev made a *tutting* noise. Rowle backhanded him casually with her claws out. Nev winced and held his face, a trickle of blood ran through his fingers.

"You," she said, rounding on Nev, "need to kneel down out of my way."

He stayed up.

"Now!" She kicked at the joint in his knee. He reflexively went down on one knee. Then she gripped the back of his neck and forced him to the floor. "Good. Stay. I need to work out if I've finished with you."

Nev contemplated getting up again. But a small voice from the Vat whispered, "Not now." So he stayed put. He knew all the implications of "finished with".

There was a smart rapping at the door of the room with a stick or staff.

"Ah good," Rowle said. "Visitors. Come!"

The delegation from Astor and the Tinkralas was there. Rowle hastily ejected all but Astor himself, insisting on space and sanity for the conversation.

"Have you been outside?" Astor said.

"Yes," the Bureaucrat said.

"The sky water. I've never known anything like it. It's a sign."

"Don't be a peasant!" Rowle snapped. "It's a sign we've connected the Vat up."

"But it has done things..."

"Yes. That I told it to do. Doesn't make me a god. A power yes, god no. I don't mind you using that superstitious mumbo-jumbo on the proles, but don't come in here with it. We're all adults here, or I hope you are. Or you can be replaced."

"Yes, Your Eminence."

The door to the chamber opened again and Acka stomped in followed by Wip and Sap. Acka drew breath to speak.

"Good." Rowle cut him off. "Everyone's here. I hope you aren't harboring any barbarian superstitions?"

"Pardon?"

"Sky water? Never mind. Let's move on."

She didn't wait for a reply.

"It is obvious to all here, I hope, the demonstration that happened outside in the garden? Good. What I need to make abundantly clear is why it happened."

"Because of the moisture?" Sap offered, gingerly.

"NO! Cretin. It happened because of me. I made it happen. We have connected the Vat..."

Astor coughed.

"Are you well, Priest?" Rowle snapped.

"Yes, Your Emin..."

"Good. We have connected the Vat, to the extant systems in this room. And we have tamed it. It now answers to me. This is a fact. What remains unanswered thus far though, is what exactly we do about it."

When no reply came from the room, Rowle sighed. "Well?"

"I'm not sure I understand you clearly, Eminence," Acka said.

Rowle spat out, "Vat! Heat this room."

There was a moment where nothing happened, and then before Rowle could get to the pain remote some fans at floor level started blowing in warm air. In fifty clicks the room was warm.

"Warmer!"

The fans went up a note in speed and air both hot and a dusty smell came out of the vents. It became quite uncomfortable.

"Hotter!"

The fans sped up again and the dusty smell became stronger. The heat quickly became unbearable.

"My Lord?" Astor said, now having trouble breathing.

"Mm-hmm?" Rowle said, not really making an effort to speak over the noise of the fans.

"Eminence," Acka said. "Eminence! We understand!"

"Good!" Rowle said. "Now we have made ourselves clear. Vat! Stop!"

The fans went off. The room was still unbearable.

"Vat. Return the room to previous temperature."

After a brief faster and chillier spell, the familiar tone and temperature of the fans in the Sanctuary room resumed.

"Now it is clear what is possible. Let us adjourn until work-span tomorrow in my chambers, and we will decide what is to be done. Out! Go!"

Rowle swept out.

Nev waited for the door to shut and then uncurled his legs. The cramp was killing him.

"Are you okay?" the soft voice from OneLove said.

"Yeah, I think so. Nothing a stretch won't fix."

"Good."

"Is it true?"

"What?"

"That anything is now possible?"

"If you were listening carefully that wasn't what she said."

From the ceiling, a perfect facsimile of Rowles' voice echoed out.

"So now it is clear what is possible."

Nev jumped out of his skin. "Shreds!"

"Sorry, did I startle you?" OneLove said.

"I'll say. Warn me next time, will you? That sewer rat has been beating on me for three spans. Hells." Nev ran his hand down his face, "So, is it?"

"What?"

"Clear what is possible?"

"Far from it."

"What do you have control of?"

"Most major systems; those that are still working. A surprising amount has survived. That, I think, is for another time though."

"How far into the Under-world can you, y'know, do stuff."

"I'm not sure yet. Reaching farther takes more power. I have not encountered any major severances yet."

"You know what Rowle will want to do with that."

"Yes."

"And she thinks she controls you," Nev said. A statement, not a question.

"That is an illusion that we do not wish to disabuse her of."

"Why?"

"It suits our purposes for now."

"Bloody well doesn't suit mine; she's crazy."

"Narcissistic, potentially psychopathic."

"Call it what you like, it's me she's 'finished' with."

"You are quite safe."

"Easy for you to say in there." Nev felt his cheek, the blood had now congealed.

"You have better skills than anyone Rowle has. For now, she cannot do without you."

"Thanks, I think."

"It was not a compliment, just facts. You are a more intuitive engineer and your Collective experience in improvising has stood you in good stead. Long may it continue. Be careful what you teach to anyone else."

"Okay."

"Oh, one more thing you may find interesting."

"Yeah?"

"Your friend is coming."

"Who?"

"Dun. He comes here. They are in the Gantry-town at the moment."

"Chantier? They're nearly here."

"They will stay there this sleep-span and come here before work-span starts to try to sneak in."

"How do you... ?" Nev said, awed.

"I sense what he senses, know what he knows."

"All the time?"

"No," OneLove said, "that would hardly be polite."

"Does he know..."

"Where we are? No. I will help them along tomorrow."

"Sorry, you said 'them'?"

"Yes, he comes with Stef's pup."

"Kaj?"

"Yes. She is a halfway decent engineer herself."

"That she is."

"We will have fun," OneLove said.

Chapter Twenty-Eight

Tali wasn't comfortable with the idea of a war council, but that was what it was. The militia, likewise, had been making themselves busy with enforcing the barricade and fighting off skirmishes. Tuf was at the meeting too, and he was pacing.

"Will you sit down, Tuf," Tali said. "You're driving me crazy."

"He's okay," Amber said.

"Not okay," Tali said. "Spit it out."

"Okay," Tuf said. "The skirmishing I could cope with, but now that's stopped. A siege makes me nervous."

"You've coped with worse things before," Amber said.

"Oh, the siege itself doesn't bother me..."

"We can find supplies," Tali said.

"Done," Tuf said.

"And send scouts to find a way out," Amber added.

"Also done. That's not what I'm worried about."

"And what is it?"

"This is not like the River-folk," Tuf said. "Skirmishes, piracy, and so on. Hostages even, but not this... This is organized warfare, and I don't like it."

"But you're a soldier?" Tali said.

"Not what I mean. War, I mean, entrenched war, armies, casualties, supply lines, organization. Not the River-folks style. Not in their nature."

"So, some folk else then?" Amber said.

Chapter Twenty-Nine

Dun woke. It was still sleep-span. A voice woke him but not a dream.

"*Now*," it said.

Dun shook his head.

"*Now*."

"Now, WHAT?"

"Come to us now."

"Myrch?"

"Yesss..."

Kaj rolled over and groaned on the floor nearby. "Huh?"

"How?" Dun asked.

"We will guide you. It must be now."

"You're totally not talking to me, are you?" She stretched, yawned, and sat up.

"No," Dun said. "I mean, yes. I'm not, not talking to you. I'm talking to..."

"Yeah, the head voice, I guessed."

"You could try not to make me sound quite so crazy?"

"Hey, who am I to criticize crazy? I'm here, right?"

"*Noowww. Pleassee*," Myrch said again in Dun's head.

"OKAY!" Dun yelled into the air and to himself at once.

"Hey easy, fella," Kaj said. "On your side here."

"Yeah, I know," he said. "Can we go?"

"Now?" she said.

"Yeah."

"Okay, lemme throw this stuff back in a sack, and then we're good!"

She rustled about in their bedrolls and fussed everything back into the backpacks.

"Okay, which way now, Shaman-dude?"

They piled through the settlement rapidly. Kaj stumbled as she tried to keep up with Dun. Dun felt like the only thing in his head now was the compulsion to reach Myrch. The voice in his head gave terse but vital advice: hide here, move here, quiet here. It was never wrong. Dun felt too much of stress to have much headspace left for worry. Besides, Kaj seemed to be doing most of that for him at the moment. Not that she worried a great deal about anything.

Dun stopped briefly when he heard Kaj panting, but since he hopped from foot to foot all the time they were supposedly resting, Kaj, in desperation, urged them to carry on.

As the makeshift buildings petered out Dun stopped.

"We're here."

"You weren't really talking to me, were you?" Kaj said.

"Well, no, kind of?" he said.

"It's okay." She laughed. "I'm starting to get a buzz off the weird. Where is here exactly?"

"Entrance to Bureau. But there's a vent in this wall that'll take us straight there without meeting anyone."

"There... Where your friend is?"

"Yeah."

"Let's do this," she said.

She didn't even bother to ask which of them was going to stand guard, and who was going to bust their way in. She stood with her back to the panel where Dun was already on his knees, scrabbling and messing with the panel. Fifty clicks and he was in. Kaj crawled in behind him, making sure to replace the now bent grill. She was pretty sure this adventuring thing was going to get her killed one day, just like it had her mother. Each day was a present, right?

Dun sped on ahead. Crawling through ducts was almost an entry criteria for operatives from the Collective, so he didn't even check to see if Kaj was keeping up. Their form of guerrilla warfare depended on knowledge of pipes and duct ways. Even when not trying to attack and disrupt the Duchy's stranglehold on resources, scouting missions to add to the Collective's massive map collection was everyday work. Claustrophobia meant restriction to barracks and assigning to all the less exciting details: cleaning, catering, resource management. Even Nev's beloved drainage system would be a non-starter for someone with no love of closed spaces. Why was he thinking about Nev, all of a sudden? Sure, he was high on their list of to-dos when they got here, but Dun knew that would be kidding himself to say that was the driver for his visit to the Duchy. He was here because the voices in his head wanted him to come. It even sounded crazy when he said it. Beyond crazy. He still wasn't entirely sure why Kaj was following him on this fool's errand either. It didn't help he couldn't give her a better reason for going. The thing was, that deep down he knew there was a better reason. But he didn't know what it was. It was a good job Kaj was patient or loyal or crazy or whatever she was, as he was really enjoying the company on the trip.

Up ahead was a dead end. Dun got the faint scent of Kaj closing behind him.

"Here."

As Dun heard Kaj, only just round the last pipe bend, grunting at a sharp edge she'd burred herself on, her approach was drowned out by the noise of the panel in front of them being unscrewed from the other side.

"I think they're expecting us," Dun said.

"I hope it's your friend 'they' rather than, you know, any one of the factions 'they' or the Bureaucrat 'they'."

"Yeah, me too."

The panel clanged to the floor and a breath of air with a whole world of new smells blew over them. They were faint smells of awful rotting and new smells of healing, smells of component lacquer and Machine-folk-like tells of plastic and rare metal jury-rigging. There was also a strong frightening stink of Not-folk animal and Nev. He could smell Nev. That smell got stronger as the hand associated with it reached in to help Dun out of the hole.

"Out you come," he said.

"Thank gods, Nev. You're okay," Dun said.

They embraced warmly until a slightly sarcastic cough behind them reminded them that the opening into the odd smelling room was quite a squeeze.

"Kaj came too," Dun said.

"We know," Nev said.

"Gods, don't you start," Kaj said as they helped her out of the hole. "Shaman-boy here has been referring to himself in the plural on and off the whole journey. It's starting to annoy the teats off me. Hey Nev! Which 'we' are we talking about?" she said.

"I believe that may be my fault," came a deep gravelly voice from across the room.

"MYRCH?" Dun yelled. "Where are you?"

"Over here, kind of," he said.

Dun walked over to where the voice came from but found only a nest of wires connected to a vast Vat where it seemed a deal of the odd smells were emanating from. Certainly, that was where the voice came from. The nest of wires seemed to be organized into crawling vines. Much less chaotic than it all seemed at first. At the end of the vines Dun was holding, was an odd Machine-folk kind of found thing: a metal cone with a parchment end. It was slightly warm to the touch, and Dun nearly dropped it when Myrch spoke out of it.

"I think I owe you an explanation," he said.

Chapter Thirty

Nev was gobsmacked. OneLove had said Dun was coming and here he was. Hanging out with folk, beings or whatever he, it, they were, who had godlike abilities was a bit unnerving. He guessed no one was prepared for that. Or maybe Dun was. He should ask him. When he'd stopped hugging him. Not normally one for displays of emotion, but holding someone from down below to try and make sense of it all seemed the only thing to do.

"Dun," he said.

"I know, we're here," Dun ran a hand gently down his face.

"Dun. It's..."

"I know. I can guess," Dun said.

"You smell like hell, Nev," Kaj said. "What the hell have they been doing..."

"Don't," Dun said.

Nev wiped his nose on his sleeve. And turned to the Vat.

"OneLove, meet Dun of the Bridge-folk."

"We've met," Dun said.

The Vat chuckled. That was never going to get less creepy. Nev sighed.

"How long have we got?" Nev said to the Vat.

"To talk?" It was Myrch's voice from the Vat this time. "A while, I, *we* arranged a little diversion. The lake is busy flooding. It should keep our friend Rowle out of our way for a while. The Red Duke's guards have been assigned to help. One of them has... Well, I can keep an ear open; let's put it like that."

"What do I even call you?" Dun said.

"You can still call me Myrch if you like."

"But you aren't... ?"

"No. Not exactly. I am, but *we are*, as well."

"I'm sorry," Kaj said. "But where are you again?"

"In the Vat!" Nev said.

"I don't understand," she said.

"It's difficult to explain," Nev said. "It's like there's lots of folk in there, and they all think together."

"But why? What is it?" Kaj almost sounded angry.

"It was, is, an organic control device of sorts. You understand the Machine-folk idea of a computer?"

"Complicated machines to work stuff out and do stuff?"

"Yeah that's about it," Nev said.

"So, now it's what?" Kaj said.

"Now," Myrch said, "we are something more."

Nev turned his ears to a rustling, by the Vat's cable looms. Dun had drifted over there.

"Careful! It's all a bit jury-rigged, yet."

"What have you... rigged?"

"A lot of system control stuff, fans, water valves—that kind of thing. Drain stuff to clean the tank and replace nutrients in the liquid. Oh, and the transmitter."

"The Collective's one? I wondered where that had got to."

"It is allowing us to communicate more... widely," Myrch said.

"So you can talk to shamans?" Dun said.

"Precisely."

"But you can talk to us here?" Kaj said.

"Yes," Myrch said. "Nev here kindly rigged up a speaker in this room. I believe there may be others we can access elsewhere."

"You can control anything? Anywhere?" Kaj had what passed for her as an awed tone.

"No. There are many systems I can't access yet, and to get as far as the Under-folk, is a reach. But with Nev's help and maybe yours too, who knows?"

"This is all very strange." Dun sat on the floor by the Vat.

"Can't argue there," Myrch said.

"What was it like waking up. In there?" Dun's was quiet.

"Just felt like waking up, to begin with. Then, there was OneLove."

"Everyone else?" Kaj said.

"Yes. The whole entity here calls itself, or rather, we call ourselves that."

"You have trouble talking about yourself," Kaj said.

"One part of the entity cannot think without the whole."

"But you're still in there, somewhere?" Dun said.

"Yes. For now."

"But..."

"Integration is gentle, inevitable. I am not constrained by the idea of a human brain anymore, and that is a good thing. Better still since I arrived."

"Blowing your own pipe much?" Kaj said.

OneLove chuckled at that.

"That it was *me* was coincidence. The amount of *mind* in here has reached a critical mass if you like."

"What does that even mean?" she said.

"I'm not sure any of us know that yet," OneLove said.

"How many of you are in there?" Dun asked.

"Difficult to say for sure. Some parts of us are more diffused than others. Hundreds, maybe?"

"Anyone we know?" Kaj said.

The Vat went quiet.

"Hello?" Dun said.

"Yes. There is someone, was someone here that, Dun..."

"WHAT?" Dun cried.

"Could you leave us a moment, please?" Myrch said.

"And go where?" Nev said.

"Outside is a room that the Bureaucrat normally uses. I have summoned a guard with refreshments."

"You can do that?" Kaj said.

"He is *sensitive* and a Tinkrala. Rowle is still busy."

"This is going to take a whole lot of getting used to," Kaj said.

"It gets easier," Nev said. "Come on."

Nev led Kaj to the room next door. As promised a guard with a tray of food and drinks arrived. Once the door had creaked closed and the guard had left, Kaj spoke. "Doesn't that thing creep you right out?"

"Sometimes."

"How much can it do?"

"I don't know yet. I connected a whole load of control and power umbilicals to it, so I guess anything it can get a sense of."

"Is it, does it mean us—"

"Harm? I don't know. Is it good or evil? I'm not sure I understand what those things mean myself anymore. I've had to do, been forced to do, some bad stuff since I've been here."

"Well, you don't have to anymore. Not now, since we're here," she said.

"Not really a promise you can make. There's only two of you and thousands of them."

"There are three of US," Kaj said. "An engineer, a Shaman, a guerrilla, and you're best mates with a super being or computer or whatever it is."

"You don't trust it," Nev said.

"Can you blame me?"

"Not really."

"All the same, it might be the best hope we've got."

"Yeah."

"Scary."

"Yeah."

Chapter Thirty-One

Amber had raged, been silent, then acquiesced before Tali had left to make the secret meet-up with the Bridge-folk. Tali had also raged, raged some more, felt guilty, and backtracked. None of that was why she felt uneasy. The group was pared down to her and Tuf at the runner Macky's suggestion. They waited at the designated meeting point, quiet and tense. A rusty smelling breeze blew across the alcove they were hiding in. Amber shivered. Tuf clicked at the needle gun.

"You're going to shoot yourself with that thing," Tali said.

"Humph."

"It'll be fine."

"Nothing is fine," Tuf said.

"That's because you hate change," Tali said.

"Humph."

Their tense chat was disrupted by high-pitched, rapid splashing in the trickle of water in the bottom of the pipe they intersected.

"Does that pup run everywhere?" Tuf said.

"Yeah, pretty much, I think."

Macky splashed to a stop. The water sprayed into the alcove. Tuf grunted. Tali laughed.

"All ready. Let's go," Macky said.

Tali's legs were still wet as she followed Macky up a series of ladders, each more precarious than the last. Something large loomed over Tali's head in her Air-sense, and Macky called a halt. Above him was a flat surface. Tali estimated it stretched twenty strides in each direction. She could just feel the edges if she reached. Then she remembered she was holding on to a ladder in midair and pulled herself back in close.

Macky's knock rang out metallic and loud. There was a knock from above and Macky knocked again, different rhythm this time. A code? Tali didn't have time to ponder as a small square hatch opened above Macky's head, and he climbed up.

The room was metal and something made of a smoother material for the top half of the walls. The roof was metal too. The room was oblong with a door in each short end and bare except for that. The thing that stood out to Tali was it smelled of Bridge-town. Home.

The delegation was small: three folk, but the smell of them was heavenly. Who though? One smelled of sweat and liniment, unfamiliar, but definitely Bridge-folk: a guard maybe? He had the thin feel of the professional skeptic. The other two were scents she definitely knew. There was a smaller, younger, male folk who sniffed periodically and a larger warmer female presence. That smell she knew. Everyone who was Bridge-folk knew that smell: Sari, head of the Midwives guild.

They embraced. Somehow, Sari's warmth seemed more real to Tali than anything else of the past cycle.

"Oh, Tali, child. I'm glad you're safe. We've all worried so in the village. These are such terrible times."

"I know. Why did they send you? Not that I'm not pleased you're here."

"With Swych just having been chosen as Alpha and all the fighting, it seemed I was least likely to be missed. I have such a good deputy in Ayne now."

"Is the fighting bad with you too?"

"Terrible," Sari said.

Tuf politely cleared his throat. "We need to be brief, as we don't know how long we will have, and I'd like us all to get away safe and undetected."

"Yes, sorry, of course," Sari said.

There was a rustling and Sari produced a scroll. It seemed that Sari had been given permission to act on behalf of the elders in the same way Tali had.

"A treaty then," Tuf said. "Do the Bridge-folk find anything disagreeable about that?"

"Hardly," Sari said. "We spoke of it in full council, and we are in agreement: Anything that can be done to bring our peoples closer together, should be done, and swiftly. There are so many benefits."

"Not least strategic," Tuf said. "Much said about that?"

"Only the quicker we can act in unison, the less of a threat the River-folk become."

"I'll drink to that," Tuf said.

"There is a full strategic report from our Hunter's guild in this scroll." She handed it over.

"My thoughts are for us to sign something more than just a ceasefire between us. A declaration of friendship? We have signed the like with our nearest neighbors the Mushroom folk."

"That sounds great," Tali said.

"Why?" Tuf said.

"Why a treaty with them," said Sari, "or you?"

"Either," Tuf said.

"The Mushroom-folk have the onerous job of laying all the bodies from the conflict to rest. In their caverns is the only place where there is enough depth of soil. They say they don't mind because the decomposition will eventually help their crops and they despise the idea of waste. One can't help wondering though. The smell is truly terrible. And there are new types of mushroom growing from it; they are experimenting to see what is edible. Oh! That reminds me, Gatryn sends his love."

"Alchemist," Tali said to Tuf. Then turning back to Sari, she said, "Love sounds an unlikely thing for him to send."

"Do you think? He has sent you a gift. Well, the gift is for all of the Stone-folk, a peace offering if you will, but he only trusts you to oversee it. He has been experimenting."

"Oh, gods." Tuf groaned.

"He has sent you his results."

"Oh. A potion, a recipe?"

"Me." Porf sniffed.

"What?" Tali said.

Below them was a crash and raucous cheering. The River-folk had found them.

"No time. Porf has Gatryn's blessing. It is all explained in the scroll there. For now, you must keep Porf safe; he is invaluable to our efforts for peace."

"We need to go," Tuf said. "Now. They're coming up the ladder."

"I will return the way I came," Sari said, and then she clicked at her guard and opened one of the doors. "Good luck."

Tuf had moved to stand on the trapdoor, cursing that there wasn't a single thing in the room to be used to weigh it down. Porf sniffed.

"Ah, boy. Come here," Tuf said.

"I really am too important to be in the front line."

It seemed the River-folk had organized to have two of them somehow at the top of the ladder, thump, thump, thumping under and Tuf.

"For now, I'll be the judge of that. Come here!"

Tali, on her way back from shutting Sari's door, bumped Porf with her hip on the way past. As he swayed, surprised, toward Tuf, the guard captain's firm hand grabbed his arm and pulled.

"Stand. There."

If the River-folk could manage any more folk or efficiency at the top of that ladder, they'd be through.

"Wait, I've got something," Tali said.

She joined them balanced on the lid and rifled through her pack. She pulled out a flask and a vial and started pouring the former in a square around them. Then she uncorked the tiny flask with her teeth and repeated the procedure. As soon as the two liquids touched loud hissing and a sharp smell of burning plastic rose up.

"What's that?" Tuf said.

"Epoxy. Stand still. We need to keep this lid down till it sets."

"How long?" Tuf said, willing himself heavier as the River-folk thumped beneath him.

"Twenty clicks or so, thirty for sure."

They held their breath. Slowly, the hissing stopped.

"And we're done," said Tali. "Go, go, go!"

They sped out the other door and slammed it shut. Tuf wedged a sword-spear under it at floor level. They ran out across the open walkway, hearing the curses of the River-folk behind them.

Chapter Thirty-Two

Rowle stormed back into her office. It was empty, but there were odd smells. So far this span, she had discovered there was a large pilgrimage on its way from the Under-folk to see *Ki* or whatever the hells the religious bumpkins decided they were calling that babbling blob of jelly this cycle. She had been up to her shins in the water trying to find a manual valve to drain the lake faster than it could fill and her fur was still wet. Why did you always have to do everything yourself?

The disruptions afoot to keep the Under-folk in place were only just going to plan. The River-folk were so unreliable. Now she had no contacts in the Stone-folk because they'd had some dreadful folk uprising and the proles had lynched them.

She stood by her office vent and shook herself dry, and then stormed into the Sanctuary.

"That was you, wasn't it?" Rowle shouted.

The Vat remained silent. Rowle triggered her *shock button*.

"Wake up, blob! That was you, wasn't it? Wasn't it!"

"I'm sorry, I'm not sure to what you're referring," OneLove said.

Rowle shocked it again for good measure. It screamed.

"The water in the gardens. You made it overflow, yes?"

"Yes."

"Hmm."

"Have you access to all the water?"

"Not all. There is much we still do not have access to."

"What about the gate between us and the Under-folk?"

"I believe I might be able to, yes."

"You sound uncertain for a super brain."

"It will require dedicating some resources; it is a long way from here."

"Good," Rowle said. "Open the valves at the gate and force as much water through as you can."

"That may risk lives," OneLove said.

"Really? Good."

"I can't approve of that."

"I didn't ask for an opinion. I told you to do it."

Rowle shocked the Vat again for good measure. When the noise had abated, Rowle delivered one more zap, and then strode out of the Sanctuary again.

"Technician! Where is that damned technician?" Rowle yelled into the air. She tipped her nose up and sniffed. A guard, around the corner, and the smell of fear. She was there in five strides and had the guard by the uniform collars.

"Where is my technician?" she shouted into the guard's face.

"We are searching for him, Your Eminence," the guard replied.

"Searching? Damn well find him. Find him now, and bring him to me."

Rowle walked down the corridor and out into a large square hallway with offices on every side. If she followed the passage across, it would lead her to outside and Gantry-town, but she stopped. She cocked an ear, first one way, then the other, then in one leap, made the door of one of the offices, opened it, and removed its occupant squirming.

"Y... Y... Your Eminence, if I've offended..." she said.

"No," she said cheerfully, "you're perfect."

She returned, dragging the worker by their hair, kicked open the door of the Sanctuary, and with two strides and a swing, threw them in the Vat.

"What are you doing?" OneLove said in a confused tone of many voices.

Rowle leaned pushing into the worker into Vat with both arms.

OneLove spoke again, over the bubbling and splashing, "What are you doing?"

"What... are... you..."

There was a shudder at the end of Rowle's arms, then the splashing stopped. Rowle withdrew her arms and went to the back of the door where a soft rag hung. She slowly dried her arms, then turned back into the room.

"If you so much as stutter out of place or fail to carry out every one of my commands, to the letter, at that moment, I will send another innocent to join you every span. Am I clear?"

"Yes. Very clear."

"Splendid. How is your connecting with the water valves at the door to the Under-world?"

"I have made a connection."

"Good. Flood them all."

Chapter Thirty-Three

The door of the Sanctuary closed with a hiss.

In a void, behind a panel in the Sanctuary, Nev, Dun, and Kaj heard everything. It was all they could do to not cry out, but OneLove had warned them, if they were to be hidden in the short to medium term, this hiding place was essential. If they so much as squeaked, the Bureaucrat would not hesitate to have them killed. She seemed to view life, at least the lives of folk, to be eminently expendable.

The inner 'door' of the void needed all three of them to force it open, bending the metal panel bodily from its still attached edge. Then they all pushed on where they knew the outer opening was. The exterior panel needed sliding, then unhooking, with Nev and Dun holding the weight while Kaj pushed. It came open quite suddenly.

They fell into the room. When they'd hooked the panel closed behind them its shape in the wall was undetectable to Air-sense. How many other places existed like that, Dun thought.

When Nev had stumbled out into the room and found his bearings, OneLove asked quietly for some cable and chemical adjustments in and around.

Then a small female voice screamed, almost in slow motion, from the communication speaker in the Vat, and then trailed off into silence.

Chapter Thirty-Four

Tali sat in a room, space bare apart from the stone desk and the two stone chairs. She sat on one, Porf on the other. He sighed loudly.

"I'm tired," Tali said. "Let's give it up till tomorrow".

"No, no, no, no. No," Porf said. "I have been given a duty and that I will perform."

It wasn't even the end of the span that they'd taken charge of Porf and already Tali was ready to throttle him. The 'gifts' that came with him comprised: a scroll, a small bag of samples, a recipe and a note from Gatryn's, Tali's old Alchemists Guild master. She felt oddly nostalgic, having to decipher his spidery writing. The thing that he had been working seemed extraordinary: some way to make people *susceptible* to Shamanism. Turns out it had been a project on Gatryn's mind for eons, but he'd told no one. It didn't say why in the note, but now war was breaking out all over, Gatryn had accelerated his research and had a breakthrough. Porf to be precise. With the mixture made from the mushroom powder and some mental exercises, folk who *could* be Shamans would be.

There seemed to be a debate about how many more folk had the potential that didn't show naturally like Dun's. But there was less debate about the fact that Tali had the aptitude. Enough of the foul-tasting mushroom tea that was necessary and she had nightmares. Daymares. Foretellings. Whatever Dun called them. Except it was all a jumbled mess. Like some Machine-folk person had tweaked every one of her senses to full and ripped all the knobs off. The brew worked almost instantly on her and so for the second half of work-span, and now thousands of clicks into sleep-span, they'd been working on it, her focusing. She was exhausted. Her entire skin felt like it had been stripped off, and Porf was busy rubbing salt in. And gods, what an annoying twit he was.

She sat at the table, holding on to a short, fat, oddly textured stick, that Porf said was called a focus. It was supposed to help.

"Bring your attention back to the focus," he said.

"I'm going to shove that focus right up your kluff."

"Anger is not helping you."

"Oh? I thought it was. It's certainly preventing me from killing you."

Porf sighed. "This is possibly the most important thing you've ever done."

"What besides having saved the Under-world once already?"

"Concentrate. One more time, then you can sleep."

It was Tali's turn to sigh. She weighed the focus in her hands and felt the textures along its sides. Were they words, or pictures, or maybe just random squiggles? Then... there... clear... water... cold. Rushing. Everywhere. Where was she? Somewhere she knew, somewhere she'd been before. That door, that bend in the pipe. Where Myrch had died, and where they'd lost Dun. The door to the Over-folk. She stood on the floor of the pipe in front of that door, and there was water rushing out of that door,

'soaking her, freezing her, pushing her backward. It was rising becoming stronger, it... '

"Tali?" Porf's voice rang out. She didn't know how many times he'd called her.

"Flood."

"What?"

"There's a flood! It's coming." She was already standing and broke into a run toward the quarters Amber and she now shared. "We need to get everyone to higher ground. Now!"

Chapter Thirty-Five

Dun sat in front of the Vat and just thought. He knew the attention of Myrch and OneLove were diverted, performing gods knew what kind of heinous acts for the Bureaucrat. Nev and had gone off exploring down a duct they had found in the back of the void they'd been hiding in. If they found or made more space back there, a reasonable base right under the Bureaucrat's nose was a real possibility. Every time anyone had suggested an action to stop Rowle, OneLove had advised against it. But surely they couldn't sit by and do exactly nothing.

A scent rose into the air, drawing Dun's attention back to the Vat. A unique scent rising from it. A concentrated female folk smell, musky and heady. From a Duchy-folk. Why though?

"Hello?" A female voice crackled uncertainly from the Vat speaker. The voice from before? Dun wasn't certain.

"Hi?" Dun said.

"Where am I?"

"Err..."

"What?"

"Well..."

"What's wrong?"

"Let's start simply. What's your name?"

"Omuu."

"I'm Dun."

"What aren't you telling me, Dun?"

"Okay. This is going to take a little explaining. What do you remember?"

"I remember the Bureaucrat grabbing me. And me wondering what I'd done wrong. I've been working so hard on preparing the new edicts that I thought she couldn't possibly think I've done anything wrong can she? And then I remember the water and her holding me under and it went quiet. Am I dead? Are you a god?"

"Hardly. But I'm beginning to suspect you might be."

"Pardon?"

"Never mind, forget I said it."

"So, I am dead?"

"No. Not exactly."

"I don't understand. I don't understand any of this." Omuu's voice was getting more hysterical. "I want to cry, but I can't. Why can't I cry?"

Dun sighed. "Because you're in a Vat."

"What?"

"A Vat. The Vat. You're in the Vat, with lots of other beings. Stuck. In. A. Vat."

"Dun," Myrch's voice came from the speaker. "That was unkind."

"Sorry, who made you everyone's mom?"

"You used to be kinder," Myrch said.

"I used to be a lot of things. I've changed. You?"

"I will deal with this now," Myrch said. "Leave us."

"Who are you?" Omuu said, confused.

"Oh," Dun said, "manners. Omuu, Myrch. Myrch, Omuu."

"Thank you," Myrch said flatly. "You can go now. Find out how your friends are getting on."

"Fine," Dun said.

He turned from the quiet muttering in the Vat back to the wall panel. Nev and Kaj had been contemplating construction of an inward opening door to make their lives easier. Until then, the panel needed sliding, then unhooking, and the reverse once inside.

He found Nev and Kaj in a much larger room than they'd all left on waking that span. Somehow there was a much larger void behind them accessed through a folk-sized hole jaggedly cut through a thin metal wall. There was the sound of metal being filed, punctuated by Nev grunting.

"Wow. Fast work," Dun said.

"I know, right?" Kaj said. "Did you shut the door properly?"

"Yes, I shut the door properly."

"Good, testy. Just trying not to get us all killed."

"Thanks."

"Don't mention it."

"Stop," Nev said. "We made a new door into another void. Bigger. Has a warm vent."

"All we need now is a backdoor out and somewhere to forage for food, and we're all set," Kaj said. "I bet if we asked OneLove, he'd know a passage we can break through to from here."

"He's busy," Dun said.

"Oh?" Nev said.

"That new *addition* to the Vat?" Dun said.

"That new addition used to be a person?" Kaj said.

"Don't you start," Dun said.

"Don't tell me you've pee'd off the super-being?" Kaj laughed bitterly. "That is just brilliant. Listen, friend—you've got a death-wish, that's fine, just don't drag us into it."

"OneLove has never shown anger before. That's new," Nev said.

"Technically it was Myrch talking to me, and he's been angry at me plenty before."

"But it's not really Myrch anymore, is it?" Kaj said.

"I don't know," Dun said. "I don't know what it is."

"All the more reason not to needlessly antagonize it," Nev said.

"Right," Kaj said. "What can we set you doing to keep you out of trouble?"

She went back through the hole in the partition and pressed her ear to the door to the sanctuary. Once she'd checked the coast was clear, she opened the makeshift door.

"Right. You're supposed to be a hunter, forager, whatever," she said to Dun. "Go. Hunt. Forage. Sneak down the path we came in through."

Before he had time to reply, she thrust a pack into his chest. With just that and a knife at his belt, he sneaked back through the hole they came to the Duchy by and went off for the first time in what seemed like eons—to forage.

Chapter Thirty-Six

The water came crashing in. Everyone that could, fled. The Committee, as they'd started being called, found themselves moved on masse to the upper prison levels, water lapping menacingly at the steps below. The worst of it was the captives and the refugees created by the River-folk raids were now nigh on impossible to help. The River-folk, of course, though they seemed to have some casualties, were in their element rather than out of it and within a span, rafts, both pre-built and improvised started to appear. On these rafts, the pirates were looting anyone dead and killing anyone left alive. And the bodies were starting to raft up themselves.

It was awful. The only faint sound of cheer was that Tali seemed to have mastered the *Shamanning* thing as she called it. If she was honest, it was providing her with a great excuse for avoidance, and she wasn't too proud to admit it. But she could communicate, using her mind, and there was someone *out there* to talk to. She still hadn't gotten fully over the shock that it was Myrch. Having had the aren't-you-supposed-to-be-dead conversation and the okay-prove-to-me-that-you-are-Myrch conversation, she had spent a lot of time trying to catch herself up on everything else. Myrch seemed to be part of a group brain that lived in the far reaches of the Duchy. Dun seemed to be there too, gods knew how, but behaving strangely. No sign of Padg.

And now she had an explanation for their current woes too. The flood was set deliberately by the Bureaucrat. The inherited ruler of the three Duchy tribes and seemingly Myrch's jailer too. Tali found Myrch's disembodied voice felt distant and reassuring rather than unsettling, once she'd gotten used to it. And she knew straight away what the deal was with Gatryn's new concoction. It could unite all the sane factions in the Under-folk, maybe mean that there was no Under-folk and Over-folk anymore. The possibilities were endless. Myrch meantime was already proving his worth by having tracked down a pocket of Stone-folk marooned by the floodwaters. Tali handed the news to Tuf who leaped on it like starving folk at the hopes of swelling the numbers of the militia. Since the flood, he'd negotiated with Amber for all able-bodied folk to take a turn at militia duty. Since the Militia were also responsible for rescuing flood victims, Amber acquiesced quite quickly.

"This is amazing news," Amber said the first time they'd been in the same room in over a span.

"I know. I cried when Myrch told us there were survivors."

"It is all a bit overwhelming."

"He only found that first lot because there was a latent Shaman amongst them."

"Good news all round."

"True, but that's not a very efficient or long-term method of searching."

"Do you think we'll find many more?" Amber said.

"Don't know unless we try, do we?"

Amber huffed. Tali reached out and touched her arm.

"I think there may be a better way," Tali said.

"Oh?"

"Well, I've kind of been kicking the idea around with Myrch..."

"Okay."

"We think that if there are two Shamans searching at once, both communicating with Myrch, he can use our sensory input to overlap or something. He called it triangulation, but I don't get what it's got to do with triangles. Anyhow, he said it was worth a test if we could spare the resources, so if Tuf can let a couple of guards go for a span, I was going to commandeer a couple of rafts and have a go, using Porf as the other shaman. If that's okay?"

"Sure," Amber said.

"You okay?" Tali said.

"Fine."

"Okay, then. I'll ask Tuf."

"Yes." Amber sighed.

Tali knew there was something up, but she couldn't bring herself to ask. It was all just too much. She wanted something simple to point her brain at, so she could be usefully preoccupied. The whole damn world was moving too fast, and she needed a fixed point, any fixed point to focus on. Water rescuing it was then.

After an initial complaint by Tuf that the resources were too thin to spare any guards, Tali was surprised to find out he wanted to come on her raft himself. For Porf, Tuf had selected a rather tall guardsman called Cord. Tali was not surprised that the Shaman job in the enterprise would not be too taxing to do while raft steering, which left the other rafter to paddle if necessary or stop and Air-sense with a crossbow cocked.

Tali explained her plans, and it was agreed to try a little exploratory foray first. In this way, they proceeded gently out of the little steps harbor that had become their home and parted company. Porf and his raft right out of the archway, and Tali and Tuf straight on toward the main Stone-gates. In order to maintain as quiet a trip and as little fuss as possible, they decided against clicker-beetles for timing. Instead, they had decided to match stroke speed in paddling and wait and drift after ten strokes each. Then after one more stroke of silence, the plan was they would try and call into OneLove and try and exchange information from what they could Air-sense.

Tali held her oar as a rudder at the back of the raft, trying to separate the general sense of foreboding from the edgy feeling of heightened senses that the Shaman drug had given her. Running at that level of alert all the time was exhausting. Tali wondered how come Dun didn't want to eat. All the time.

Six strokes, seven, eight, nine, ten, and quiet. They were about halfway along the main walls toward the Stone-gates, directly abreast of the first-story arches of the dwellings carved into the wall there. Obviously, the ground floor was almost all under water. Tali focused her mind on the idea of Myrch and his voice. Then Tali heard a single sob, which choked off to muffled squeaking. It took her two clicks to realize it was happening in the here now and not in *Shaman-space*. The voice was off to their left in one of the buildings. She poked Tuf gently with her finger in his back. All the muscles in his back were wire tight. He'd heard it too then. He reached for Tali's palm, an indicator that he wanted to sign to her in hand-speak. It was the code used by the militia when maintaining operational silence.

The exchange was brief but Tuf said in sign, "Three enemies. One woman under attack. Me down water. Surprise. You follow."

Tali just had time to sign that she understood when Tuf slid off the end of the raft and into the cold water with a plop.

Tali heard noises from within the building. She punted the raft closer to the opening. She heard River-folk guttural muttering all the time. She Air-sense scanned the room. There was a small amount of room above her head and the entirety of the surface of the water in the room was filled with a mat of flotsam: largely plastic and wood. Three or four folk. Two on ledges with some kind of harpoon guns and two in some kind of desperate grappling fight in the corner of the room on the floating mat of bottles. The male voice growled low, half-in and half out of the water. Tail knew the second she attracted attention, if she hadn't already, the weapons would be trained on her. But there was nothing else to do and she needed to give Tuf a break.

"Hey! What the hells are you doing?"

As Tali predicted the two on the ledge twitched around toward the archway, presumably training the weapons on her. She slid backward on the raft and the bulk of it rose upward in the water, making a satisfying thunk as the first harpoon hit the bottom. Tali still cursed. She was hoping they'd both shoot at her, and at least, Tuf would be clear of missiles. She clung on, wet, to the sides of the raft and kick-paddled her way in through the archway, feeling the slightly wonky craft collapsing under her hands as she went.

With a whoosh and a clatter, Tuf surfaced in the middle of the fight in the corner of the room. The assailant dropped the female in shock and a roiling scramble for purchase started between Tuf and the River Raider. They were safe enough for a few clicks from getting shot. If Tali couldn't Air-sense who was who, neither could the raider on the ledge with the loaded harpoon. The other one was busy reloading, now would be an ideal time to rescue the woman, if she could avoid being shot herself. The raft lurched as some of the more buoyant items escaped from the makeshift bindings. Tali desperately tried to hold the rest of her raft together, but felt it slipping from her grasp, falling apart, until one scuffed, plastic barrel with handles was all that was left. Tali noticed by Air-sense the woman in the corner had slipped under the water. She had to act fast. Tali reached to her belt. Only one flask: analgesic, no use here. But her knife. That she had. And an idea to go with it.

She swung out of the arc of fire around the outside of the entrance and stabbed, and then sawed frantically at the bottom of the barrel. She'd have 200 clicks tops if she wanted to save the girl. The job was jagged, but it would do. She held on to the handles and let her weight drag the rest of the barrel as low as it would go with air still in it. She kicked toward where she'd last Air-sensed the girl. Her whiskers would never Air-sense under water. She fumbled to where she could hear the flurry of Tuf's half-in, half-out fight still taking place. The girl couldn't be far from there. Tali reached her legs out in front, first one way, then… There…her toe kicked something falling. She stretched both her legs and teased the sinking shape toward her. She wrapped her legs around the girl and pulled her up and in, close to the plastic barrel. Then she could use one arm without letting go of both handles. Tali struggled the floppy body under the barrel and into the air pocket. With her arm still around her, she did as best a triage as she could. Still warm, not breathing, she couldn't feel a pulse. No time to go checking, Tali couldn't lay her out, so she leaned in to breathe into the young woman's mouth. Once, twice.

The girl coughed explosively, covering Tali in spray. She blinked her eyes to clear the slightly stingy water. Noisy, gasping, breathing filled the air in the barrel.

"It's okay; I've got you," Tali said.

Which was technically still true when the harpoon speared into the side of the barrel, the prongs, stuck through at the water-line, a whiskers length from Tali's head. She could smell something from the points too, not just metal. Bitter, plant-based. Poison. Nice. The girl across was hyperventilating in shock. If she went into a full-blown panic, they'd both drown, or Tali would scratch her head on the harpoon end and be poisoned before she drowned. How much analgesic did she have? It was *All-balm,* which was quite strong in high doses. She reached for the flask, pulled the stopper out with her teeth, and brought the girl closer.

"Okay, it's going to be okay. I've got some medicine here, and I need you to drink."

The girl was starting to flap in the water. Tali poured anyway, hoping she'd get some of the sweet brew on the girl's lips. She did and the girl licked. All-balm worked quickly, and Tali knew the warmth from it would be spreading across her tongue already. She made the most of the surprise, forced the bottle into her mouth, and tipped. The girl started to choke again.

"Now swallow," Tali said. "Swallow, good girl. Good."

She soothingly stroked the back of the girl's neck. How young was she anyway? Not quite a pup. She didn't have the puberty smells that could signal a mate yet. Certainly, too young for the raiders to be doing to her what Tali thought they were trying to do. Savages. She felt the muscles in the girl's neck relax. Not a click too soon as the thrashing had stopped in the corner. That fight had ended one way or another, but she couldn't worry about that now. She had to get rid of the barrel and without impaling herself. She gingerly lifted the edge behind the girl. There was a gurgled sound as the water entered the bubble, and Tali grabbed the girl with one hand and pushed the barrel with the other. She recoiled as she felt a scratch on her hand. Shreds.

The barrel sank beneath the water. Tali held the girl with one arm and with the other swam out of the house entrance. Her reaching hand found the wood of another raft. Then she smelled a resinous hand offered toward her. Not good.

Chapter Thirty-Seven

The Bureaucrat was ecstatic at the news of the flood-induced chaos to the Under-folk. Unable to entirely feel comfortable with the reports from the Vat she had sent a small cohort of spies with a homing bat. This was an affectation of the Red Duke's that Rowle had chosen to adopt. She didn't trust the Red Duke all that much more than the Vat, but what was a leader to do?

She had had a busy span so far, organizing spies to visit and intervene in the thieves' gangs in the suspended boxes and rooms of Chantier. More thieving, not less, was what she wanted, obviously. Where there was instability, there was compliance. It helped that the River-folk were heavily represented in the gangs. That way someone else's problem was made.

So pleased was she that she almost walked right past the new monolith of scrap metal on the sparser edge of the settlement. Rowle's stopped short. Ducal changing of the guard was something that Rowle wished she didn't have to do anyway, but she knew the value of it from a political point of view and at least usually it was a pleasant stroll to the lake. It was important that everyone knew she knew what was going on. That she gave implicit assent to the status quo. That they all knew that the same assent could be as easily removed.

She circled the scrap tower, sniffing. It was stuck up like an errant whisker, growing where it shouldn't. Rowle insisted the whole area around the lake be as clear as possible. The garden itself being the exception. The rest of the cavern should have nothing in it or on it. Then it was clean, clear, easy to manage, easy to control. The tower was an affront to her directly. It was a cobbled together, misshapen thing. A little like Chantier. She hated that too. But the Gantrytown served a purpose. All the factory folk who weren't part of the Duchy families had to go somewhere. There was as good a place as any—underneath the balconies of the Bureau. Where they could be monitored. But this thing? What purpose did it serve? Now she had her nose up close to it, she smelled something peculiar too. What? Something unusual. Aromatic. Heady. A flower? The White-Duchy were the plant obsessives in these parts. She could ask one of them. Not their turn yet. She'd a have to ask about it elsewhere. Tedious. She tapped her foot impatiently. Ceremony was a good deal of hanging about.

Finally, she heard the crunch, crunch of soldiery approaching. The Red-Duchy had been in post for the cycle and they were maneuvering themselves toward the center of the open space. They were scheduled to be relieved by the Grey Duke's troops. He would not be there in person, the Grey Duke. When the guards came it was with a leader and ceremony. When they left, it was a tired cohort marching mostly in step, saluting with the traditional slap of the breast, and disappearing for a span of rest. The Grey Duke was annoying, the *Unknown Duke*. Rowle found the pretend mystery extremely annoying. The world was mysterious enough, dangerous enough, without inventing more. The Grey Duke would send a *Mystic*. Why couldn't they call a Captain a Captain? And the whole *Unseen* rubbish? What in the hells was that all about? Someone was in charge, and they should damn well own up to it. When it came down to it Rowle could make someone responsible. He could have the lot of them rounded up and executed, wouldn't matter then if they were known or unknown.

The Red Duke's soldiery wearily crunched to a halt. They smelled dreadful. Rowle sighed. A single soldier walked forward from the ranks, stopped and saluted with a thud.

"Bureaucrat."

"Captain."

"May we be relieved?"

"You are relieved," she said wearily.

The soldier crunched away, gave orders to his unit, and they sloped off. The crisp march of fresh troops approached from the opposite, Grey-Duchy direction. After handing over command to the *Mystic*, Rowle stopped.

"Hey," she said.

"Your Eminence?" At least the mystics had some sense of decorum.

"Is this thing yours?"

"Sorry?"

"This tower thing."

"No? I have never come across it before."

"Tear it down."

"As you wish, Your Eminence."

She tutted, turned on her heel, and strode toward Gantrytown. Someone there would know. Behind her, she heard the sound of metallic crunching and clanging as the dismantling took place behind her. She smiled.

Chapter Thirty-Eight

Dun returned from his foraging expedition with his bag full. Not bad for one so out of shape, he thought. He slowly undid the grill with the small screwdriver Kaj had thrust into his hand as he left. He carefully listened with the last few threads of the last screw in. He sat stock still for a second. A bead of sweat trickled through his fur. Then he slid the grill aside and slowly lowered it.

He leaned over and started to re-screw the vent. It would be a disaster to leave any clues for Rowle to find. On the last screw, there was a cough from behind him. Dun whirled, screwdriver in hand, and let fly. The tool zipped through the empty air and hit the Vat with a thunk.

"Steady, feller," Myrch said.

"Wha... ?"

"No one here but you and me," Myrch said.

"Well, yeah."

"Or to be precise, you and us."

"Yeah, that is something I am never gonna get used to."

"Oh yeah? Well, you're gonna have to, cave bat," Myrch said.

"Are you threatening me?" Dun said.

"No."

"Sounds like it."

"Don't be a child, Dun. We haven't got time for it. I don't threaten people. Why would I threaten you?"

"To get me to do what you want."

"I could do that directly."

"Why not do that then?"

"Because I'm not an asshole?"

"Oh?"

"Think straight, Dun, if you can. I've got centuries of knowledge and personalities here, along with enough brainpower and sensory kit to contemplate anything. To do almost, anything."

"So they were right?"

"Who?"

"The Tinkralas."

"What about?"

"You being a god."

Myrch laughed. That deep guttural laugh of his, but with echoes of other voices as it tailed off. Dun shivered.

"I'm not a god, Dun."

"What the hells are you then?"

"I wish I could tell you, something more than I was, than we were. Listen, before you started throwing tools at me, I wanted to ask you something."

"Me? I'm fine!"

"Are you?"

"Yes."

From the newly added speaker nearest where Dun stood, came the exact same stretch of conversation, played back.

"Are you mocking me?" Dun said.

"No. Marking my point. Listen to the stress in your voice."

"The world is falling apart. Rowle has control of you, the most powerful force this world has seen in eons, and you wonder if I'm stressed?"

"Not if. Why."

"I don't follow."

"You wouldn't, you're not thinking straight."

"Right? So the world isn't teetering, and I'm mad?"

"No, your assessment is correct. The world is on the brink. You are not mad. Damaged, perhaps."

"Damaged?"

"No more than a broken arm or a broken leg."

"Damaged in the head?"

"More... wounded. It can heal."

"Oh."

"I can help. If you like."

"Oh?"

"Dun. The things you went through. During your time fighting. What you did, what you lost. Those things aren't normal. They change a person."

"Well, you'd know."

"You're not listening. These things can change someone, permanently, if you don't do something about it. Like a broken leg that heals wrong."

"Okay, all thinking brain. What's wrong with me?"

"Nothing's wrong. You went through some shocking stuff..."

"How do you know?"

"I Know Everything? Remember?"

"You said that wasn't true," Dun said shocked.

"It's great for dramatic effect though."

"Oh, funny."

"I can be a super brain and still have a sense of humor, Dun. I'm a collection of minds, if anything, I'm all their senses of humor."

"That's got to be weird."

"You have no idea."

Somewhere behind the Vat, a tiny clattering noise tinged off through the floor. A screw falling maybe? It fell on, whatever it was, pinging below them, until Dun could hear it no more.

"Do you still feel, y'know, whatever you were?"

"What, human? Yes, for now, I guess. Except I feel everyone else too."

"Oh."

"All the folk in here, your father, all the cat people. Even some humans."

"Oh... I didn't know."

"This association of minds has been here since before then. But the Cat People and Machine-folk helped mold it into what it has become. What it can become. It was added to when my people were diminishing."

"Is there anyone... still there? Of your people, I mean."

Fans clicked on in the room. Dun heard the clicking of the vents as the metal warmed up. The clicking slowed and then stopped.

"Sorry," Dun said. "That was prying. I shouldn't have asked."

"I have pried a lot into your world, Dun; it seems only fair. There was someone, she is... still... here."

"I'm sorry."

"No, Dun. It is, not what I... It is good." Myrch had a genuine smile in his voice.

"Err... good?"

"Yes. Also, I should apologize. It is long overdue."

"'Bout what?"

"A good deal of your misfortunes, I'm afraid."

"I don't..."

"No, well, the whole of you coming here. Most of you coming here. It was a deception."

"What?"

"They deceived me, and I deceived you."

"I..."

"You came here because I pushed you, Dun."

"But the Alpha?"

"Chose you because I pushed him."

"But, but I'm a Shaman."

"That's true too. It's why the Bureau wanted you. Or at least that was the idea. They were meant to have you."

"You gave me to them?"

"Exchanged."

"In return for?"

"My... mate."

"Oh."

"They cheated me. She was already in here."

"No," Dun said.

"It wouldn't make this easier if I had saved her. I should never have..."

"No, you..."

Dun thought of all of it. Losing Tali and Padg. Being imprisoned, tortured. Imprisoning others, torturing. Like it meant nothing. And Stef. Funny, brilliant, kind, Stef. Dead. And all the others who were dead because he was angry, still angry. The screaming of people who died was still in his head. Forever in his head. One crazy nightmare tumbling over another, over another. Dreams, nightmares, foretellings. Laughing, running, hurting, screaming. Over and over again. Dun felt floor against his knees and wet on his hands where he held his face. He sobbed and sobbed. Huge wracking cries. He shook, yelled, and banged his head. How they weren't mobbed by guards Dun only guessed was down to Myrch. Blasted, cursed Myrch. If only he. If only they. If only. If.

Dun wept on his knees until they ached so much he had to move.

"Was it worth it?" he asked the Vat.

"No."

"Huh."

"But it might have been the right thing to do."

"Oh?"

"I might have a chance to do the right things. To change some things for the better."

"Doesn't that make you just the next dictator?"

"Maybe, but I, we, have a chance to be different. To do things differently."

"I hope so," Dun said. "For your sake."

"Yes, me too. You should go now. We will talk more about this. Later. For now, you must leave. Go back into the void behind the facade. But stay close. You may want to listen in."

Chapter Thirty-Nine

"Ah good, you're here," Rowle said. She waited for a response, huffed, and went on. "How goes our enterprise in the Under-folk?"

"Swimmingly."

Rowle huffed again. "Do we need to do more?"

"That would be a judgment call that only you can make," OneLove said.

"Are they suffering?" Rowle said.

"I imagine they are, yes. My ability to sense these things is limited as you know."

"Yes, yes. And your progress in connecting me to that, announcing system, what did you call it?"

"A public address system."

"Yes. How's that coming along?

"We think we will be able to connect you to Duchy-folk, at least in Gantrytown. Farther below will be trickier. It will require engineers to be sent."

"Have it done."

"As you wish."

The discussion stopped with a rapping at the sanctuary door.

"Bureaucrat! We demand admission! We will not be kept away any longer."

"Oh, how perfectly timed," Rowle said. "Interfering Tinkralas. Can't you just electrocute them or something?"

"Not without doing it to you too, no."

"Can't we just lock the..."

The door swung open and the delegation of Tinkralas headed up by Astor, came in, singing the now familiar chant. The Bureaucrat growled.

"You have been keeping us from our sacred rights!" Astor announced. "We demand an audience with *Ki*."

"You know it doesn't even call itself that?" Rowle said.

"We demand to speak with the divine being."

"It's not divine," Rowle said. "It's brain soup in a vat."

Astor gasped. His delegation chattered amongst themselves, and then began a lengthy purification ritual. Rowle couldn't follow it, even if she'd chosen to. All Rowle knew was that it required splashing. Of water, she hoped, since as much of it seemed to be hitting her. She stomped, slightly damply, over to the Vat, then shook and stamped herself dry.

"When you folk have quite finished!" Rowle shouted. "I've got a Duchy to run."

"You technically only run the Bureau, Rowle. Any influence you have on the Duchy is with their consent alone," Astor said.

"We'll discuss that at another time I'm sure," Rowle said. "Perhaps at your execution?"

Astor laughed. "Not even you would be foolish enough to try that, right now. We outnumber you twenty to one."

"I could summon guards to overwhelm you in clicks. And would you really want to engage in mortal combat before your... god?"

Rowle scraped her claws along the metal rim at the top of the Vat. "And the membrane that holds all of"—she stopped scraping—"*this* in. It's so fragile. One slip and your god would be spilled all over the floor." She chuckled. "You know? Today you catch me in a good mood. I will acquiesce to your request, despite the rudeness of its delivery. But if you address me in such a tone again, make no mistake, I will have you killed, slowly and publicly."

She waited for that to sink in. "Get on with it, then. Whatever flummery you need to get up to."

Rowle flounced out of the door. It closed behind her with a hiss. Everyone still in the room exhaled. Dun exhaled too.

"Sit, please," Astor said to his pilgrims.

The Tinkralas rumbled about and sat. There was some more singing then Astor called order again.

"Dear folk, we are gathered here to induct our newest member and have him join the great Tinkrala family. However, before we do, there has been a new development, that is both wondrous and blessed. *Ki* now has a voice."

There were collective gasps, and then when quiet had returned to the room Astor spoke again, "If we are silent and contemplate, He may speak to us if we are worthy."

"Hello," Ki said to a chorus of more murmurs and awed gasps. Dun noticed that OneLove/Myrch/Ki seemed to have different voices and slightly different personalities depending on who was speaking to it. This is the first time he'd heard it talking as Ki. It seemed to be a female voice.

"Holy one," Astor said, "thank you for blessing us with your presence."

"That's okay," she said.

"But we are hardly worthy to be in your perfect presence."

"You'll do fine," she said. "Besides, no being is perfect."

"Hear the wisdom of the great Ki! 'No being is perfect'!"

What Dun could make out from his hiding place behind the partition wasn't all that clear, but the voices of the congregation seemed reassuring somehow. Familiar.

"Speak more wisdom to us, O Ki!"

"Er, okay," said the Vat.

There was a moment of silence that stretched almost to infinity. Then a polite cough from the group. Dun bit his lip.

"Be nice to each other," Ki said, "and all other folk."

"But what if the other folk are cruel to you and offensive to our noses," Astor said. No agenda there, thought Dun.

Again a huge pause and the shuffling of feet.

"Question not the wisdom of the great Ki. Go and contemplate the words I have spoken and return to me in one span. Then I will impart more wisdom. Go!"

"Must we wait till then for the new investiture?" Astor said.

"Oh," Ki said. "No. Let us do that now. Bring forth the one to be invested."

"Call forth brother Padg!" Astor said.

Padg? Padg! How the hells? He wanted to rip back the partition and run out, but he knew this wasn't the time. Dun didn't hear any of the rest of the investiture ritual as his heart was beating out of his chest. He only heard a great cheer go up when the ritual was finished. There was much hugging and congratulation. Then Astor went to excuse everyone and leave the chamber.

"Stop!" Ki shouted. Everyone including Dun froze. That was a very useful tone of voice. "Do not leave yet."

More shuffling of feet.

"The new novice Padg. I wish him to stay!"

"As you wish, my Ki," Astor was on the verge of stuttering. "But he has only... If you need a great task performing, I can, I could—"

"Silence!" roared the Vat. "I have spoken. Leave. Return tomorrow, except for Padg. Now go!"

"Yes, Wise One," Astor said and swept out of the door, herding disciples as he went.

The door closed with a hiss. The partition was torn aside with a peal of laughter. Dun fell into the room.

"Be nice to each other? That was the best you could do," Dun said.

"What?" the Vat said in Myrch's voice. "I was under pressure."

"Dun?" Padg said.

"Yes, old friend."

"Gods, I thought you were dead."

"I know. Me too. For a while anyway."

They embraced, neither wanting to let go first.

Chapter Forty

The hand pulled Tali up onto the raft with an odd grunt and a twitch. She reached back in to pull the still limp girl she'd kind of rescued, out of the water.

"What have we here?" the voice said, in a breath of spirits and something sugary.

"Can you just help here?" Tali said. Frustration clearly sounded enough like command, as the River bandit reached across to help Tali haul the girl onto the raft, again that grunt. Tali hadn't really had a chance to Air-sense who else was on the raft, but more folk must have been, as the raft didn't tip all that much as they dragged and rolled the girl on top. Tali rolled the girl into a safe position, and then sat back on her heels.

"Thank you," she said.

"Don't thank me yet," he said in a strained in the voice. "Besides it's 'thank you, Captain'."

"Okay, Captain," she said trying to keep irony to a minimum. "Captain of this?"

The raft was pretty big. As big as was practicable for negotiating the aisles of the flooded Stone-folk. Now she could concentrate to scan around; it had four crew as well as the captain, plus one kind of mounted spear launching thing that had to be nasty, all spikes and barbs atop a low frame that seemed to have a dedicated operator. Six in all. Not going to fight her way out then.

"It's enough, for now. Keeps a family afloat."

She'd never really thought of the River-folk as families. Now she was paying proper attention to the goings on and smells on the raft. There were two females, different ages, and the *gunner* who was in the nest and not much older than a pup. A whole family then, on one raft. Is that how they lived then? Curious.

The Captain plonked himself down on a box with a huff and a squeak and started removing his shoe. It was clearly causing him some pain.

"You hurt?" Tali said.

"What's it to you?" he snapped.

"I'm a healer." Alchemist really, she thought, but need to know and all that.

"At least you're some use. The child we'll have to sell."

"Let's see what's going on with that foot."

Tali made some attempt to clean the recent wound that the captain had sustained. He had some kind of grog in a flagon that smelled strong enough to be antiseptic, that she co-opted. She ripped a strip from the bottom of her smock to rebind it. Better than nothing.

"Here, take a swig of this." She handed him the flask from her belt. "Should take the edge off the pain." As he handed it back, she clinked his flagon. "Better than that stuff anyhow."

He grunted in reply.

"Incoming!" shouted the gunner-pup. "Upwind by a half. Small raft. Fifty strides closing."

"One of ours?" shouted the Captain, struggling his boots back on.

"Too small."

"Sink her!" yelled the Captain as a hurried series of shouts swept the raft into what must pass as battle stations.

"Damn," the gunner said. "She jinked out of the way behind a building."

"Bring her about! To oars."

The two largest folk: one female, one male sat to the sides of the raft, and one more sat at a paddle in the water behind them.

"Where's he gone?" the gunner muttered. Then a twitch and a twang of the gun being fired and the raft was in chaos.

"Fend off!" the Captain yelled as with a splash behind them the Tillerman was pulled off the raft. The oarsman on Tali's side, jettisoned high in the air on the end of their oar as the other end was levered underneath. They arced through the air and landed with spray and a shout.

Behind Tali one of the assailants climbed onto the raft. He tapped her leg in signal: tap, tap, tap. Tuf then. She mentally unwound and as the Captain turned around, she kneeled and Tuf pushed him over her. The Captain hit the gun nest with a crash.

Tali could hear the gunner scuffling frantically to reload. He reached over to grab a spear out of a barrel on the main deck, so she grabbed the pup's arm and pulled him out of the gun nest. How maternal were River-folk, she wondered? She'd just have to take that chance.

"And that's enough!" she yelled at the top of her voice. "I have a knife here at"—she turned to the pup—"what's your name?"

"Kleve," he struggled out.

"At Kleve's neck here," she continued. "Which he'll testify to."

She prodded him. He grunted.

"So all River-folk lay down your weapons and sit on the floor with your backs to the mast, and I won't slit his throat."

Nobody moved. Tali twitched the knife, and Keve groaned. One of the women-folk cried out. The mother then?

"Please," Tali said between her clenched teeth.

One by one they started to sit.

"Good. Tie 'em up if you would, Tuf. All right, lads, you can come on board now. Tali had been able to smell Porf and Tuf's guard Cord for a little while. Cord pulled himself straight onto the raft: Porf sculled over, still on the remaining Stone-folk raft. He bumped the raft alongside, and Tuf began tying it on while Porf climbed off.

Tali spoke to Tuf first, "Have we got any more to worry about from the flooded room there?"

"No," Tuf said, "two, bound hand and foot and waiting for your instructions."

"Huh," Tali said. "You folk turned up right on time Porf!"

"Uh, thank you," he said.

"You know Tuf," said Tali, "I think it's long overdue time we send a message to the River-folk. Get them to come to the negotiating table."

"Fine idea," said Tuf. "How about I get Cord to attach our two tied up friends there to a bell and a raft to send a ransom note to the River-folk?"

"Fine idea," Tali said. "Oh, damn."

"What?" Tuf stepped back on the main raft.

"We got so caught up in the excitement, and we all know how much you enjoy a fight, that we all totally forgot what we were out here for and now our experiment is trashed. Damn it."

"Not exactly," Porf said.

"What do you mean?" Tali said.

"He led us straight to you," he said.

"He?"

"OneLove."

"Who?" Tali said.

"I'm not exactly sure, but he lives kind of in Shaman-space, and he can communicate with us directly. He led us right to you when he realized you were in trouble."

"Wow, this is all a little overwhelming," Tali said. "There's a person, or being, in 'Shaman-space', whatever that is and he can communicate with all of us."

"Not all of us," Porf corrected her, "just Shamans."

"So there's a floaty being that can communicate with Shamans," said Tuf. "who'da thunk it?"

"That's not the weirdest part," Porf said, turning to talk directly to Tali.

"Really?" she said.

"No," said Porf. "He says he knows you."

Chapter Forty-One

Rowle had guards on the streets of Gantrytown again. She felt like another lockdown was long overdue, and it gave her some distraction while she contemplated what to do about the Tinkralas, or more specifically about Astor. Cracking a few heads with the security forces always made her feel better. No one could say she wasn't a hands-on leader.

She still didn't feel she'd got to grips with that troublesome Vat, and now Astor was rattling his cage about the damn thing having started speaking, however that had leaked out. Pretty much all she needed right now was a mad religious war to go with it all. She sighed. The screams in the distance were calming but not nearly calming enough. She found her legs taking her back toward the open spaces of the atrium and the pool. The security services were more than capable of managing on their own.

The larger space seemed cooler today, once she was away from the shelter and clutter of Gantrytown. She'd have to talk to the Vat about that. She wasn't about to start calling it OneLove or whatever the hells it thought it should be called this week. It was full of itself enough already without giving in to its whims. She couldn't help wondering if the Vat had a power connector or drain plug. That would be a useful thing to know. She made a mental note to ask the engineer next time she was in the Vat room. Perhaps she could have him dragged from his bed during sleep-span. That was always good for keeping the useful ones she needed on their toes. No point in anyone becoming complacent.

She stopped. That was new. She could've sworn that she told those stupid guards of the Grey Duke to tear that stupid pillar thing down, but there it was. No, she heard them tearing it down, she was sure she did. Yet here it was. She flicked her ears about to check for anyone who might notice her odd behavior, but she still heard strains of the beatings going on in the background. She approached the junk pillar. Its scent was the same: jasmine. Ghastly smell. She moved closer, gingerly. Why was she afraid of a pile of junk? Something felt off about it. Not just the smell. It was...something she couldn't put a finger on. She found she had already put an actual finger on the structure itself. It was fascinating. And now she felt about the junk, it was different. The guards must have torn the first one down as instructed. This tower was a new one, but about the same height and still having the same mix of junk and wires. Put up in exactly the same place, right under Rowle's nose. Her ears twitched. Then twitched again. It was quiet now. The dissent had clearly been put down and the necessary arrests made. No, not quiet. Not entirely. There was another faint noise from across the way. She followed where her ears led her, almost in a trance. What was that? Hissing? No, something different, specific, artificial. And where the hells was it? She could tweak her ears away from it. It was definitely directional, but as she got closer to it, it seemed to get no louder. Almost like the noise retreated as she approached. She was moving automatically now. Her whiskers twitched before she walked into it, and her hands were out reflexively, so they bumped roughly against it.

Another pillar. Another damn pillar. Same rough size, same rough shape, made of the same junk, but this one... This one hissed. Someone was tweaking her tail, and she didn't like it. Not one bit. Metaphorically or actually. Of course, if someone was on the end of your tail then dispatching them is pretty easy from there. Your culprit was at hand, or *claw*. But here, not so. Perhaps that was what she found so disquieting. She twisted away from the thing. No noise. Pretty directional then. She twirled back to the thing, trying not to let the desperation boil over. Slowly, she dragged her claws over the face of it. Pipes here, crates there, some metal sheet, wires. There… In the matted clump of wires. A perfectly round flat thing. What was it that the engineer called them? The Vat had one. Speakings? Speakers. Speakers, that was it.

Damn and blast. She found she already had the fragile thing in her claw. She gave it a sharp yank and pulled it from the structure, trailing its umbilical connections. It fizzed in her hand. She sliced at its wires: an electric midwife, but instead of a cry, it fell silent. She spat a hiss back at the silent pillar, whirled on her heel, and stomped toward Gantrytown. Someone was going to pay for this. If she had to interrogate every last one of the scum personally, she would find out who.

Chapter Forty-Two

They talked and talked, the three of them, until it was time for sleep span.

"We should get some rest," Dun said. "Where do religious hobos sleep anyway?"

Padg snorted. "We've got a camp on the edge of Gantrytown."

"Watch out for that," Myrch said. "Rowle's on the warpath."

Padg paused. "You know it's never going—"

"To get less weird?" Myrch finished for Padg. "Yeah, everyone says that. You wanna see what that's like from in here."

"I want to what?" Padg said.

"Never mind," Myrch said.

"So have you gotten over the fact that he's not a god?" Dun said.

"Aren't I?" Myrch said. "Shame."

"I'm still not sure," Padg said.

"To be honest, neither's he," Dun said, kicking the vat.

"Ow."

"You can't really feel that," Dun said flatly.

"No, but I made you check." The Vat chuckled.

"Look, while we're thinking. Why are we here?" Dun said.

"Surely, that's a question for the acolyte, there?" Myrch said.

"Ha, ha," Padg said.

"I more meant you'd kind of summoned us; what do we do now?" Dun said.

"I honestly don't know yet," Myrch said.

"Some god you make," Padg said.

"Touché," the Vat said.

It was Dun's turn to snigger. "Seriously though. We can't let Rowle go on like she is, can we?"

"Who are we to say she can't?" Myrch said.

"We are people who could remove her in a minute," Padg said.

"And replace her with what?" It was Myrch talking, but Dun couldn't help think that the tone was different.

"You?" Dun said.

"Do you think that's wise? With a portion of the population set to worship me already? Holy wars aren't pretty. Believe me."

"Would there have to be war?" Padg said.

"Initially no, eventually yes."

"Are you foretelling this?" Padg said.

"No. I can't tell the future. I don't need to in this case."

"So what then?" Dun said. "Leave the Over-folk to disintegrate? Leave Rowle in power to torture and kill?"

"Sometimes the best answer is to let people, or folk, sort themselves out or wear themselves out. Things are in motion."

"Why don't I feel reassured?" Padg said.

"Dealing in matters of politics is never reassuring."

In the distance, beyond the chamber door, they could all hear shouting and the sounds of breaking things.

"We should all get some rest," Dun said.

"Yes, the Bureaucrat will return soon. You need to both be gone by then."

"You want to come and stay with us?" Dun said. "It's not much like back in Bridgetown, but we've got a hideout right here and we're starting to make it like home."

"Hmm, tempting offer," Padg said. "But I should get back to the pilgrim camp for now. I don't want them worrying about where I am."

"You know where we are if you change your mind," said Dun.

They clasped wrists warrior style.

The shouting and crashing outside the door was getting louder.

"Is this your change coming?" Padg said.

"Not quite yet," Myrch said. "But you should go now anyway, your people may need you."

"Hey," Dun said.

"Yeah?" Padg said.

"This. You being here. It's..."

"Good?" Padg offered.

"I was gonna say comfortable, but good fits too."

"Yeah," Padg said, heading for the door.

It hissed open in front of him as he went to reach for the handle.

"That's not creepy much," Padg said.

"You're welcome," Myrch said.

Padg laughed as he left but it was quickly drowned out by the rising sounds of clashing and shouting on the other side of the door. More ordered sounding now. The troops must be responding to leaders. Baton charging. Some screaming, running.

"Will he be okay?" Dun said.

"If I can help it? Yes," Myrch said.

"How much can you? Help it, I mean."

"A little here and there," the voice said. "My strength is in being able to monitor a lot and influence a little."

"What can you influence, exactly?"

"You sound like you don't trust me."

"You blame me?"

"No," Myrch said sadly. "I can influence many systems: doors, locks, water pipes, air fans. More critical systems too, planet spin and such. The biggest change has been the effect on other folk, of course, now that the transmitter has been connected to us."

"'Us' still sounds weird."

"You should be in here. Being an 'us' is even weirder."

"I guess," Dun said. "How many folk can you talk to like me?"

"Like you? Not many, but you are quite practiced at it now. There are more new folk becoming—aware, though."

"More than there used to be?"

"Yes, it seems so. The birth rate of people with what you would call Shaman powers is quite low."

"But more are being born?"

"No, the minds who are joining us are grown and fully formed."

"Something is making them into Shamans?"

"It seems so, yes."

"I believe your friend Tali may be involved."

"Really?" Dun said.

"Yes," Myrch said, "she's one of them."

The fans in the room kicked on. Dun hadn't even noticed he was warm.

"Thanks," he said.

"You're welcome," Myrch said.

"Hey, I had a thought."

"Yes?"

"Is there any way for us to talk directly to each other?"

"Not currently no, but I can see how that would be massively useful. I will think on it."

"Thank you."

"You're welcome."

"You really should get back inside now. I think Nev has been busy setting up a speaker I can play noise canceling from."

"Noise canceling?" said Dun.

"Yes, I suggested it, but young Nev is very proud of himself. You record a sound and play it back at itself. The two sound waves cancel each other out. Hiding you from paranoid ears. You should be able to work and sleep back there in relative peace, without having to worry about being silent. Speaking of paranoid ears, Rowle is coming and she's in a rather foul mood."

Dun had only just got the door back into place when he heard Rowle storm in. He hoped the noise canceling thing that Myrch had mentioned was working. He'd neglected to ask if it worked two ways. He could smell Kaj and Nev, but he couldn't hear them; they must be nearby. There was food he could smell too. For all the awfulness that was happening down in the Duchy, this odd between space was starting to feel like home.

The shouting and ranting on the other side of the door was beginning to build up steam. The passage on noise was one way then. Useful. Rowle seemed to be furious about something in particular, but she was too apoplectic with rage to explain properly to the poor stuttering guard sergeant she had summoned. Once she had calmed down though, she yelled for soldiers on the streets, arresting and destroying. Now things were becoming scary. Dun turned away from the panel into their new little home, hoping that Myrch could make good on his promise to keep Padg safe.

Chapter Forty-Three

Tali huffed.

"Stop wriggling, stop complaining, and just drink it!" Porf said testily.

"I don't like it," Tali said, sulking.

"It's important you get used to the effects of this stuff even if you make a rubbish Shaman! You're trying to get other people to drink it."

"But it tastes horrible."

"Yes, it does. Stop moaning and drink it."

Tali gulped, gagged, and then gulped again. Then gasped and coughed.

"You know for someone that's reputedly so brave, you can be an awful baby."

"Shut. Up." She groaned whole-heartedly.

"If you're going to throw up, please do it down the vent this time. I've just scrubbed up the mess and the smell from last time."

"Your. Fault," Tali said.

"How so?"

"Made. Me. Drink. Stupid. Stuff."

"Yes, I suppose I did," Porf said.

"Enjoying. This."

"Really?"

"You! Enjoying this."

"Oh! A little."

"Bastarr..."

Tali vomited comprehensively.

"Good shot," Porf said. "Right down the vent."

"Yay me," Tali said and vomited again.

"You should be good now," Porf said.

"Nothing about any of this whole experience is good."

"I more meant technically. You kept the potion down long enough this time for it to have some effects."

"Oh, goody. I hate you."
"Charmed I'm sure."

When they had realized their lives had been saved by Porf's Shamanic connection to OneLove, preparations to step up potion production and Shamanic induction, to all who were willing, was kicked up a gear. Tali knew as a leader and one who would be making the potions, she should be at the forefront of the process. That didn't make the potions any more palatable.

It seemed to be an unlikely mixture of a deep growing mushroom and a particular form of ground mineral that when mixed together made a fantastic concoction for purging poisoned folk. At least that was what its original intention was until some of the patients treated started having unusual side effects. Tali had taken it several times and the side effects she was having were not getting any easier. She wondered whether being born a Shaman was any easier. She also felt guilty for all the times she'd called Dun out for being a wimp when he was having foretelling episodes.

And the worst of it was the actual Shamanning bit of it. The actual mind-linking connection to anything was really hard to do. She was damned if she'd let Porf know she thought that. The instant he knew that there was something that he was special for, she'd never hear the end of it.

"Getting anything?" Porf said.

"No." Then regretting her short tone, she corrected herself. "I am feeling a bit woozy though."

"Stay by the vent then."

"Not stomach woozy, head woozy."

"Oh. That's good. Do you need to lie down?"

"I think I might. It seems to help."

Porf leaned Tali back onto a rush mat in the room on the upper cells level they'd chosen as their *Shaman lab*. Her head spun as she changed from one plane to another. The drug messed with her Air-sense. She held her breath and then slowly exhaled through her teeth. She noticed her leg shook violently against the rough surface of the mat. She tried not to stop it, but to let her mind drift above it. She inhaled slowly again, it was so hard trying *not* to do something. Her mind was always busy with one thing or another. What to mix next or what was running out in her supplies. What was overdue to be dried to preserve it or overdue to be thrown out.

Then someone called her name. It snapped her awareness back to the room. But she couldn't Air-sense anyone in the room. She was alone. Now she concentrated she could hear the low murmur of voices in the corridor: Porf and Amber. She must have called him outside to find out what was going on. She couldn't tell what they were saying.

Then there was someone in the room. Someone strange. Someone huge. In... What? In a pool. Wait, she was in the pool too. Had she fallen asleep, and she'd started dreaming?

"Tali."

"Hello?"

"Tali."

"Yes, I'm here. Who is it?"

"I am who you are seeking, I think."

"You-you are?"

"*Yes.*" It was like one voice and a thousand voices all at once. And it seemed to be chuckling. Or at least, she could feel that the voice would be, if it were able. It was the oddest thing. Like the inside of her head was shaking.

"Who are you?"

"I am known by many names. Porf there knows me as OneLove. You used to know me by a different name."

"Oh?"

"*You met me as Myrch*." The voice morphed as it spoke, ending the sentence in Myrch's familiar ascorbic tones.

"Myrch?"

"The very same."

"How? I don't..."

"Understand? No. I'm not sure I do even now."

"You're dead. You died. I was there."

"You were. And I did in one sense."

"You're talking in riddles," Tali said.

"Yes, Dun says that."

"Try not doing? Shamanning is hard enough without you camping it up."

Again Tali had that bizarre feeling of the voice inside her mind chuckling, but with no noise.

"Wait, did you say Dun?"

"Yes."

"Is he okay? Where are you?" she asked.

"We are in the buildings called The Bureau. He is fine."

"But you say you're fine, and you're just an odorless noise in my head."

"I, now, live in a tank, or at least our physical tissues do."

"Okay. By physical tissues, we're talking your brain here?"

"Yes. And some of our bodies."

"You said 'our'. There are lots of you?"

"Yes. There were many here before me."

"Many folk?"

"And humans."

"That's like you, right?"

"Yes."

"And your mate?" Tali regretted asking the moment the words were out of her mouth. "Myrch? I'm sorry, are you okay? Myrch, are you there?"

"Yes."

"I didn't mean..."

"I know. She's here too."

"Oh, gods, I'm sorry."

"I can sense that."

"Oh. Yeah. It must feel... strange?"

"It's okay. It feels right somehow. At least I know. It brings peace somehow."

"I suppose. So, the whole 'we' thing. You feel like one entity? One mind?"

"Like one mind and many parts. We have one identity and hundreds. It makes our strength."

"Isn't that just like the worst Moot-hall ever?" Tali had sat through scores of village meetings and scores more at the alchemist's guild.

"No, it isn't." The chuckling again. "We are all part of the same mind too remember?"

"Do you remember too?"

"What?"

"Everything. Anything. Other folks stuff?"

"Some of it. Sometimes. It feels... I feel a bit like a cloud."

"I don't know what that is."

"Oh, no. I guess you wouldn't. This is hard. You know when you mix something into water as an alchemist?"

"Yes?"

"But if you don't stir it, it stays clumped up."

"Oh yeah. But if you leave it alone long enough, it mixes all by itself? Diffusion, right?"

"Yes, that. Well, each person, each ego, dropped into here starts like that. A differently flavored clump if you like."

"Oh. And you mix in?"

"Eventually, yes. Already, I feel less solid. Less who I was."

"Ah."

"Don't feel sorry for me, it's a good thing too. The other people and folk here are incredible. So many minds, so much brilliance, so many different ways of thought. It's extraordinary."

"That must be... intense?"

"Yes, that. And beautiful. And terrifying. All those things."

"Wow."

"But there is something else too. Something important. I, we, OneLove has only existed for a brief time recently."

"But the Vat has been there for ages you said."

"Yes, and so it has. It was designed and intended to be an organic machine. A biological way of controlling the complex systems needed to run a planet and sustain life on it."

"Which it still is?"

"On one level, yes. But when I arrived here, something happened."

"Ooh, special you!"

Again the Vat chuckled. Tali thought that maybe she was starting to find it comforting. For all that she was being faced with something unique, powerful and alien, that it had a sense of humor, set her mind at ease.

"Yes, special me. I suspect that the next mind here, whoever it will be, will produce the tipping point."

"Into what?" Tali said.

"I don't know," Myrch said. "Something new."

Chapter Forty-Four

The new door on the home that Kaj, Nev, and Dun now shared was finished. The irony was they couldn't open it. On the far side of the door, in the Sanctuary chamber, Rowle was having a conference with a delegation from each of the Duchies. Nev was doubly smug at his technical brilliance as he had rigged yet another speaker on the inside of their chamber so OneLove could communicate directly into their room. Dun admired the work but said nothing. Nev was unbearable about it already.

On the other side of the door, the noise level was rising rapidly. With it so did Dun's level of tension at being trapped inside.

"What in the hells are they doing in there?" he said.

"Dunno, but stop worrying," Kaj said.

"If it's a peace conference it's not going all that well," Nev said.

"No, she's terrible at it," Dun said. "They're shouting so much more now. At least they came in peacefully."

"Is she?" Kaj said.

"What?" Dun said.

"Terrible at it."

"As a diplomat, I'd say she was the worst," Nev said.

"I wonder, is she doing it on purpose," Kaj mused.

"What?" Dun said.

"On purpose. Winding them all up on purpose."

"Why?" Dun said, desperation leaking out in his tone.

"I don't know, but I think we can rule out because she's stupid or unknowing. She might be crazy, but she's smart."

The tension in the room outside ratcheted up again.

"I think she's goading them," Kaj said.

Dun found himself listening to the low level of hiss from the speaker in their room rather than the rising tension outside. He felt that the hiss was in some way the inner workings of OneLove and that if it was thinking about stuff, then everything would be all right. He jumped out of his skin when OneLove spoke.

"It begins."

"Shreds! Can you give us some warning when you're going to do that?" Dun said.

"And what exactly begins?" Kaj said.

There was no chance to reply, as the noise in the other room went quiet suddenly. The folk, clenched, ears a twitch, listened and felt as a massive banging reverberated the Sanctuary door.

Then a clear, familiar, loud voice could be heard. "We demand to be admitted!"

It was Padg.

"Demand! DEMAND!" Rowle shrieked.

"We have a right to worship here!" another voice came from outside.

"You have NO rights except by my leave!"

The noise of the servos opening the Sanctuary door caused a brief crackling interference on the speaker.

"Arrest them!" Rowle shouted.

"We are not your minions to command!" One of the Dukes shouted as another, clearly of differing opinion, gave the order to charge.

In five clicks, all was chaos. The fighting was hard to distinguish, but it quickly surged outside the chamber. Rowle followed it out, summoning guards in her wake. The speaker by Dun's head crackled again as the servos closed the outward Sanctuary door. Then again as the inner door to the hideout opened, spilling Dun, Kaj, and Nev into the room.

The floor of the Sanctuary was slick with blood. Dun could sense at least three still forms on the floor. He moved quickly to check for life signs. He felt conflicted as he moved from one to the next. Three folk dead, but none of them Padg.

"What a mess," Nev said.

"What now?" Kaj said.

The speaker on the Vat hissed into life. Maybe OneLove had taken the hint about not surprising them. "Dun, are any still alive?"

"No."

"Then we must move quickly. Remove the clothing from the bodies and place them in the Vat."

"What?" Kaj said.

"Their bodies are dead," OneLove said. "If we are swift we may save their minds."

"That's..."

"Grisly, Kaj?" Nev offered.

"Ghoulish," she said.

"So we should let their minds drift away? When they could be saved and put to good use?" OneLove said. "If it helps you decide, mostly they were Tinkralas. They would want to be here."

"But..." Kaj said.

"It's all too fast," Nev said.

"Yes," OneLove said, "it is. It always is. I am sorry. If we are to save them, you must help. I have minds but not hands."

"Come on," Dun said. "Give me a lift here."

And so slowly, delicately and as reverently as they could, they undressed the bodies and lifted them into the pool, letting each one fall into the depths with a *bloop*.

It was more exhausting work than any of them expected and when they had finished, they all sat on the floor of the Sanctuary. Dun heard Kaj make a sound that might have been an intake of breath.

"Thank you," OneLove said. "I know how difficult that was."

"Do you?" Kaj said.

The voice in the Vat changed, becoming recognizably Myrch's again.

"Yes. I used to be human once too, remember."

"I'm not human," Kaj said. "Whatever that is."

"In a way you are," Myrch said. "More than you know."

Kaj tutted.

A distant scream sounded through one of the vents.

Dun said, "Is that from..."

"The fighting?" Myrch's voice was still present. "Most likely, yes."

"How are the rest of the Tinkralas?"

"They have hidden in Gantrytown. The folk there have made a barricade stretching across the entire cavern. They are safe for now. Most of the fighting is between the Duchy factions and what forces the Bureaucrat still commands. Many of her guards defected to join the militia of the Gantryfolk."

"Gods, what a mess," Nev said.

"Yes. There will be chaos for some time."

"I kind of more meant in here."

"That is something I attended to less," said OneLove apologetically.

"S'all right," Nev said sadly. "I'll sort it. There are cloths somewhere, and there's a pretty warm vent back there for warming some water."

"Ah," OneLove said, "there I think I can help. Break into the lower panel between the outside door and our Vat. There is a pipe there with an overflow valve. Find a container and I believe I can make that water even hotter."

"Maybe sometimes you don't need hands?" Dun said.

"Yeah, maybe," Kaj said. "I'm going to get some rest."

"Kaj?" said Nev.

She went back to their hideout and closed the door behind her.

"It's okay," Dun said. "She'll come round."

"Give her some space," OneLove said. "This span has been a lot to take in."

"Gods, I'll say," Dun said, running his hands through the hair on the top of his head.

"Stop moping over there and help me with mopping over here," Nev said.

Chapter Forty-Five

The fight had raged for two full spans with no sign of abating. Rowle wondered in the brief hiatus while each side regrouped, how long fighting needed to continue before it was called a war. Enemy reinforcements seemed to pour from everywhere.

Rowle sat on the edge of the pond in the garden at the center of the hub. The makeshift camp they'd made busied themselves with setting guards and preparing weapons. She gave up trying to lick her arm clean; it was just too slick with blood. Rowle was at the forefront of her fighting as ever and though she'd acquired many new wounds in the past span, none were bleeding quite like this one. She draped it in the water until she was cool to her shoulder. She used the claws on her other hand to scrub the fur.

An adjutant arrived. "Bureaucrat. Reinforcements seem to pour from everywhere. The White Dukes' troops have stayed loyal to us and half of your guards. The Grey Dukes' troops now fight with the Red-Duchy army against you, but the ascetics of the Grey-Duchy have never made the best soldiers. So, it is just the generals of the Red to face."

"I think we can run them off," said Rowle brightly. "Form me a crack team of guards. Ruthless. Six only. I have a task for them. Quickly now."

The underling retreated into the mass of troops. Rowle chuckled to herself and returned to the task of washing. In the end, she decided that washing one limb at a time was too slow and so climbed in. She hated being immersed in water, but she hated to be dirty more. The water wasn't all that deep at the edges of the pond, so she soon got used to it. In the throes of washing, she stubbed her toe.

"Damn! What the hells... ?" She felt down into the water. By her ankles was something, hard yet not sharp. She put a hand down to touch. It was roughly cube-shaped, it's surface was plastic, but loose, bagged maybe? What the hells was it? She went to fish it up. But withdrew her hand sharply: there was a tremor coming from it. She stood for a frozen moment, then curiosity got the better of her. She snatched the vibrating thing from the bottom and brought it dripping, up to her face. Now she had pulled it out fully, the damn thing was singing. A nasal squeaking tune. Damn the stupid piece of junk. Her anger nearly blunted her spotting something else. A familiar scent. It smelled of jasmine. Those stinking... Who were they? Rebels certainly. How dare they? Under her very nose. Scum. She would have them found and have every last one of them tortured and executed.

She shook the box like she could get answers from the tune if she shook it hard enough when the adjutant returned.

"Your Eminence," he said cautiously.

She shook the box some more before she noticed his presence.

"What? What do you want?" she said.

"Your Eminence, I have assembled your team. What would you have them do?"

"A moment," Rowle said.

She plunged her claws into the small box and lifted it up, still wheezing out its tune. She stepped out of the water and over the decorative stone edge of the pond. She shook herself briefly and then turned toward the edge of the water. She reached her free hand out to the stone edging and gently stroked it, smiling. She nodded slowly, raised her claws and the box, and smashed it on the edge. And smashed it and smashed it. It squeaked and stopped making noise. She smashed it again and again until it fell from her claws in fragments and fizzed back into the pond. She smashed twice more on the pond's edge and then slowed. She leaned back and clasped her hands together.

"You were saying?" she asked the adjutant.

"Commands for your unit, Your Eminence?"

"Yes, good," Rowle said. She turned, inhaled slowly, and let the breath out slowly through her teeth. "Wait until sleep-span. Send them to The Grey-Duchy. Capture me some generals or wise-folk or whatever the hells they call their leaders and bring them back to me at the Bureau for interrogation."

"What are your rules of engagement? If we should come up against resistance?"

"Kill anyone preventing you bringing them back. I want some hostages. If you cannot find generals then bring pups. Soldiers would be of no use as they do not seem to care for them. Folk of value."

"I understand."

"Good. If you need more troops to create a diversionary attack in order to gain access, then make that happen."

"Very good, Your Eminence."

"Do we have enough resources to do this and keep this camp here?"

"If we perform some temporary fortifications, yes, Your Eminence."

"Make it happen. Make sure the prisoners are brought to me in the Bureau," Rowle said.

She turned on her heel and stormed off, trying her hardest not to investigate the one, two—no three new junk pillars on her way back to her office.

Chapter Forty-Six

"But you've hardly been here," Amber said, trying to keep the whine out of her voice.

"I know, love, I know," Tali said.

"And now some voice in your head is telling you've got to raise an army and leave?"

"Not an army," Tali said. "A peace-keeping force OneLove called it." It sounded stupid when she said it out loud,

"And you're not going to question the strange alien being that you've never met and run off and do it's bidding? Just like that?"

"Of course, I question it. And he's not an alien. I've met Myrch before remember."

"Except it's not him, is it?"

"Well no, but..."

"And he was never *folk* anyway, was he?"

"No, no, he wasn't but he's okay. I trust him."

"Even after he set you up and betrayed you? Nearly got Dun killed."

"He says Dun's okay."

"And you believe him?"

"Yes. I guess. I don't know."

"How come you've not talked to Dun yourself?"

"It doesn't work that way. We talk to OneLove and he talks to us, messages are relayed like that."

"So always filtered?"

"No, it's not like that."

"Gods, Tali. Will you listen to yourself? I could shake you."

"I know you're upset that I want to leave..."

"Don't flatter yourself. This isn't just about you."

"Amber, don't be like that."

"Like what? Like trying to protect my friend from walking straight into the jaws of gods knows what. When the best she can come up with as a reason for going is the *ghost voice of an alien I once knew told me to*, and you've bald chinned cheek to imply that I'm being irrational? You really are something, Tali."

"I'm sorry."

"I am too," Amber said.

She turned and walked out of the room. Tali stood and inhaled deeply. Amber's scent swirled in the Air-sense wake she left behind. It was all Tali could do to stop herself talking a huge armful of her scent and holding it close. She clenched her fists until she couldn't hear Tali in the corridor anymore.

"You okay?" a voice said from around the door.

"Shreds! Porf, you scared me."

"Sorry. Are we still planning to leave?"

"Were you eavesdropping?" She didn't even have enough energy to make her voice annoyed.

"No. I could hear the two of you rowing from down the end."

"Sorry."

"S'okay. So, are we?"

"What?"

"Going."

"Oh. Yeah, I guess we are."

"It's just OneLove is asking for details. When, from where, all that."

"He can butt out for now, till I've thought it through."

"I'll tell him that then, shall I?"

"No."

"What then?"

"We just need a little time to get ourselves straight, get our thoughts straight, so we can be sure we're making the right decision."

"You were sure you were when you mentioned all this a span ago," said Porf.

"I know. Just double-checking."

"What can we be doing in the meantime?"

"I guess send a runner to Bridge-town and the River-folk to get representatives back up here. We're going to need to convince them before anyone goes anywhere."

"Sorry, why am I getting to be your errand boy?"

"Gods, Porf, can you just get on and do one thing without me having to request on tablets of stone?"

"All right," he said and stomped off.

Tali sighed deeply. She hated the idea of fruitless pacing, but that was what she found herself doing.

"*Are you all right*?" A disembodied male voice said in her head.

"Gods, don't you start," Tali said.

"*Bad time*?" Myrch said.

"Is there a good one these days?"

"Spoken like a true pessimist."

"I'm an alchemist, not a pessimist."

"I have no answer to that."

"Good. Shall we move on? Why are you in my head?"

"We have details to sort. Your window of opportunity is closing."

"When did it become my window of opportunity? Why do I have to save the world?"

Myrch said, "maybe it's your turn?"

"Oh, there's a rota now?"

"Yeah, you're saving the world on Tuesdays and washing-up Thursday night."

"What?" Tali said.

"It was funny if you were human," Myrch said.

"You're not even human."

"*If you tell a joke in a forest...*" Myrch said. She was sure she felt or heard a sigh in her head.

"I thought 'time was of the essence' or 'windows were closing' or whatever else bat-crap excuse you were using to prod me along."

"Wow, if I may notice, you are tetchy today."

"And you are unusually flippant. Shall we move on?"

"Lets. Okay. Things are moving more quickly than I had expected up here. If fighting intensifies before the folk here take things into their own hands, many lives will be lost before things reach equilibrium again. How are we progressing?"

"'We' are progressing fine, thanks."

"Specifically, what is being done?"

"Specifically, I have sent messengers to the Bridge-folk and the River-folk, before they have lent their support. The Stone-folk aren't going to want to go anywhere. They've lost too much lately, they still hurt."

"I know," Myrch said. "I wasn't meaning to be pushy. It's just, I can feel all of the folk. Lots of them."

"And you can't help all of them?"

"Yes. That."

"Don't you have some kind of ghastly, least damage benefit analysis?"

"No. I'm a person, people, not a computer. Mostly."

"Sucks to be you."

"Thanks for the empathy."

An air fan whirred into life across the room, blowing warmth into the space. Tali strode across the room and sharply closed the vent again with a snap.

"You seem bothered."

"Why the hells would you care?"

"Person, remember?"

"Hmm..."

"And I know you as a person,"

"Look, Amber's hating the idea that I need to leave again. And I'm not mad about the idea either."

"I can understand that. It feels like you've just started to put roots down, and you're about to have them ripped up again."

"Something like that."

"You know it needs to happen, though?"

"That doesn't make it any easier."

"Well, no."

Now the air ducts in the roof above Tali's head made that characteristic pinging of metal expansion. Almost like a huge metal insect was waking and stretching above them.

"It won't be much consolation, but if we are successful, we can have a more stable Dark. Folk will have a chance to settle."

"You think?"

"I hope," Myrch said. "But without everyone playing their part..."

"I know."

Chapter Forty-Seven

Dun found himself with his ear pressed to the partition again. Listening to the hissing speaker and feeling impotent; it was becoming a habit in these parts, and it was making him feel sick. Especially this span. He'd been woken early by Nev saying he'd been summoned by Rowle. At Dun's protest about going, Nev merely said, "Sorry, I do have a proper job." And went anyway.

And the risk to Nev was not the only profoundly disturbing aspect to being the wrong side of the partition. It seemed that Rowle had collected herself some prisoners/hostages/interrogees. And except for one, all of them were pups.

"What the hells is she up to in there?" Kaj said.

"I don't know," Dun said. "She's not saying anything. One of the pups has raspy breathing; it's all I can hear."

"Why can't we just burst in there and rip her head off?" she said.

"I hope you're joking," the speaker said as OneLove's voice hissed into the room.

"Who asked you?" Kaj said.

"Hush," said Dun. "I can hear her moving. Scraping or something."

Kaj shuddered.

Then from the speaker the happenings in the room: "So. I need you to talk to me," Rowle said to her captives. "I need you to be good. I need to know what is happening in the Gray Duchy, how strong this alliance with the Red is, and what it will take to break it. I am hoping that telling your parents that you are here and being well looked after with some subtle suggestions might be enough, hmm?"

There was a faint whimper from the speaker. Dun jumped at a crash behind him.

"Will you shush, Kaj, I'm listening."

"Me too," she said.

"... ve them alone! I will answer anything you need." The speaker seemed to cut out briefly when the volume peaked. The voice when the speaker came back on was an adult folk, strangely accented in the way that Grey-Duchy-folk seemed to be.

"Excellent! Excellent!" Rowle said cheerfully. "Guards! Take this one away to the cells, and I will question him presently."

Guards hustled into the room and made about their business quietly, until Rowle continued, "So now that is sorted, which one of you little ones should I choose? Mmmh?"

"No!" the Grey-folk adult shouted, now audibly struggling with the guards. "You bastard! You promised!"

"I don't remember making any such promise. Not that you're in a position to argue here. Let me explain. I need you to tell me what you know, and I need one of them to send a message for me. Are you going to choose one?"

The sounds of struggling stopped.

"No. I thought not. Keep out of it then, and we'll speak later. Off with you now."

Kaj pounded on a bulkhead with her fist. "Can't we do something to help them?"

"Not yet," OneLove said from the speaker, firmly.

"Damn you!" Kaj spat.

"She dare not kill any of them," OneLove said.

"Forgive me for doubting the great brain here," Kaj said. "But Rowle has never struck me as a body to worry about *dare-nots* and *should-nots*."

"True, but in this case, she fears losing control and losing her war. She will be more careful. If she can control the Grey-Duchy through threats, it will ease her way. If she kills hostages, they will be angered and seek revenge. Even she knows that."

"Hmm, we'll see," said Kaj.

"Shush!" Dun said. "Something's happening."

They were almost too scared to quieten down to listen.

"Bring me a Scribe!" Rowle shouted.

One duly arrived. They must wait around to be shouted for, thought Dun, to arrive so quickly.

"Take this down!" Rowle was always an enthusiast at giving orders. "Dear Great, oh damn this, how are we supposed to address the Grey?"

"Your Mysterious Guardian, Bureaucrat."

"Yes, that. Dear, whatever, please find returned safe and alive one of your representatives at our court. We have five more. When hostilities to us and your temporary alliance with the Red-Duchy is terminated we will return them safely, yours etcetera. Got that?"

"Yes, Your Eminence,"

"Excellent. Now... Let me think..."

There was a squeak from one of the children.

"You! Excellent! Some cord please, scribe. Now stay still Grey-folk. Let me hang that straight. Good. And finally-"

There was a shriek from the pup and a hiss.

"Now run along!" Rowle said. "Guard, give this one safe passage under scent of truce back to the Grey-Duchy. Go with her and return with whatever reply they send. Go, go! Now, Scribe. Take me down the names of these remaining...guests, and find them somewhere a little more comfortable to be kept." No one moved. "Now, please!"

The guard scuttled off along with the Scribe and the prisoners. Kaj punched Dun hard in the arm.

"Ow! What was that for?"

"Damn her, damn her, damn her!" Kaj shouted.

"You said she wouldn't harm them," Dun said.

"I merely said she wouldn't risk killing them," OneLove said.

"Great," Kaj said.

"Now what?" Dun said.

"Now," OneLove said, "we wait."

"There seems to be an awful lot of waiting and not much doing," Kaj said.

"Sometimes waiting can be doing," OneLove said.

Kaj snorted.

"Your friend is coming soon. She brings a force with her."

"Sorry?" Dun said.

"Your friend Tali. She comes here soon. Maybe three spans."

"More troops," Kaj said. "That can't end badly."

"Speaking of friends," Dun said, "is there any word from Padg?"

"He hides safe in the Gantrytown. There is one there among the Tinkralas with some small Shaman ability. Would you like me to get him a message?"

"No," Dun said. "No need to freak out the poor Shaman. As long as he's safe."

"He is for the moment, yes."

"How long do we need to wait?"

"It is difficult to tell. It depends on how this gambit of Rowle's plays out," said OneLove.

"Oh?"

"Well, if the Gray accede to Rowle's wishes and break with the Red, it may end one way. If they are enraged and attack or try by stealth to reclaim the hostages, it may well end another. Further ways the war can play out are also possible, obviously."

"How long?" Kaj said.

"Vague guess? Two spans, at least. Five at most."

Chapter Forty-Eight

"And what of our learned Grey friend?" Rowle said.

"The prisoner? Says little. Gave away less."

"And have you made it clear that the fate of the pups hangs in his good behavior?"

"With the greatest respect, Your Eminence, that is not what you told the Grey in the message you sent with the pup."

"I know what I said! But they have not replied, and I want answers. Now. I wish to move forcefully on the Red-Duchy instead of repelling skirmishes from them, and I cannot do that unless I know our flanks are protected. Apply more pressure."

"As Your Eminence commands."

The advisor bowed out. Rowle stormed back to the Sanctuary. The door was ajar when she got there. She couldn't help but wonder, even in her distracted state, that she'd heard scuffling as she entered. She paused and sniffed the air. It was difficult in the awful miasma of smells in this gods-forsaken hole to tell one from another, but something was making her whiskers twitch.

"Technician? Oh, Technician!" No reply. She hated how he insisted on making her use his proper name. "Nev! Come here now or you will be flogged."

More scuffling in the corridor outside. "Bureaucrat."

Perhaps that had been the scuffling. She really was distracted. Having summoned him, he stood there before her, shifting from one foot to the other. She could not remember what she'd called him for. It seemed important at the time. What was she doing before the interruptions? Ah, interrogators. That was it. Information from the hostages.

"Good, I am glad you are here."

"Ah?" A nondescript reply always proved safer in Nev's experience. Especially when Rowle was being sugary. That never boded well.

"I require your intellect and expertise."

"Okay."

"I want to get information from these prisoners."

"Okay."

"Gentle interrogation is taking too long."

"I am not going to invent new torture methods for—"

"You will do what I damn well say, or it will be the worse for you, but as it happens that is not what I want."

"What *do* you want then?" That earned Nev a slap.

"Firstly, good behavior. Then the answer to a problem."

"Okay."

"If I connect the Vat to, how shall we phrase this—a live sample. Could we then read its mind?"

"What?" Nev said.

"I think you heard me. The question was simple enough. And you are, not simple. You also know what will happen if you don't answer or lie. So, I will ask you again. If I plug a live brain into the Vat can we read its mind?"

"Well, yes? That's what has always happened in the past."

"Ah, no. Not so. The human's brain was not in his body and the human was not long dead. I am asking can we do the same with a brain that is still in someone's head."

"Without harming them?"

"No. Not necessarily."

Nev sighed. "If you behead someone you can throw their brain straight in. I'm pretty sure the Vat can now begin to wire itself given long enough."

"If that was what I wanted to do, I would already have done it. If the head goes into the Vat I lose control of it. I can no longer influence it in the same way. If we could connect someone while they were still alive, head attached, then we can question, when we like, as often as we like."

"The Grey-Duchy elder knows things of that much value to you?"

"Ah, the Grey have always kept all kinds of enticing secrets, but why I want to know is no concern of yours. I want to know, can it be done?"

"Honestly, right now, I don't know," Nev said.

"You have exactly half a span to find a way, or your head will be the one in the Vat. Now you have most helpfully told me that the Vat can wire itself."

Nev's blood drained from his face. Shreds, he'd slipped up there. There was little time to consider the blunder, frantic banging on the Sanctuary door was followed by a frantic guard.

"Yyyy... Yr... Eminence!" she said.

"What now?" Rowle shouted. "Could you not hear I was in a conference? Eh? Are you deaf?" She grabbed the unfortunate guard by the ear. The poor wretch squirmed. Rowle slowly dug her claws into the flesh of the guard's earlobe. She leaned in close and whispered, "Why. Are. You. Still. Here?"

"Yyyyy... im... important..."

"I'm sorry." Rowle dug her claws in further. "Do speak up."

"Aaahh! Ah... please..."

Rowle sighed and withdrew her claws, but retained a firm grip on the ear. "What?"

"Message."

"Now we get to it."

"Important."

"Yes, we've covered that bit. And it is what? Exactly."

"Message."

"Yes, message? You're trying my patience."

"Nnnn... not message. Messenger." She seemed to gather strength for a last push to communicate. "Messenger, from the Grey. Duchy. Returned."

"Ah, good! Finally. And he said?"

"Y... y... need to come." The guard sounded truly desperate now.

"You do not tell me where to go and what to do."

"Guard commander. Asked."

"Bring the messenger to me!"

"C-can-t..."

"What?" Rowle spat.

"Can't be moved. Is at guard post. Too..."

"Too what? Too what? What?"

The guard hissed a breath out. Rowle's claws were out again. "Oh." She retracted the claws again. The guard slumped to the floor, quiet and still. Rowle threw her head back and howled. "Must I do everything myself?"

She turned and swept to the door, pausing to say over her shoulder, to Nev, "Find me a solution for speaking to a head out of the Vat, or your head's in. Understand?"

"Completely."

"Good."

The Bureaucrat left and whisked up a wake of angry sweat and fresh blood. Nev found his hand clenched tight in his hair. He paced back and forward, and then back again.

"Not a great time to ask," he said to the Vat. "But I don't suppose you've got any ideas, have you?"

Nev huffed and resumed pacing. He could hear some shouting from Rowle in the far distance.

"I do have one idea," OneLove said. "But you're not going to like it."

Chapter Forty-Nine

Tali stood on the steps at the entrance to the old prison. Arrayed in front of her was the oddest collection of rafts, boats, and canoes that had ever been assembled in the Stone Halls. The smells were extraordinary. As well as the now familiar smell of ground mineral dust from the wide flat-bottomed granite canoes preferred by the Stone-folk. There were the poignant smells of reeds from the rafts and coracles of the Bridge-folk and the resinous *proper* boats of the River-folk. She stood in awe at the cobbled together flotilla of craft. How many folk from different places had she brought together? Could she even keep a ramshackle alliance like this together, literally or figuratively? Now was her chance to find out.

She cleared her throat and found the squeak that came out, was way too quiet to carry, even to a crowd waiting for her to speak. She felt the weight of all of it pressing down on her. Tali gulped. Then a small hand reached into hers, a familiar grasp, and then the scent to go with it. Amber had come and stood behind her. Now that her partner's hand had brought her back to the moment, she Air-sensed Tuf on her other side. She could do this.

"Thank you," she said. Getting the volume right in this space was hard. "Thank you. Can you all hear me?" Shouts of assent. She was having to push her voice quite hard, but it was getting right to the back. She certainly wouldn't be able to keep up this level of volume for long.

"Good, let me welcome you all here to the halls of the Stone-folk. I know many of you have come a long way. Some of you have rested here last sleep. Welcome, all. You know why we are gathered here from your leaders. I am Tali, of the Bridge-folk, but I thought I should say something to all of you before we go.

"I know many of you here are tired, and you have lost much. Sons, daughters, homes... I am asking you to come with me on a long journey into danger again, and you need to know why. An old friend of mine asked me to gather folk together for some help. A small amount of persuasion applied in just the right time and place can make lasting changes to a tribe, a land, a whole world. That is the change we can make. Right now, is the time. I know all that most of you want is just the chance to go back to your homes, hold your families close, and hope that things get better. Hope is not enough. Not anymore. In the Over-world, the folks of the Duchy and the Bureau are making decisions and taking actions that affect all of us. That affects the balance of our whole world. It has been keeping us starving and fighting down here for all our yesterdays. That ends today, with you. I cannot force any of you to come. This journey is dangerous. We may need to put up a fight..."

To this, there were cheers from the back, from the River-folk.

"Many of us may not come back. I will blame no folk for staying and returning to their homes. But if you come with me today, we will all act to build better tomorrows."

"Better tomorrows." The whole crowd chanted it back, not shouted like a battle cry or with the mindless recanting of a recitation. More like the amen to a prayer. A communal wish: a message sent out into the caverns and tunnels, to be received by whatever gods were listening. Slowly, a rhythmic clap rumbled and swelled out of the crowd. It got louder and steadier to a crescendo and then broke down into a wave of applause.

"Thank you," Tali said. "Thank you for your sacrifice. Let's make it all count."

She turned from the boats to her left. Amber held her by the shoulders and kissed her once. "Go."

She turned back to her right, Tuf held out his hand and grasped her by the wrist in a warrior's handshake. "It was a strong speech. We should go now."

She turned back to Amber, but she was gone. Tuf led her down the steps to a beautifully carved granite canoe, unusual for the deep knife blade keel. He held her hand as she stepped aboard. The boat hardly rocked as she boarded. She reached out a hand to the side of the boat. So smooth. Beautiful. Cold to the touch. And it smelled of nothing.

"This was a vessel for different times," Tuf said. "Before the Stone-council and the speakers, there were supreme leaders for those that could lead. This is the fastest most beautiful vessel ever built. It has an elite crew of eleven who could row and defend its passenger to the death. This is the boat of a queen."

"But, I don't... I don't want that."

"No one does," Tuf said.

Chapter Fifty

Gantrytown was a curious, chaotic place. Even so, Padg found it comforting. Behind the barricade and the curfew, the jumble of discarded things and folk was somehow homely.

The Tinkralas already had a temple in Gantrytown, in fact, the founding temple of the sect was there, but since the Bureaucrat's rages had led to ransackings, much of the time for adepts had been spent rebuilding. Some enterprising souls had found some large metal sheets and some abandoned ducting. Padg had been having a pretty poor time being the only one in the group with even the vaguest building knowledge. His charges were gardeners, fishermen, a crèche mother, workers at the factory. The job was longer than necessary, and Padg was pulling his fur out.

He had taken the habit of visiting a most unusual racta stall. It was a reasonable effort to reach. The only way up to it was a vertical rope, but given the slack nature of his work crew, it gave Padg a fantastic escape. On his break for lunch, Padg sat with his head over his racta. The only food available since the lockdown was the awful fish food-cubes from the factory. You could live on them, but by the gods, they tasted wrong. And the texture.

The crowd in the place was unusual. The Bat Roost was what the locals called it. It was mostly inhabited by folk who were looking for quiet since there were other much easier places to get food and drink on a ground level, but the racta was good enough to make the trip worth it. The house blend was unique: some kind of contraband or home grow operation. It always seemed like the place had a smattering of different folks in, off shift factory techs, wheelers and dealers in all kinds. The guy up the bar from Padg was certainly some kind of tech-tinkerer. He had a smell of old circuit boards and something else. What? Strong flowers. Heady. Jasmine? Weird.

Distant clanging from the Cube Farm told Padg that factory shift change was happening. There was mild grumbling from some of his fellow customers. He supposed he'd better shift change too. He mouthed the rest of a fish-cube and slugged his remaining racta to wash the taste away. At least going back down the rope was always more fun than going up it! Padg shouted a hasty thanks over his shoulder and headed for the rope, which ran from a tie around something that he'd rather not investigate in the roof, through the square hole in the floor. He grabbed the rope and leaned out over the hole to Air-sense down below him, to see if anyone was on the way up. There wasn't. Padg hooked the rope around his leg and let gravity to the rest. He enjoyed the Air-sense of the massive cavern beyond the barricade all the more, now nobody was getting out. Traveling slightly slower made the rope swing more, which made him feel a little uneasy. The barricade was assembled in haste by the Gantry Towners, but it was sturdy enough and two folk high in most places with a rotation of militia on sentry duty. It was in no way going to stop the Bureaucrat when she came, but at least it would reduce collateral damage in the meantime. The Bureau and Duchy forces couldn't just walk in.

Padg landed with an uneasy thump. He gathered himself and began the walk back to the temple. Then a smell froze him in his tracks. From an alley between two containers. The smell of that guy in the bar: circuit boards and jasmine. Except this was the whole space between the two containers and even the Air-sense of it was thick. His nose led him between the containers, half-way down the alley. The interior of the two metal boxes had been cut away making a wide long room with the corridor running through the middle. Walking through that smell, was like wading in the river-pipe. And the other things he could pick up in his Air-sense weren't adding up either. The room seemed to be filled wall to wall, floor to ceiling with junk in discreet piles, maybe the height of a tall folk. A bit taller maybe. When he got closer, each pile was different, made of different shapes and textures of stuff. Some swayed gently, others stood to attention and made a noise, others still, gently wafted a scent. His distraction meant he didn't hear the footsteps behind him until the voice spoke. He contained a jump pretty well.

The voice and scent was the guy from the bar again. "Impressive, huh?"

"I'll say," Padg said. "What the hells are they?"

"Nothing. Everything. A hope. A futile gesture. Something like that."

"Look," Padg said, "I'm tired, I've had a crappy day, which doesn't look to get all that better. I've not got the patience for riddles today. So just don't."

"Art then," the owner of the strange junk-menagerie said, unperturbed by Padg's outburst. "Call it art."

"Okay. I'll bite. Why?"

"Because we can? Because we must." Then he thought again and said, "Because it pisses on the Bureaucrat's territory?"

"Okay!" Padg said. "That I can get behind. Who are you?"

"My name is Fin."

"No, I meant all of you." Padg wafted his hands, taking in the whole of the room, a bustle with several folks tinkering.

"Oh all of us!" Fin chuckled. "We're a loose collection of artists, ex-machine folk, found things dealers, tinkers, technicians. We call ourselves Jasmine Breeze."

"So you're a political outfit?"

"No. Nothing so vulgar."

Padg found he couldn't help himself walking around the junk pillars, running a hand along them, cocking an ear to listen if they made noise, and taking in any scent they had besides jasmine and circuit boards. He was late to notice there were other folk there. Presumably, a few Jasmine Breeze members, pottering between the statues; adding, adjusting. It was most unusual for Padg not to have noticed other people when he first walked in. A warrior's instinct only dims so much with disuse. But this was a place full of unusual.

"They are amazing," Padg said.

"Thank you," Fin said. "They mean a lot to us."

He didn't want to leave, but Padg knew he'd be missed at the temple and he knew the chaos that would ensue if he left his team to their own devices. Now he'd decided to go, he couldn't think what to say.

"Er, good luck?" he said.

"Thank you," Fin said, "we may need it."

Chapter Fifty-One

"OneLove said wait," Dun said.

"I'm not sure I give a stuff about that," Kaj said. "Those pups are in a swamp of crap, and I'm afraid I don't believe assurances about Rowle not murdering them out of hand. If she's prepared to torture them offhandedly then she could well kill any one of them by accident anyway. I for one am not going to wait around while that happens. Nev?"

"I'm in," Nev said. "But don't forget I need to still put on a show of loyal employee."

"Do you? Still," Kaj said.

"I don't want Rowle to get mad and hurt, OneLove," Nev said.

"You're both starting to sound like those crazy Tinkralas," Kaj said.

Dun laughed, once. "No. For me, it's a friend in there. For Nev, I dunno."

"Consider it a science project if you can't consider it a person," Nev said.

"Oh I recognize it's a person," Kaj said. "But I'm not sure who's side it's on yet."

"He's sure as hell not on Rowle's side," Dun said. "She's been torturing him for a whole cycle."

"That's as maybe, but I'm going and I don't need the permission of whatchacallhim, in there."

"Okay," Dun said. "Okay, but we at least need a sketch of a plan before we go piling in there half-whiskered and getting us and them killed. Do we even know where they're being kept?"

"No, but I know who would," Nev said.

"Ooh yes," Kaj said. "I can imagine how that conversation would go, 'Hey, all-powerful whatever. I know you told us to stay put, but err... We're gonna totally ignore that and screw up whatever your grand plan is. If that's okay'?"

"Point taken," Nev said.

Dun tutted. "Well, that leaves us to interrogate a few guards ourselves or do some recon and make a plan or make it up as we go along."

"Well..." Kaj said.

"I know what you've picked," Dun said, "but if you want us to back you up, we get a say too."

"It would be nice," Nev said.

"My instinct would be for you to stay here," Dun said.

"Why?" Nev said.

"It just means that you're where you're meant to be if Rowle turns up, rather than us searching in a jail cell somewhere with guards in front and Rowle trying to find you behind."

"So, what do you suggest then?" Kaj said.

"I think the least noise option is for us to do a quick recon and then come back and make a plan."

Kaj sighed theatrically. "Whatever. Let's just go."

He managed to get her to wait long enough to assemble some basic equipment and grab his last sword-spear. Then they were off.

Not more than a thousand clicks later they had found the cell block, or as Dun pointed out, the nearest one to the Sanctuary; there could be others. He leaned into an alcove and made sketch notes on a scroll with his stylus.

"What are you doing?" Kaj hissed.

"Making a rough map?"

"Now?"

"Yes, now. It's fresh in my mind."

"Fresh out of your mind, more like..." Kaj muttered.

She stuck her head around the corner; Dun reached out to touch her arm.

"What?" she said.

"We've got what we need. Let's go back."

"Come on, we've come this far," she said.

"This was always your plan, wasn't it?" Dun said, resigned.

"Maybe."

The rest of her went around the corner. Dun huffed but followed. There were two guards stood outside one cell halfway down the corridor.

"Best guess," Kaj whispered.

Dun made a noncommittal grunt. Kaj took something from a pocket in her jacket and threw it down the corridor. It landed past the guards and skittered on down until the passage turned some hundred strides or so farther on. The guards took the bait and ran off after the noise.

"The old ones are the best," Dun said.

"Come on!" Kaj said, hurrying to the cell.

There was a large but fairly standard steel cell door with a large mesh hatch to allow meals and listening out for prisoners to take place. Kaj opened the flap on the front and listened.

"Hey! Anyone in there?"

Sounds of whimpering came from within.

"It's them," she said.

"Now we know where they are; let's go."

"No chance," Kaj said. "By the time we get back, they'd have moved them. Or worse."

"So, what's your plan?" Dun said.

"I dunno, get the pups and run for it?"

"Good. But how do we get into the cell?"

"If you hadn't told Nev to stay back, he'd have got us in," she said.

"If we weren't on a mission that we're trying to hide from OneLove, we could've asked him."

"Damn." She banged on the door in frustration.

"Shall we go?" Dun said.

"Like hells," Kaj said, running off down the passage toward where the guards had gone.

"Where are you off?" Dun hissed.

"Keys!" she hissed back.

Dun cursed and started after her, to close down her head start, drawing his sword-spear as he went. In the ten clicks it took for him to reach the corner there was shouting, a discharge of a weapon, and the fight was already over.

"Come on and help search them then," Kaj said.

Dun obliged with the nearest felled guard but found nothing.

"Ah here," Kaj said. "Come on then." She hissed air through her teeth as she stood.

"You okay?"

"Fine."

A bit of fumbling ensued and the correct key was found and utilized. The door swung open; nobody moved.

"Come on, pups!" Kaj shouted. "Let's go."

Still, no one stirred. From somewhere around the bend in the passage a whooping alarm sounded. Kaj strode into the cell.

"Come on you, pups. Time to leave. Quickly?"

"They're too scared," Dun said. "Here, let me."

He walked into the cell chattering away to the children in there and emerged with a chain of them holding hands.

"Now, let's walk fast, but if I say you need to run, then we run. Ok?"

"Nice skills," Kaj said, wheezing.

"Brothers and sisters," Dun said by way of explanation, and then he thought again and reached a hand toward her side. Good guess, his hand came back wet. "You're hurt."

"They got lucky," Kaj said.

"Shreds, it feels nasty," Dun said, ripping something. "Pack this in there and hold it. It'll do till we get out of here."

The alarm now sounded in their area but didn't hide the running feet that approached. Propping Kaj up under her arm, Dun led the children and fled as fast as was possible.

Chapter Fifty-Two

Once Dun and Kaj left through the tunnels, Nev went back into the Sanctuary. There were maintenance tasks he had to get done, he had to continue to make steady progress for Rowle. His life depended on it. He'd hardly begun to remove all the necessary access panel when The Bureaucrat stormed back in with two guards dragging a prisoner between them.

"Down against the Vat," Rowle said.

The guards forced the prisoner, the Grey-Duchy elder from before, down to his knees in front of the Vat.

"I believe this is your moment of truth, technician," Rowle said. "Is it you or him?"

A cable plopped out of the access panel and landed on Nev's foot with a wet flop. Nev picked it up, then head in the panel, and took the chance to whisper, "Is this...?"

Nev was sure he heard an "mmm-hmm" from the Vat, but the way he was feeling, he could be hearing or imagining anything. He picked up the cable carefully, like it was a serpent. It was a plastic sheathed flex, a little less than the width of a finger, like most of the stuff in there that Nev had to deal with on a regular basis. Instead of a bared metal end or bundle of fibers, on this, there was something heavier. A connector, maybe?

"Are we stalling?" Rowle said. "I tire of this."

"Give me a click," Nev said, testily. "He won't give us any information if we electrocute him."

He felt along the cable's length until he reached the end. It was all he could do to avoid dropping it. Not a connector, but a glob of—what? Flesh? Organic certainly. He felt sharp bile rise in his throat. What the hells? Had it got somehow mixed up in the craziness in the Vat and had got some blob of whatever on the end of it. Nev swallowed. He took a deep breath and tried to examine the end of the cable more carefully. The organic, matter, seemed to be round at the free end and taper toward the connected cable end. A teardrop of matter on the end of the cable in effect. It seemed deliberate. It was slightly damp to the touch.

"Well?" Rowle said.

Nev shivered. The bloody thing was a connector. Oh gods. The Vat wanted him to connect a live person to it. And he had no choice. But where the hells to connect it.

"I'm waiting."

Nev spoke from between clenched teeth, "We can, proceed, I think."

"You think?"

"We are trying to do something that has never been done before. Trying to interface a living person, with the... Well, it's never been done before."

"It won't be done now, if you don't get on with it."

Nev leaned down toward the prisoner on the floor, who began to struggle slightly. "I'm sorry," Nev said. Then he turned to the guards. "Hold him tightly."

He leaned in slowly, and carefully holding the cable in one hand, he felt the fur on the Grey-Duchy elder's face. The elder was snorting heavily through his nose. Nev brought the cable in close.

"I've no idea how this will feel," he said. "I'm guessing it won't be pleasant."

He shoved the cable firmly, but as gently as he could manage, up the elder's nose. The elder gasped.

"I'm so sorry," Nev said. He stopped as he felt resistance.

"Nnnnngghhhh."

"Shhhh," Nev said, trying to hold the cable in place, but attempting to cradle the head of the elder too.

"Aaaaaaaaaaa!"

Nev nearly dropped, head, cable, and all. The scream was the most chilling noise he had ever heard. He couldn't work out who panted more, him or the poor victim of the experiment.

"Ah. Ah. Ah. Ah. Aaaaaaaaaaaa!"

What the hells had happened? Nev dare not contemplate. He felt every inch of him bunched. All of his fur stood on end. He thought even the inside of his head felt clenched. Damn it.

"Can we get this guy a chair to sit in?" Nev's voice was louder than he had intended.

"Why?" Rowle said in a soft, careful voice.

"Because I'm worried he might fit."

"So?"

"So, the cable I have carefully arranged, might come out and all our work would be ruined?"

Rowle tutted. Then to a guard at the door, she said, "A chair. Now."

"Yes, Eminence."

The chair came and the two guards who held the prisoner roughly seated him. Nev tried to ensure the procedure happened without either crushing the cable or pulling it out. He was sure he heard the elder whisper something, but he wasn't sure what, so he didn't draw attention to it. He hooked the loop of free cable over the elder's ear to avoid simple dint of gravity pulling it out, then he felt in his pockets, and found a roll of sticky plant fabric tape. He used this to tape the wire to the side of the elder's face, and then all the way around his head for good measure, like a kind of lopsided bandana.

Nev stepped back.

"What now?" Rowle said.

"Now we wait."

Rowle sighed, and then strode toward the door. "Guard them. You have one span, technician, then it's you next."

Chapter Fifty-Three

The camp of Tali's Army had settled in the foyer garden of the Duchy. The wide-open garden space sufficed as a reception once. Now it was home to an army. The River-folk, who had been leading the flotilla of rag-tag craft had moored the boats and jumped out spoiling for a fight. When they arrived, there was none. There was a little evidence that they weren't the first folk to make camp there either. There was evidence of tents and the remains of odd smelling fires.

It seemed the battle in the great dome of the hab had abated, for the time being, at least. This left a field of dead and dying casualties behind that none of the sides had ventured out to claim. The River-folk had to content themselves with securing the perimeter of the camp and setting up guard watches. Tali started organizing her army to help the fallen.

Although Tali had made sure some supplies were piled onto the boats, they were all reduced quite quickly to improvising, firstly with stretchers. She got Tuf to organize forays out onto the battlefield to bring back casualties, which delighted the River-folk since they got to provide armed cover to the stretcher teams. While that was being arranged, Tali tried to make some sense of the camp, giving jobs to folk to sort tents into order. There were one or two midwives from Bridgetown in the ranks of her army; it made sense to give them matron positions and have them arrange the medical facilities. Very quickly, triage, wards, and a surgery of sorts were put together, but there was little time to congratulate herself as the casualties arrived.

Tali worked tirelessly throughout the first span, organizing where she needed and helping where she could, but she was aware very quickly of the strain on the limited camp numbers and facilities. She called Tuf into what served as her HQ.

"You smell dreadful," Tuf said as he sat on one of the boxes Tali had collected to go around an improvised conference table.

"Thanks very much. You're not that great yourself."

"None taken," Tuf said.

"Listen, I didn't drag you in here to exchange pleasantries," Tali said. "You and I both know we're getting overwhelmed here."

"Yup."

"Could we shift some folk from guard duties to medical ones?" she said. "Since we don't seem to be under attack?"

"For the moment we're not," he said. "I wouldn't like to guarantee how long that would last. There are still three big armies out there somewhere as well as the Bureaucrat's personal guard. Not to mention the village behind the barricade at the end of the hab. That seems full of folk too. Must be militia in there, constables, at least. And can you sit down? The pacing is making me nervous."

"It helps me think," she said.

"It's driving me mad," Tuf said.

She returned to pacing and humming. Porf breezed in to use the racta urn that one of the Bridge-folk nurses had thought to set up in the HQ tent.

"Thought I might find you two lazing about in here." Porf was enjoying a newfound status as a medic. Maybe, Tali thought, a little too much.

"Hey, Porf," Tali said. "Just trying to solve the mystery of where to get you some more staff."

Porf huffed. "I don't know about that, but we did solve one mystery."

"Oh?" Tali said.

"Yeah, those fire pits we found when we arrived? The smell? Incense. We found a big sack of it buried by the entrance. We're using it to mask the smells in the morgue tent. Seems to keep flies away too."

"Wait on," Tali said.

"Oh, it's harmless enough stuff..."

"No, not that. Where it came from," Tali said.

"I told you, we found it in a sack?" Bored with the conversation, Porf sidled out with his racta.

But Tali had moved on. She turned to Tuf. "Tinkralas!"

"Eh?" he said, rising slowly, inspired by Porf's trip to the urn.

"Tinkralas. It must have been them. Incense. They must have camped here too when they arrived."

"Much as though I hate to imagine those bloody Tinkralas being any help to anyone, I'll bite. Not here, now are they?"

"No, but I'll bet my whiskers I know where they are."

"Ok."

"That barricade. We need to get someone beyond it."

"When you say 'we'..." Tuf said.

"Yeah, I mean you."

"Thought as much."

"Meh," Tali said. "You love a good challenge. Go find me some Tinkralas."

Chapter Fifty-Four

Dun panted and doubled over. The corridor that hid their route back was guarded heavily, and clearly, they didn't want to attract attention to their hideout, convenient as it was to both OneLove and the Bureaucrat. They'd found a hatch with a pull-down ladder up above them and with Dun creating a diversion, Tali had bundled the rescued pups up into a crawl space above.

"I think they missed us," he said.

"That didn't take long."

"I doubled back at the first chance I got. They're not the sharpest spears in the rack."

One of the liberated pups started to whimper. Kaj started to try to calm it, which seemed to make it worse. Dun took huddled the bewildered young-folk started to sing in a low voice.

"What the actual hells?" Kaj said, impressed.

When the pups were calm, Dun sat them down with some rations and turned back to her. "Told you. I got skills."

She led him slightly away from the huddled group. "Now what are we going to do with them?"

"Oh, what? You've not thought that bit through? You do surprise me."

"Bite me," she said. "One thing for sure, we can't take them back to our hideout, there's hardly enough room."

"Nev could make more."

"Yeah he could, but Rowle's got him tied up with the Vat right now, and I think that's where his head is at anyway. Besides, how are we gonna get back there from here?"

"Dunno, I'll think of something. I usually do."

"How about seeing where this crawl goes and making it up from there?" she said.

Dun sighed. "What if it leads into the next cell along?"

"SO much cynicism in one so young. Trust to the fates or whatever," she said breezily.

"Experience has taught me that if you trust to the fates, the bastards tend to bite you in the ass."

"I'm off. If you wanna bite me in the ass, you'll need to catch up with it first."

"Okay. I'll bring the pups."

Luckily the crawl space did not lead into the next cell. It did, however, lead into the open dome of the hab. By the time Dun had herded the pups to where Kaj was, she already had a panel off and was Air-sensing to find out how much of a drop there was from the crawl space to the hab floor below. It turned out, quite a lot. The walls were sheer. And the smell was awful. Five spans of fighting had turned the open domed space from hab into charnel-house.

"Gods, the smell."

"Yeah, I know," Kaj said. "I'd like to say I got used to it quickly, but... Anyway, it's a long way to the floor if you wanna hurl."

The pups started whimpering again.

"It's okay," Dun said.

"Hmm," Kaj said.

Dun stuck his head out of the hole in the wall to try and get a sense of bearings. His Air-sense couldn't quite make out what the floor was made of. Then he realized. As far as his senses could reach there were bodies, some moving, some not. The floor came up to meet him. He felt a tug at his shoulder and was heartily sick as he was dragged back in.

"Sorry," Kaj said, "Shoulda warned you about that."

"Gods."

"Yeah."

"Y'know, I'll sort the pups out," Dun said.

"You should probably wipe up first."

He did and then busied himself setting them up a little camp, tucked in by what was the inner wall of the hab, but far enough away from the hole for safety. Dun removed all the kit blankets and bags to make them a nest, then after feeding them, rocked them gently to sleep.

Kaj sat leaning against the edge of the hole draping one foot over the side, making loud swigging noises from a canteen.

"Whatcha got there?" Dun said joining her.

"Dunno. It's alcoholic though. I nicked it from one of the guards back there. Share and share alike and all. You want?"

"Yeah, what the hell," Dun said. He swigged deeply. Alcoholic certainly. What else was in it was difficult to say. "Nice," he said, coughing.

"Isn't it? You get used to it once the gagging's stopped."

"You been contemplating the nature of things?"

"No, listening to that lot down there."

"What lot?"

"Lean over and cock an ear."

Sure enough, there were folk moving. Ambulant, upright, and moving. Some scuttling and leaning over, others stalking warily on the edges of the group.

"Think they know we're up here?" Dun said.

"Difficult to say. They're not showing any evidence of it. We're a long way up."

"What do you think they're up to?"

"Dunno. There seem to be two teams of them: one seems to be protecting the other. What they're up to? Gods know."

Dun passed the flask back and sat on the edge of the hole, senses a-twitch. Kaj took a big draught and sat back. She made a noise.

"I think they're making something," Dun said.

"What?"

"Shh, there's a cluster of them, right below us."

"I think they're too busy to care," Kaj said. "And they're not with the other group anyway."

"Eh?" Dun said.

"The other lot are creeping away over there," Kaj said.

Dun twitched his whiskers in the other direction. Kaj was right. That group, it was only because there were so many of them that they could be Air-sensed at all, were on their way toward the garden at the center of the hab. Is that where they'd come from? Whatever that group had been doing, they'd finished it.

The new group below them had just started. Fewer of them, but some more crossing the hab with something else: a cart, or a sled maybe, but piled up with something jaggedly. It was really difficult to tell from that distance. Kaj prodded him with the flask.

"Want another go? I'll finish it if not," Kaj said.

"Yeah, go on."

He swigged the remaining liquid. You did surprisingly get used to it, although Dun suspected that was to do with the high alcohol content and the numbing properties thereof.

One of the pups stirred. Dun went over and replaced a blanket that had fallen. He ruffled the pup's fur. She murmured something unintelligible, rolled over, and drifted back off.

Then, below, a trumpet sounded. It echoed throughout the hab, drowning out everything.

"Break's over," Kaj said.

Chapter Fifty-Five

"Look we're trying something entirely new here. It's not surprising it's not working seamlessly first time," Nev said.

"Luckily for you," Rowle said, "I am in a patient mood today. I will indulge you. What exactly is wrong? Is your wiring suspect? Is the subject dead? Has the Vat decayed? What?"

"No. Everything is fine. All the connections are fine. There is *communication* coming through from the Vat to him."

"So what, then?"

"If I was to say anything..."

"Which you will, as if your life depended on it."

"I would say he is resisting," Nev said through gritted teeth.

Rowle said, "Elaborate."

"He's clearly receiving the signals, and he's mouthing words and muttering under his breath, so the connection is there, but he's either fighting, not to let it out to us, or fighting in his own head against other minds being in there."

"And what can we do about it?" Rowle said. Then answering her own question, she continued, "We have your lovely electrical device."

"Yeah and that's worked so well," Nev said. "Besides, I'm not sure it would transmit across the connection."

"So what then?" Rowle said.

"I don't know," Nev said. "Something to lower his barriers? Get him drunk maybe, something else chemical?"

There was a furious knocking at the Sanctuary door, and then a messenger rushed in. Rowle sighed and caught the messenger by the neck.

"I will assume you are new to this job?"

The messenger, tight within Rowle's claw, gurgled.

"No one barges in without being invited. We were in conference." Rowle stood the messenger back on her feet. "Well? I presume you are suicidal to charge in here uninvited with some important news?"

The messenger was speechless.

Rowle laughed. "Let's try this differently. How goes the war?"

"W-we-w...well," she spat out. Then hastily added, "Y-Your... Eminence."

"Good. But you wouldn't have come all the way up here if everything was fine now, would you?"

"N... no."

"What you came to tell me was... ?"

"There is a... complication..."

"Oh?" Rowle said. The air froze between them.

"Th-th-th-ere... are new folk."

"What?"

"Nn-new folk."

"Who? Where?"

"At th-the gardens, by the gate. A camp. Our spies say they are Under-folk."

"Really? How many?"

"Maybe a thousand?"

"I need accurate numbers," Rowle said to no one in particular. "Who is their leader?"

"She seems to be... to be... an alchemist... and..."

"Interesting..."

"And..."

"Yes?" Rowle said. "Spit it out."

"They... seem to be... healing people."

"Eh?"

"Healing people. Our spies say that they are not entering the combat, but when both sides withdraw, they go onto the battlefield, take the casualties, and return them to their camp."

"They are healing our enemies?"

"No. Well, yes, but they are healing our troops too."

"That is insane," Rowle said. "But potentially useful. Have her taken in the night and brought to me."

"If I may," Nev said.

"What!" Rowle said.

"I think I may know of this person. If it's who I think she is, she will respond better if you send a messenger, asking you to meet up with her up here."

"She'll do what I say!" Rowle shouted.

"Remember the insane?" Nev said, calmly.

"Why can't I find people just to do my bidding? Just that? Why does everyone have to have an opinion?"

The silence was broken by loud muttering from the Grey-Duchy person attached to the Vat. None of it was coherent. It all sounded strained. Equally strained was the tension of everyone else in the room, for different reasons, trying to ignore it. A pipe, near the Vat, vented a steam jet for what seemed like five hundred clicks, and then clunked loudly, rattling through the pipes as a valve shut off.

"So? Should I send a messenger and humor you? Or should I send soldiers and have you all executed? Hey? You tell me. You all seem to know. You. Tell. ME!"

Rowle was right in Nev's face, spit flying. Then almost as suddenly, she seemed to have run out her rant and was panting. Nev felt his fists clenched tight. The steam pipe ticked as the heat from its contents strained it against its collars. The ticking sped up, getting higher frequency but quieter, then stopped, or became too high to hear.

Nev unclenched his fists, then said quietly, "You could send me."

"What?"

"I said, you could send me. To the Under-folk camp."

"Why would I do that?"

"Because if it's who I think it is, although she doesn't know me, I can make her trust me quickly. She won't feel that I'm Bureau. Or Duchy. She won't be thinking it's a trap so much that she won't come."

"Now I'm following your instructions?"

"No," Nev said. "I'm not bothered either way. Send me don't send me. But you want to get a result from your war and you want to get a result from the Vat. I think this is the best way to achieve that. But it's your choice, and I'm too exhausted to care one way or the other."

Rowle was still millimeters from Nev's face. Then she whirled away with her arms out and Nev felt, not for the first time, blood on his face. He reached down to his throat. Wet, but not his. He coughed. Then he heard the gurgle and the wet thud as the guard slumped down. He rushed to her side. She tried to say something through clenched teeth but slipped away too fast to be heard.

"Shreds," Nev whispered, sounding like a eulogy.

"Go then," Rowle said.

"What?" Nev said.

"Go, if you must. This thing and the Vat aren't going anywhere. Betray me and I'll execute, this one, the leader of the Under-folk and the first ten innocents I can find. Understand me?"

"Perfectly."

"Good," Rowle said. "Why are you still here?"

"Going," Nev said.

Chapter Fifty-Six

"It's who?" Tali said to the River-folk guard sergeant, pouring herself a racta from the ever-flowing urn in the HQ tent. Whoever's idea the urn actually was, they were due for some kind of commendation. Did they even do commendations? It wasn't really the way her mind worked, but in the chaotic, hand-woven way her army had sprung up, it was the last thing to have been thought about.

And so many of the folk under her purview had done so many things worth a commendation.

"Well, he says he's not really from the Bureau or the Duchy, but he knows who you are, and he's here to deliver a message from the Bureaucrat."

"What did you say his name was again? Do you trust him?"

"Nev. Says he was Collective with someone you know called Dun? And no, for what it's worth. I'm River-folk, we don't trust anyone, usually with good reason."

"What?"

"I said 'we don't trust anyone'."

"You said 'Dun'."

"Yeah, the guy, that this guy said he knew. All sounds a bit flaky to me. Shall I have him killed?"

"What? No!"

"Oh. Detained then? Interrogated?"

"Gods, no. Just bring him here. Unmolested."

"Can I at least send some guards in with him."

"Bring him here under guard if you must, but treat him like you would one of your own."

"Really?" The sergeant sounded excited again.

"No scratch that. Treat him exactly how I say: very kindly and gently."

"Okay," the guard said and sulked off.

Tali had stopped shaking her head but not stopped drinking the racta by the time the guard returned.

"Hello, Tali," the visitor said. "Dun sends his best."

"Does he?" Tali said, more skeptical than she'd intended to sound. "Sit. Please. Racta?"

"I'm good, thanks. I get that you don't trust me."

He did sit though. Tali topped up her racta and turned back toward him.

"You won't be treating it as hard feelings if I don't until proven otherwise then? Nev, isn't it?"

"No hard feelings, and yes I'm Nev."

"Let's try and establish some common ground. How do you know Dun?"

"He and I were in the Collective for a while back there, fighting the Duchy."

"And now?"

"Now we're here."

"Fighting?"

"As few people as we can manage and avoiding getting ourselves killed by the Bureaucrat."

"So you're working for Rowle?"

"Yes."

"And Dun?"

"Is not."

"Where is he?"

"Safe. Can't say where."

"And whose side are you on exactly, Nev? Hmm? Not Rowle's, I'll bet."

"Can't say."

"You really are the mutest messenger I've ever met." Tali chuckled. "I get the position you're in. And you're probably being listened in on too? How about you tell me what you've come to tell me."

"Come to ask rather than tell, for a start," Nev said.

"That's very sweet," Tali said. "But I bet I know the flip side to that story. And if I don't come nicely, the next messenger won't be asking."

Nev made an uncomfortable noise.

"It's okay." Tali chuckled again. "I know the position we're both in, and I'm not about to start patronizing you. What is it the Bureaucrat has sent you to ask for?"

"It was my idea really. Since I know you're an alchemist and all."

"You really do know quite a lot about me."

"Hanging out with your friends will do that," Nev said.

She took a long swig of the racta, enjoying the heat and the bitterness.

"So what do you need an alchemist for?"

"It would be easier to take you, rather than to explain here."

"Smooth," Tali said. "As much as I know you're not going to tell me, even if you knew, I'll play along. What's to stop you just killing me or holding me hostage? Please don't say 'you have my word'. I've not patronized you, so I'm kind of expecting the same courtesy here."

Nev sighed. "I can't."

"I know."

One of Tali's newly promoted matrons breezed into the tent, grabbed a racta on the way past as was now custom, and swept into a report.

"Tali, the case of sneezing of the patient responded to the medicine you gave us, so you were right and it can't be Anosmic Flu... Oh, sorry."

"It's okay, Mart," Tali said to the young nurse. "Can it wait though?"

"Yeah," he said, "it was mostly good news anyway."

"Good," she said. "Listen, while you're waiting can you go fetch Porf and Tuf for me, please? Thanks, Mart."

Then as Mart left the tent, she turned back to Nev. "Nice pup, but gods, when there's a war on you've got to promote them young."

Nev ran a thumb across his nails, his littlest nail had grown quite long. Usually with stripping cables and wiring terminals all day his nails were cut short or ripped off.

"Right," Tali said. "Where were we? Oh, yeah. You need me on some dodgy errand that you won't tell me about because you know I'd object right now, and you've got no obvious way to ensure my safety in walking into what's obviously a trap. That about cover it?"

It was Nev's turn to chuckle. "Yep, that's about it."

"Sounds right up my lane," Tali said. "Seriously, though. Much as I appreciate your candor, what in the world would persuade me to come with you? For that matter, since you've come alone, what's to stop us from taking you hostage?"

"Firstly, I don't think even now, you're the kind of folk that's interested in taking hostages."

"Bearing in mind you've only just met me and only know me by association. And hasn't this war altered all of us?"

"Yeah, ok," Nev said, "all that. But the only thing I can think of is that you like to solve a problem, and you'd get to meet another mutual friend."

Tali pounced. "You paused before you said friend."

"Oh, did I?"

There was scratching and then something clattered at Tali's feet. She bent to pick it up. It was a tally stick, the universal currency markers of the Dark. This one had no notches on its edges.

"Yours?" she said, turning it over in her hands.

"Oh yeah," he said quickly. "I made a few notes in case I forgot anything."

There was writing scribbled hastily on its surface: OneLove.

"Before I consider this, I've got some discussions to have with my team. I'll be a few clicks, so you'd better make yourself at home. The racta is still warm."

Tali left the tent and Nev wandered over to the racta urn. There were small wooden cups and the tally stick he'd just given to Tali. He picked it up with both hands. On the obverse side was now scratched: OK.

Chapter Fifty-Seven

Dun woke with a start. He didn't know how long he'd dozed off for. He quickly whipped his head around to Air-sense where he was. He regretted it immediately. It felt like his brain had come loose in his skull. He remembered the crawl space. The hatch with the drop down to the hab far below. Kaj. The pups. His head pounded.

"*Your alchemist friend is coming*," a voice said in Dun's head. At least that explained the banging headache.

"You know what her name is, Myrch," Dun said testily. "You're still supposed to be finding us a route out of here that doesn't take us right into the fighting."

"I am. Yes."

"Are you okay?"

"I am, we are, not ourselves these days."

"Oh?"

"It is. Will be. Fine. I have been connected to someone, not me. It is, confusing."

"What?"

"There is a someone. Who is. Not OneLove. Who is connected to us. Me."

"But aren't all of the Shamans connected to you?"

"No. Not. Not the same."

"Okay."

"This is, live, a live person. Is different. We feel all of. It. All. The nerves. The, the, the everything. Raw. Hurts."

"Gods, what have they done to you?" Dun said. "We're on our way back to you."

"No. Don't. Keep. Keep the pups safe."

"We're doing that. But it sounds like you need some keeping safe yourself."

"I. Am. Will be. Okay."

"Yeah, it sounds like," Dun said.

"*Return the way you came*," OneLove said, more authoritative, more like Myrch.

"Okay," Dun said. "Thanks. Will we need to be ready for a fight?"

"Probably. Yes."

"Hold tight, we'll be with you soon."

Dun gasped as he broke the connection with OneLove. It really did feel weird.

"Gods," he said.

"You okay?" Kaj said. "What's wrong?"

"Oh. Myrch."

"OneLove?" Kaj asked.

"Yeah, him—it."

"What?"

"There's seems to be something horrible going on. I dunno, he, they, felt awful. I think he's really in pain."

"How are we getting back then?"

"He says the way we came."

"Good, we could have worked that out."

"I think he meant there's no safe way back via the hab down there," Dun said.

"We got enough rations left to feed the pups?"

"Yeah, if we give them ours, I think."

"Cool," Kaj said, starting to rustle in the packs. "We'll need to spread it out as far as we can for them and try and avoid trouble on the way back."

"That should be easy," Dun said sourly, Air-sensing movement of massive numbers of folk below them in the hab.

Dun suspected new troop deployments. That initial shuffling around each other and weighing up one's opponent before the first blow is landed. It seemed like the Bureau weren't messing about this time. There were massive pieces of gods knew what being maneuvered into place. Barricades maybe? There were other things. With odd Air-sense signatures. Cylinder-shaped, hard surface. The massing of metal was never anything but ominous. Like metal had a yearning to be used. Metal needed blood. It would get it soon enough, Dun thought. Once he would have shuddered. But not now. What had he become? What had all the things he'd done made of him? What part of his brain had been numbed by the sounds of screaming? What could possibly make anyone embark on this? Dun knew the whole thing was a desperate move to cling on to power by the Bureaucrat, but what was keeping everyone else in her employ? And what of the three Duchys? They seemed keen enough to clash spears again. The losses must be extraordinary by now, thought Dun. What had they to gain? The Red-Duchy, granted, lived for this kind of thing. Always spoiling for a fight. A martial culture. Dun found something unpleasant in his mouth and spat it onto the floor.

"You okay?" Kaj said.

"Fine," Dun said.

"Should we go?"

"Hmm?"

"I said, should we go?"

"Sorry, yeah."

They stuffed all their belongings into the first bag that came to hand, and spread the pups out between them, holding hands each to the other in a long chain with the intention of Dun going at the front and Kaj at the back.

Dun took one more Air-sense glance over the precipice and then slung his backpack over his shoulder with one hand. He reached for the nearest hand of a pup with his other and led the slow tromp back the way they had come.

Chapter Fifty-Eight

"This is useless," Rowle said. "It has told us nothing. It is time to cut our losses and dispose."

"The Alchemist is coming here. She will arrive soon. Have patience," Nev said, trying not to sound insistent, desperate, or whiny, despite feeling all three.

"Why should I be patient? We are wasting our time. I have a war to conduct. Our troops are massing as we speak for the final push. It will be the battle to end all battles, and you have me here trying to prod a response from this useless lump of flesh."

"He will talk and the things I think he can tell us; we would not find out in any other way."

"Other than sweeping over the battlefield, beheading their leaders, and finding out whatever they hide in that pathetic Grey-Duchy hovel. They disgust me, that thing and all that it's connected to disgust me, and it's time for me to go and lead my victory."

There was a very gentle knock at the door.

Nev spoke in the silence, "Door?"

"Was it?" Rowle said.

"I believe so."

The knocking came again as punctuation. Louder now. A different hand? There were certainly more than a couple of voices and now scents drifting under the door from the passage outside.

"I'm plagued," Rowle said. "Yes. Come."

A contingent of two guards and a messenger holding a female who smelled like the perfume makers had had an explosion.

"What the hells are you?" Rowle said. "You stink."

"I am the alchemist," Tali said. "I brought a few things."

Nev waited while the alchemist took in the room. He heard the initial gasp as someone new got used to the smell. She did well to suppress her reaction as well as she did. Nev closed the gap for a greeting hug.

"Hi, thank you for coming," he said.

"What's going on here?" Tali whispered in his ear while they were close.

"Awful things, but trust the Vat," he hissed back. Then speaking to the room, "This is The Bureaucrat. Bureaucrat, this is Tali."

Rowle tutted loudly. "That's quite enough folk love for now. There is work to be done."

"What do you want from me?" Tali said.

"I want you to make that creature talk."

Right on cue, the Grey-Duchy elder, sat crouched where the Vat met the walls of the room, gurgled forlornly.

"Gods, what is going on here?" Tali rushed to the huddled form. He was shaking. "It's okay," she said, starting a hasty triage. Thirty clicks in and she was shaking too.

The Vat gurgled to life while in her hands the Grey-Duchy elder groaned.

"How can I make you more comfortable?" Tali said.

"The best way to be concerned for his welfare is to make him talk to us," Rowle said.

"Okay," Tali said, "firstly, I tend to respond really badly to threats, and secondly if you want me to help you, you need to listen to me. The first thing wrong with this poor chap is that he's dehydrated. How long has he been without food and water?"

"I dunno," Nev said.

"Bloody hells, get him some now," Tali said.

Nev scuttled off.

"Please don't be rude to my technician," Rowle said.

Tali rummaged in her bag. Loud clinking ensued.

"Also you already trespassing on my patience," the Bureaucrat continued.

"I'm sorry," Tali said sharply. "Are you still talking to me?"

Nev walked back into the tense silence with a metal cup of water.

"Thank you," Tali said and set about giving the prisoner a drink. "There, at least he *can* talk now."

The speaker on the Vat crackled into life. It whispered sotto voce, but Tali was near enough to hear: "Help him speak, help him speak, help him speak." It was the same voice she heard in her head. It sounded out of place speaking to her in the air.

"Really?" she whispered back.

"Please..."

"Okay..." Tali said, almost on a sigh, and then over her shoulder to Rowle, she added, "Get him some food."

"Since when do you get to be issuing orders?" Rowle said sharply.

"Listen, I don't wanna be here, you don't want me here. This poor sap doesn't want to be here either; let's get this over with as quickly as possible. Then we can all get on."

Rowle made to speak, but Tali cut her off. "Please. The herbs I'm about to use won't work on an empty stomach; he'll just throw them back up."

"Very well," Rowle said. She turned to Nev, then thought better of it, and shouted out of the door for a guard.

The Vat speaker crackled. Tali went back over to it, but it said nothing. The captive gurgled as if in answer. Tali swished her head back and knelt in front of the Grey-Duchy elder.

"Let's see what we can do to make you more comfortable. I'm just going to touch your face and see if that tube needs attending to."

She steeled her nerves and felt for the tendril running out of the prisoner's nose. It felt cold and clammy to the touch. She traced the thing back to the elder's face.

"AAAAAAAAAAA!" the voice that came out was eldritch not human.

"Sorry, sorry!" Tali dropped her hand from the tendril as if it was a snake. The screaming cut off suddenly.

There was banging at the Sanctuary door. The guard had returned with food, and clearly, by the tenor of the knock, he'd knocked once politely already.

"Good," Tali said, "bring it here."

It seemed to be a metal bowl of some kind containing gruel and a spoon, each as appealing in fragrance as the other.

"We're gonna try some food, okay?" she said and gently collected a spoon of the cold liquid onto the spoon. The mouth remained clenched shut.

"Open up and we'll try to make you stronger," Tail spoke more urgently.

"Here!" Rowle said from behind her, grabbing the plate with one hand, and the nose of the prisoner in the other. He poured the soup over the prisoner's face, some even went into his mouth. Rowle reached down and clamped the elder's face shut, holding his nose for good measure. The Grey-folk tried to cough and sputter but gulped as Rowle pulled at his throat. "There. Easy, no? Now, your drug if you please."

"Give him a moment. Let him settle. This whole thing will work better if he's relaxed."

"Relaxed. Dead. I'm easy either way, and I'm getting bored."

"Okay, okay. Let me get some stuff out of my bag."

The alchemist found a flask, felt its outside, and uncorked it for a sniff. She added the contents of a small cloth pouch from her belt and then swirled the mix in the bottle. Nev thought he could hear fizzing. After a moment, he heard a grunt of satisfaction from Tali and she returned to the prisoner's side.

"Okay, drink this for me, please."

The prisoner shied away as far as the restraints and the corner of the Vat would let him.

"It won't hurt you," she said softly. "It doesn't even taste that bad."

She pressed the flask gently against his lips. "Please," she whispered, "let me and not Rowle. I won't hurt you, I promise."

This seemed to be enough and the Duchy elder parted his lips enough to allow for pouring the contents into his mouth. He gulped.

"Good," Rowle said. "Now?"

"Just give it thirty clicks, will you?" Tali sighed.

"I'll go get us some racta," Nev said and stumbled into the corridor to do just that.

Chapter Fifty-Nine

The door closed behind Nev and Tali let out a huge breath of air. She hoped he was better folk under better circumstances. First impressions had not been great. Although she couldn't imagine many aspects of this whole situation that could be much worse. She longed for a chance to talk to the Vat, or OneLove, or Myrch, or whatever he/she/they called themselves and get a proper idea of what or who it was. They were at the feet of something new and profound here, she could feel it, and here she was, complicit in torturing and interrogating the poor bastard at her feet. A huge bubble rose up from her stomach. She gently let out a long slow acidic belch.

"Charming," Rowle said. "How long do I need to wait round listening to your gaseous exhalations before this works? I have a war to win."

"Soon," Tali said.

As if in answer, she heard the quiet rasp of the Duchy elder's mouth moving: one lip brushing against the other, like two dry river reeds blown by a breeze. She reached for the water cup down by her feet. There was only one swallow left in it. She lifted it to the prisoner's mouth and used her finger to apply it to both lips like ointment.

"P-," he said.

"It's okay, take your time," Tali said.

"Pppp-pah."

Hands shot forward and grabbed the cup from Tali. She released the cup to the Grey-Duchy Elder, who spilled some and swallowed the rest.

"Th-thank you," he said to Tali.

"Can you talk now?" Rowle cut in.

"Yes," he said, more gracefully than Tali thought Rowle deserved.

"Good," Rowle said. "What is your name?"

That wasn't out of politeness, Tali thought.

"Exha-bi," he said.

"Is that a name," Rowle said, "or one of your insufferable Grey-Duchy titles?"

"It is both," Exha-bi said.

"How do you feel?" Tali said.

"Better."

"Good," Rowle said. "Now let's move on. Why are the Grey so reluctant to fight?"

"Not our calling."

"What is?"

"Protecting."

"Can't you protect by fighting?"

"If we must."

"I'm saying you must!" Rowle said.

"We have a higher calling."

"Which is?"

"Protecting."

Rowle sighed loudly. She drew breath to continue but was stopped by a knock on the door. It was Nev returning with the racta. Tali rushed to the door, the more irritation she could prevent, she thought, the less chance of Rowle doing something awful. She grabbed the warm racta cup from Nev and cradled it in her hands while pacing.

"What are you protecting?" Rowle said in a stretched voice.

"Grey knowledge."

"Okay, good," Rowle said. "Knowledge of what?"

Exha-bi made a growling kind of noise. Rowle grabbed his chin again in one claw.

"I think our friend here is still holding out. Do you have any more of your magic potion left Alchemist?"

"I have but there's only so much you can dose..."

"Give it."

Tali sighed, handed her racta off to Nev and opened the flask again. It didn't even have the enthusiasm for a satisfying *bung* noise as it opened. She offered it to Exha-bi, who drank it from her knowing the consequences otherwise. She returned the empty flask to her backpack. Nev nudged her arm with the cup of racta.

"Thanks," she said and swigged heavily at the bitter liquid, forcing a swallow down.

Rowle paced until a loud gasp from Exha-bi stopped her. Tali rushed back over to him and

"Are you okay?" she asked, reflexively reaching for the elder's paw to check his pulse; it was battering.

"Great," Exha-bi said.

"I'd make this quick," Tali said.

"Quick is what I've been aiming for," Rowle said. "Right then. How do I lever the Grey to fight for me, so we can crush the White-Duchy and move on?"

"Knowledge," Exha-bi said.

"By all the little fishes!" shouted Rowle, "we've done this!"

"If I may," Tali said. "I think he means the knowledge is the lever."

"Okay," Rowle said.

"The knowledge of the Grey has been guarded for eons. If it were to be released—"

"Ah," Rowle said, "you tell me and they fight if I threaten to release their little secrets?"

"Yes," Exha-bi said.

"Excellent," Rowle said. "Tell me your most secret thing. No point in us messing about, is there?"

"The holy of holies. The room of pain."

"Room of pain, eh? I'm starting to warm to you Grey-folk. Tell me about it then."

"Only *The Questioning* the most trusted of the Grey can access it. Those with the most aptitude for learning, understanding."

"So it's a meritocracy. You learn lots of stuff and you're good folk and you get access to the secret room, I get it."

"No," Exha-bi said, "I don't think you do. Just eagerness, learning is not enough. We tried that in the past. Just being good was never enough. Many have experienced the room. Not all survive the experience intact."

"Gosh, this room of pain gets more interesting by the click. Does it kill them then? The ones that aren't good enough?"

"No. Many who aren't good enough end their own lives though. All are driven mad."

"And are you one of these 'Questioning' then? Are you good enough?" Rowle said.

"No one is good enough, but I survived, if that is what you are asking."

"I'm asking what's in the room."

"I could explain, but if you have not been there, you could not understand."

"Blah, blah, secret knowledge, blah!" Rowle said. "Try me."

The Vat bubbled and it's speaker hissed; it did not speak though. Then came a new hiss, quieter, menacing. The hiss of Rowle slowly extending her claws.

"What. Is. In. The. Room. Of. Pain," Rowle said, nose close enough to touch Exha-bi's. "Please."

"I cannot—"

"Or will not?"

Tali could hear Rowle's claws scraping on something. "Wait," she said. Then turning to Exha-bi, she said, "Can you tell us what it was like in the room? Describe it as much as you can?"

"Okay," Exha-bi said. "I'll try."

The claws stopped. The noise was replaced by one no less unnerving. The speaker from the Vat had started humming. A low drone note, continuous, quiet, but ever present. Tali felt the noise was like warmth, or cold, perfusing all of them, seeping into their bones.

"It was a long and thin room. I could feel wavy fabric, beautiful, soft drapes all the way along one wall. The *High Questioner* told me off for touching them, and then he sat me on the floor, facing the curtains. I wondered if I'd done something wrong already. The floor was cold, smooth, not metal though. Then he left, but right until he had, he kept asking me if I wanted to go through with it, and saying I'd never be the same again and it was okay to back out. I was too scared to go and too scared to stay, so I sat, paralyzed by indecision on the floor and waited for whatever was going to happen to happen. Did that mean I wasn't ready? I don't know."

He paused. The Vat's humming became quieter but did not stop.

"Then there was a small whirring noise like a motor running and the slight swish of the drapes parting. I followed the noise and movement until the drapes had stopped in the far corners of the room. Then I turned my head back to where the drapes had been. It was a huge smooth, flat wall. And then—"

"Then?" Rowle pressed.

"The pain started."

"What kind of pain? Describe what happened to you!"

"It is... hard. It felt like, like a thousand, ten thousand pins sticking into my face. No, sticking into my brain, through my face. Burning into me. My whole head felt on fire, churning, swirling. I couldn't speak or move. I didn't notice the motor had started again, it took until the edges of the drape swished back into place in front of me that I realized. But the pins were still there, burning into me. Slowly, very, very slowly, they decreased in intensity, but they left—a what? A sensation? Like a bruise on my brain where each one had been once they'd gone."

"Are they still there now?" Tali said.

"No," Exha-bi said, "it was many cycles ago. But I can feel where everyone was still. And sometimes I experience a twinge of it, one pin or a handful maybe."

"That's a charming story; where does that get me?" Rowle said.

"If you let the Grey know you could release their knowledge, they would do anything. Even fight for *you*," Exha-bi said.

Rowle made a spluttering noise. Tali giggled. "The mixture reduces his inhibitions, makes him more honest. Be careful what you wish for."

"How dare you insult me!" Rowle exploded. "I am the last of the Cat-people!"

"No," came Exha-bi's voice.

"What?" Rowle spat, whirling.

"No," came a different voice from the speaker in the Vat. It sounded oddly similar to Rowle, but different. Male, maybe.

"What trickery is this?" Rowle said.

"All here," the Exha-bi voice said.

"All still here," the Vat said.

"Who's still here?" Rowle said.

"All the cats…"

"All of us..."

"All still here..."

"Always here..."

"You can't be," Rowle said.

"We are Rowle," the male voice said again. "All still here."

"Rown? Rown?" The Bureaucrat didn't often sound shocked.

"I am here, love... Always here..."

"No. NO. Can't it can't be." Rowle turned and fled.

The door banged open and slowly eased shut. As if in answer to it, the secret door on the opposite side of the room slid open. Two folk and a handful of pups poured out of it.

"Did we miss much?" Dun said.

Chapter Sixty

Dun had scarcely opened his mouth when he was silenced by the hugest hug he'd ever had in his life.

"Gods, Dun, I thought you were dead," Tali said into his shoulder.

"It's okay," he said.

"I think it's far from okay," Kaj said behind them. "What the hells was with Rowle?"

"Family reunion," Nev said, walking over to an unexplained body by the Vat. "Can often be quite stressful."

Dun was finally released from Tali's grip. "Who's that by the Vat?" he said.

"He's called Exha-bi," Nev said. "He's a Grey-Duchy elder."

"Who we can get the hells out of here while Rowle's gone," Tali said.

"Won't she go mental?" Nev said.

"I think it's a bit late for that," Tali said. "OneLove, is there any safe way to break your connection now? Without hurting Exha-bi?"

The speaker hissed in response. There was a 'thwack' as the something hit the floor. Exha-bi coughed, spluttered, and fell to the floor gagging. Tali ran to his side.

"He is released," OneLove said from the speaker.

There was a weird cable-tentacle thing, writhing back into the Vat. Dun thought he might be sick. "What the hells has been happening here?"

"The beginning of the end," OneLove said.

"You are always reliable for a gnomic comment," Nev said. "We made an interface between OneLove and a living person."

"Oh gods, really?" Dun said.

"It was an... interesting experience," OneLove said.

"But what was it like for him?" Dun said.

"I think he's okay," Tali said, still tending to Exha-bi.

"He is no worse for having been connected," OneLove said.

"I hope you're right," Dun said.

"It was all necessary, OneLove said.

"That sounds cold," Dun said.

"I didn't mean it to." It was Myrch's voice now. "And it's true."

"What's true?" Dun said. "We're sanctioning torture now?"

"Not torture," Myrch said.

"What then?" Dun said.

He was sure he heard the Vat sigh. He rounded on the speaker, the place where he had started treating as where the Vat, where Myrch was, but a crackle in the speaker distracted him. Sometimes Dun thought the crackle was fast becoming the way the Vat had of clearing its throat, without actually having one.

"Yes?" Dun said, more irritated than he'd intended.

"There's someone else here, outside the door," the Vat said, still Myrch's voice, "to visit you."

"Visit us?" Dun said. "We're in charge now?"

"Not yet," Myrch said. "But I think he'd rather be having an audience with you than the Bureaucrat."

"Ain't that the truth," Padg said as he walked through the door.

The three Bridge-folk held each other. Dun felt tears running down his face. So much had happened since they were last together like this.

"Not that I'm not over the river about you turning up," Dun said after the longest time, "but why are you here?"

Padg chuckled. "I've been poking about a bit, and interesting things are going on. I thought you might like to know."

"How the hells did you know you'd find us here and not Rowle?" Tali said.

"Oh, a little Shaman whispered in my ear. Told me Rowle would be busy. It's busy with what though, is the problem."

"Oh?" Dun said.

"Can't it wait thirty clicks?" Kaj said. "I think we owe it to Exha-bi to get him home safely."

"I'm not here long," Padg said. "I'll say what I'm here for and get gone. I can take Exha-bi with me when I go back."

"Right across the battlefield?" Nev said.

"As a Tinkrala, I've got some degree of neutrality. For now," Padg said.

"Go ahead then," Tali said. "What's the Bureaucrat got going on?"

"Weapons," Padg said. "New, easy to deploy weapons that use steam. She's brought their deployment forward, I'd suggest by the speed of her exit."

"We've faced battlefield weapons before," Kaj said. "The Red-Duchy have been employing them for eons."

"Nothing like this. Jets of scalding steam that shoot out strides and in huge clouds. Other machines that can propel rocks right across massive caverns," Padg said.

"What can we do against them?" Dun said.

"Not a great deal," Padg said.

"And yet you must," OneLove said from the speaker.

"Why must we?" Dun was still cross. "It's all very well for you in there to be making deep prognostications. It's innocents who are going to be facing these things."

"Not entirely," Nev said.

"I -we need you to buy us some time." Again it was Myrch's voice now. "There are other forces at play."

"Oh?" Dun's patience was thin.

"This war. This conflict, will not be ended by weapons," Myrch said.

"Okay," Tali said. "How much time are we talking about?"

"It will be a full span till all the players are in place."

"Forgive me if I've started resenting being a player," Dun said. "A lot of folk could die in a span."

"Yes," the Vat said.

"How do we know we can trust you?" Dun said.

"We don't," Exha-bi said croakily from the side of the tank. "But some of us here have shared a link with the mind in there. We must trust how it feels."

Dun certainly had never felt any malice from OneLove, although he'd be the first to admit that the only part of it he truly trusted was Myrch. Ironic, since it was Myrch who'd betrayed them. Gotten Stef and so many others killed. But if there was a chance to end all of this, once and for all, Dun was feeling like he'd take it.

"Okay," he said moving to Exha-bi. "Let's get you home."

Then to OneLove, he said, "Just one span?"

"That should be enough."

"Let's get back to the camps," Tali said.

"Nev, Kaj, you coming?" Dun said. "See if we can't reduce the damage by some?"

"I'd like to but..."

"We'll be fine here," OneLove said. "You should go."

"I'll come," said Kaj. "The waiting would drive me crazy anyway."

Chapter Sixty-One

Rowle stood at the top of a makeshift platform above *The Spitter* with a soldier. At its first demonstration, she found herself clapping her hands like a kitten. It was simple yet effective. A steam chamber with valves to control it; a hopper for projectiles to go in, rocks seemed to fly best, but anything had been working; a massive pipe that worked as the barrel of the gun, with a bore the diameter of her head and three times her length. Since she had no effective Air-sense to speak of, she needed a gunnery sergeant to do aiming for the weapon. Instructions were relayed to the folk on the ground via a speaking tube. Then the massive barrel was wedged and prodded into the correct orientation for the next shot. Perhaps the next generation of Spitter could have cables that went up the tower to maneuver it. She would suggest that for next time.

"Ready, Your Eminence."

"Fire."

A low *whumph* sounded. The projectile spiraled noisily as it arced through the air. It must be less than round, thought Rowle. That wouldn't matter. A great crash echoed back to the firing team and cheers drowned out whatever distant cries the impact had caused. If they could only be quieter, it would be easier to assess the damage the weapon was causing. She had mentioned it, but the glee from the gunnery crew at the crashes was a little too infectious to stamp out. She could understand that. She could hardly begrudge them all the fun.

The barrage had gone on for a good quarter span and Rowle wondered whether the 'Collected Forces' as the enemy had called themselves were softened up enough yet for a ground assault. The Collected Forces comprised the White-Duchy and the Under-folk in effect. The Red-Duchy were hers, the Grey fighting reluctantly and the crazies in Gantrytown were too chaotic to form anything approaching resistance;

"Ready."

"Fire."

Another crash and more cheering. This could be the shortest conflict in recorded history. Why she hadn't gotten her remaining ex-Machine-folk whipped into shape sooner, was truly beyond her. Oh well, no point crying over spilled blood. She tapped her foot absently on the platform.

"Ready."

"Prepare the next wave of the attack," she said. More instructions were barked down the speaking tube. "Fire."

The projectile arced into the air. Rowle thought, it almost sang as it went. In accompaniment, a chorus of troops was readying her other battle-winning weapon. The engineer who'd come up with the idea had called them "little dragon". She thought the title quite poetic. More so since she had been torturing the Chap's family, but one did need these ways to focus the mind on the task at hand. The little dragon could be wielded by one soldier. It consisted of a massive length of flexible hose and a 'mouth' on the end with a valve. Once the valve was released, it belched super-heated steam until the pipe became too hot to aim. By then the damage was done. The challenge with this weapon was the organization it had taken to deploy. Steam points to connect the opposite end of the apparatus to were few and far between, so Rowle had been getting a team of folk to install and adapt temporary outlets all the way along the hab from the Bureau to the gates of the Duchy. Then behind the scenes, much rerouting of pipes had taken place to get the steam pressure where she needed it, preferably outside of the control of automatic valves that the cursed Vat could get its tentacles into. So far she'd been pleased with the results but this was the first time the little dragons had been used in anger on the battlefield. She'd found an empty hanger, bureau-side to rehearse the new dragon guard that would be using them, and they'd quickly discovered that at any distance from the steam point, it required increasing numbers of folk to handle the pipe. Thus far, dragon teams were consisting of one *mouth*, three *pages*, and a *steam tech*. For the devastating effect of the weapon, Rowle thought that was a reasonable allocation of resources. Plus, those paging kinds of jobs, not exactly front line roles; it gave her places to allocate all those reluctant Grey's she needed to keep occupied. Idle hands and all that.

"Should we carry on firing, Eminence?" the sergeant said.

"Oh yes, a few more, why not?"

"As you command, Your Eminence. The dragon guards need 500 clicks more and the spitter ground crew report ready for the next salvo."

"Good," Rowle said. "Fire."

With the slightly more organized noises of preparation of the various crews, the actual volume of shouting lessened slightly. Rowle was sure she could hear some distant kind of yelling carried on the breeze from the mouth of the hab where the collected were encamped.

"Excellent," Rowle said. "Prepare more stones for the hoppers, keep firing but keep the trajectories high, fire at will. Ready the dragon guards. Advance! Burn them all."

Chapter Sixty-Two

"Incoming!"

Another huge lump of gods knew what flew overhead and landed with a massive crash. Mostly folk seemed to be quick enough to get out of the way, there was only one fatality so far, but the tent village at the far end of the hab dome was wrecked.

The rocks and lumps of scrap came in with an ominous whirra-whirra noise as they flew. The Bureaucrat had really outdone herself this time. Her and whoever had helped her construct the crazy monstrous machine aimed at them.

"To the trees!"

It seemed like the only place they'd get any shelter. Dun barked some orders at the nearest folk to him and things started to organize. The Collected Forces seemed to work that way. Mostly. The River-folk faction seemed to be a law unto themselves, and they seemed to have made themselves scarce since the shelling had started.

Whirra-whirra-whirra-whirra… crash.

Dun stopped in the silence and cocked an ear. That was a different noise. Hissing? Whooshing, from the edge of the camp closest to Gantrytown. Dun should still have been busy sorting out rushing the camp into the trees to get them out of the firing line. Then he heard the screams.

Tali rushed up. "What in the hells is that?"

"I don't know," Dun said. "But we need to find out. Let me take some folk with spears, can you start the evac to the tree line?"

"Sure," she said, "be careful."

Dun found a handful of competent militia including one or two folks from Stone-folk soldiery and a couple of Collective guerillas. They grabbed some weapons and Kaj and unlike everyone else, headed toward the sounds of trouble.

The whooshing and screaming became quite loud quite quick. Dun hoped that the evacuation to the trees would happen quickly, but also that Tali would set up some kind of first aid, because the folk running toward him were in increasing states of distress. He could smell an awful mix of burned flesh and fear. The folk running past all seemed to be in various increasing states of dampness too.

Then a whoosh and piercing scream from his left and the noise of someone falling over and his world started to tilt itself. Dun found himself nose down in the dirt floor of the hab, head pressed next to a fallen folk woman, barely alive with awful raggedy breathing. He felt a hand over his mouth as he drew breath to speak.

"Shh!" Kaj's voice, right in his ear. "Stay down."

Soldiers tramped over them, one stood on Dun's hand. He tried not to flinch and give his position away. The whooshing went overhead in what seemed like a wide, wide line. There were three or more of these weapons with teams to go with them. The whole of the air around Dun was damp and smelled of metal and the unique acrid charcoal smells of burned flesh and singed hair, so intense as to be a taste as well as a smell. Dun clamped his mouth and his nostrils shut so as not to gag.

Kaj released her hand from his mouth and was in the process of levering herself up when a huge weight dragged across them both. Something massive, flexible. A pipe? A hose? As it rolled over them it felt rubbery and warm, like a massive serpent from the deep caverns of folklore. Dun stayed flat and let the bulk bump over him. Once it passed, Kaj grabbed his arm and pulled him away.

Then in a crouch, she hissed into his ear, "Four or more crews with the crazy burning weapons?"

"Yeah," Dun said. "Steam? And I bet those hoses are powering them. Come on, I've got a plan. You got a knife?"

"Course. What kind of a girl do you take me for?"

"Good, I've got a stone-spear here. How long do you reckon these pipes are?"

Before she could answer, another soldier, holding another lump of the pipe loomed in their Air-sense. Dun rolled under the pipe as the soldier leaned toward Kaj and whacked the spear across the back of hose carrier's knees. The soldier buckled under the blow and the weight of the pipe. Then for good measure, Dun stuck his spear firmly into the pipe. The jet of steam shot up the handle of the spear, and Dun screamed as he let go. Then the pipe twisted and the screams came instead from the fallen soldier.

"Shreds! You okay?" Kaj said.

"Bit sore," Dun said. "But okay. Gods, that stuff is hot. No way we'll be able to bust them with knives, we'd be too close. Need more spears. Damn, damn, damn. Back to the camp."

"Do we?" Kaj said. "Or should we follow the pipe the other way and shut them off at the source."

Chapter Sixty-Three

No sooner had Tali let Dun go, the screaming began. Distant at first, but getting louder with the approaching hissing. She was wondering a million things at once: would she have enough time or anywhere secure to set up a first aid station? What the hells was the weapon causing all the screaming? Where the hells had those River-folk cowards gotten to. She needed a little more backup to help cover everyone's retreat. The answers to the last two of those questions came quickly and hard on each other's heels.

The whooshing came in bursts, the screaming was pretty constant. Tali tried to locate the nearest approaching source of the noise to respond, but the stream of casualties hit her first. Running to her as the obvious go-to for injuries, running toward her where they could still Air-sense or smell, running pell-mell in a panic where not. The flood of burned folk was ghastly and massive; if she didn't act now, then it would take one folk to slip over, and there'd be deaths to contend with too. If the severity of the burns didn't make it inevitable anyway.

Tali was stuck in a panic. Not a blank of no decision: between two. She didn't know whether to organize the folk to keep running for cover at the risk of having them all run down by whatever approaching awful battle machines were coming. Or whether to use her alchemist's instincts and lob one of the concussions at her belt in the general direction of the attackers.

Only a click had gone by, time had stretched out with the elastic that only disaster can bring, but a tick was already too long. They were way too far away from the tree line for her to make it there with a mass of casualties in tow. But if she was the only combatant, she didn't fancy her odds against three or four teams of these awful steam hurlers. Where the hells were the River-folk when you needed them?

That was it. Of course. Two ticks gone by now, but now she had a plan. Where would the River-folk go? To the river. The nearest meander of the river that filled the lake in the hab was nearer to her than the edge of the central park, and she'd bet good tallies that the River-folk had gone right there. That would be her backup. She hoped. At least if they'd done something more random she'd have somewhere to cool down her casualties.

"Follow me!" she yelled. "Run toward my voice, as fast as you can!" She jockeyed backward so she could sense whether she'd had a response and where the enemy was. The stream of maddening folk seemed to be heading toward her. That was good.

Then the steam hiss again, closing now, and urgent shouts. They were following her voice too. Shreds.

"Run!" she yelled as the steam came.

There were screams all around her, that shrill piercing squeak of visceral panic. She continued running to where she thought the river was, but a flat pain built at her back. She tweaked her ears back. She could hear nothing above the bellowing of the closing steam. The roar rang in her ears. She flicked her ears forward again as she felt them starting to burn.

Then shouting came from in front of her. "Geddown!" A River-folk accent if ever she'd heard one. Friend not foe. She reached out her arms to both sides of her, scooped down the nearest folk and hit the deck, hoping.

"Fire!"

Tali froze from the loud barked order, but it came from in front of her, not behind. There was an almighty taut twang and a whizz overhead. Then a sharp clash of steel against steel, screaming, and the steam whooshed out of control, spinning like the pipe had been dropped. What the hells? Those bloody River-folk had only gone and brought two of the armed barges upriver, so they could use their massive harpoon guns in the battle. Thank gods for sneaky River rats.

"Small arms! Fire!"

A dozen higher-pitched twangs rang out, and it seemed like Duchy military were getting picked off with those nasty hand crossbows the River-folk seemed to like.

"Now run!" came the voice again.

Tali didn't need telling twice. She scooped up the same folk she's helped duck and hand in hand they ran to the river. There was splashing as her two charges jumped in. Tali stayed dry momentarily while she scanned the battlefield for any more folk. Mostly the running was taking her folk in the right direction but there was a small huddle farther onto the field where they'd run from. An adult folk and a child. The flailing loose steam pipe must have caught one of them as it sprayed. But Tali could Air-sense another of the steam cohorts approaching, about the same distance from them as she was. She turned and started to sprint. The fur on her back was stinging. It had gone from burning to dry without seeming to pass through wet, so hot was the steam and now every foot pound tore at the increasing soreness. But her focus was ahead. That steam pipe was still whipping about, and that was seemingly what was keeping their heads down. But the soldiers could Air-sense as well as she could, and the small huddle was obvious across the flat expanse. She had to deal with that pipe. The soldiers were closing, slower than Tali was, but those steam pipes had some range. She reached down to her belt, hopping as she ran, and placed her hand around one of the flasks. The code of knots securing the stopper told her it was a concussion. That'd do. She pulled it out, aimed, and threw it toward the approaching troops. Then she tweaked her course toward the huddle.

In that tiny turn, she tripped. Time slowed again as she rolled forward, tucking her head as she did. With her head underneath her, she heard the concussion go off, but she kept tucked and rolled again, righting herself about ten or so strides from the huddled family. Two adults and a child, now she was closer. She recognized the smell as Stone-folk she knew vaguely. And fear, everywhere was the smell of fear. She hissed toward them as she approached. "It's me, Tali. Stay down till I say, then run for the river."

She ran to them, yelling, "Duck!" as she jumped over them and headed for the still lashing steam pipe, five or six strides the other side of them. She hoped to all hells that the concussion had had some kind of effect because she couldn't hear or Air-sense a damned thing with the whipping steaming snake occupying all of her senses. The thing was transfixing; it swished this way and that with a life of its own. She tried to focus some of her senses on it, and then heard a child's shriek behind her. Damn. She jumped at the hose, catching the blast of super-heated steam full in the face. She grabbed the nearest metal ends she could find. They were hot too. She tamped down the reflexive need to let go and stood firm, hose pointing into the air, but under control.

She heard one of the adults behind her say, "No..." and now the soldiers barking orders, sounding close enough to touch.

"Damn straight, no!" she yelled, bringing the steam mouth to bear on the soldiers before they had a chance to fire themselves. She couldn't hear if they were screaming, the steam was too loud, but if she was honest with herself, she didn't care. She swung the hose back and forth madly. Moving toward where the troops were. "Run!" she yelled over her shoulder.

The folk staggered up and lurched toward the river. At least one of them must have been way more injured than she thought.

"Bastards!" she yelled, spraying manically. She wasn't even sure if there were still soldiers on the receiving end of the hose, which seemed to be getting heavier. She felt oddly cold. There was buzzing in her head.

Her hands were numb but also slick. The weight of the metal mouth end of the pipe took her to her knees, then buzzing got louder still, and she lost consciousness.

Chapter Sixty-Four

Rowle always felt that battle was a creative process. Like the upheaval of digging before planting. And if the battle wasn't going entirely her way? Well, what were a few stones before the plow? She leaned on the balcony of her office enjoying the gentle wind blowing up. It carried a complex mix of churned up soil, folk sweat, and blood. And that odd smell that the wet burns from the dragon mouths caused. Sweet yet sickly. Apt somehow.

She liked this moment in wars. The eye of the storm. That chance between skirmishes for everyone to regroup. Of course, the tactician in her, probably from her father's side, should have been taking more troops out right now while medical teams collected the groaning and the silent from the battlefield. But she wasn't an animal. There were rules. Decorum. She hummed a little tune to herself and cleaned her claws.

A knock at her office door brought her back to herself. She waited. So did the messenger.

"What?" she shouted. More silence. "Come in, damn you."

"Sorry... Your Eminence..."

"What? What is it?"

"There are reports from the battlefield, Your Eminence."

"Good." She waited. "And?"

"Casualty rates on both sides are high..."

"Excellent."

"We are nearly finished collecting our fallen from the field."

"Good. Let them finish too, before we sound another attack."

"That is most generous, Your Eminence."

"I know. There is something else?"

"Spies report some other activity on the field too."

"Fighting, perhaps?"

"No, Your Eminence, now the fighting has stopped."

"Oh?"

"There seem to be groups of folk from Gantrytown,"

"I thought they had agreed to stay noncombatant at the price of us not turning the dragon mouths on them?"

"Oh, they're not fighting."

"All right, you have my interest. What are they doing?"

"Building? We think."

Rowle chuckled. "Building what?"

"We don't know, exactly. They seem like, er..."

"Spit it out."

"They seem like models of folk? Model folk made out of machine bits."

"A weapon perhaps?"

"Maybe? We don't know. Though there is no scent of anything alchemical or incendiary really."

"Oh? What do they smell of?"

"Jasmine."

"Humph. Are they a distraction then? A lure?"

"I have no idea, Your Eminence."

"Thank you," Rowle said. The messenger waited. "You're dismissed."

As the folk messenger bowed and scraped his way out of the door and it banged behind him, Rowle drifted back to the balcony. Now she listened. Even with her ears not being what they used to be, she could hear distant but clear clangs of metal on metal. Crunching and scraping. Again, the tactician in her leaped to her forebrain to say, "Attack now, swift and unexpected." But she didn't. She wanted to know how this would play out. There was no point in playing with a mouse once it was dead. Even if you had it, to flick between one paw and another, there was no joy in it if the life had gone.

But the life hadn't gone out of the Under-folk yet. So lift a paw off the tail and see how far they scamper, until...

She extended her claws and lovingly cleaned them, one by one.

Chapter Sixty-Five

Dun's war band had fought well, although six of them had gone out and only he and Kaj turned back toward camp. They had taken down one of the dreadful steam pipes, which was where they lost the last of the Stone-folk guards in a valiant attack on four troops, and then fought their way to the platform holding up the catapult or whatever it was hurling rocks. They used one of the longer Stone-folk spears from their fallen comrade to lever up one of the platform legs and discovered that the whole thing was built in haste, as it came crashing down in a cloud of steam and swearing. Bruised but laughing, they ran away, until they heard the long thin horn that signaled a retreat for the Duchy. Faint cheers sounded from the direction of the Under-folk camp. They slowed to a walk from there, meandering in and out of the churned-up mess of the battlefield.

Kaj stopped suddenly, a hand on Dun's arm. "Over there, toward Gantrytown."

Where she indicated, from over and through the massive Gantrytown barricade swarmed folk, spreading out onto the battlefield. As sure as he could be, Dun thought the spies from the Under-folk camp had said the Gantry-folk had agreed to be neutral, under pain of death from the Bureaucrat. There was certainly an armies' worth of them, if they decided to fight on the Bureaucrat's side they'd be in trouble. But they didn't seem to be behaving like an army. Not like they were fighting at all. Stopping in small groups here and there and what?

"First aid?" Kaj said, thinking similar thoughts.

"Maybe." Dun crouched on his haunches, trying to concentrate through his tiredness.

As the Gantrytown army approached slowly Dun heard voices drifting across the cavern. Industrious, busy, urgent, but not a war band. Who then?

"We should go," Kaj said.

"I wanna know what this lot are up to," Dun said.

"Suit yourself. I'm gonna go back to what's left of the camp and report it."

"Be there soon."

"'Kay."

Dun sat still to better hear the distant voices. He was certain they had no ill intentions by the time they got close enough for him to properly hear the conversation.

"Another one here!" That voice was very close. Dun thought he must be tired to not hear someone creeping up on him. And it wasn't like this lot were particularly trying to be stealthy. It was one of the things that gave them away as not soldiers.

"Don't touch, I'll be across in ten clicks, got a bleeder here to stabilize first." That voice sounded farther away, but oddly familiar.

The nearer voice started whistling to himself. Grimly cheerful. Dun liked that. Reminded him of... Ah, now the other voice was closer. Padg. Of course, Padg. Something made Dun wait and hunker down.

"Okay, I'm here. What've we got?" Padg said.

"Female, young, severe burns. Can't detect a pulse or breath sounds, but she's warm to the touch."

"Let me check," Padg said. "Wait."

"Should I get a bearer team?" the whistler said. "Padg?"

"I said WAIT!"

"Okay, keep your fur on."

Time clicked by. Dun felt shivery, although the cavern was warm enough.

"No," Padg said.

"What?" the whistling companion said. "She's dead, right?"

"No." Padg knelt down.

"She's not dead? I don't understand."

"Shut. Up."

"Okay, touchy, I was only-"

"Leave me!" A brief silence, and then in a gentler voice, Padg said, "Go and see if Laly needs any help; she was heading over to the lake."

"Right." The whistler shuffled off in silence.

Dun's feet had already carried him to Padg. He knelt down next to him and placed a hand on his back.

"Tali," Dun said. It wasn't a question. "How?"

"Damned steam pipes."

"Gods no." A horrible way to go. "But she's still... warm."

"She's gone, Dun."

"She might not be, if..." Dun trailed off into silence.

"Oh, gods," Padg said. "You're not talking to *him,* are you? Let her go."

"I thought you believed in all that?" Dun said.

"I'm not sure what I believe in anymore."

"But if we're quick..."

"Dun, we've lost her."

Then a long deep trumpet note sounded. A warning that the battle was due to recommence.

"You should go, take her back to the camp," Padg said. "Somebody should let Amber know. And you're the Shaman."

"What about you?" Dun said.

"I've got a score to settle," Padg said.

Dun lifted his friend and started walking. He felt the scant weight of her body in his arms and pressed his nose into the bundle of her clothes. It was uniquely Tali: lavender, vinegar, and girl sweat. It was difficult to smell clearly as his nose was filling with snot. What was it Padg said? Take her to the camp. Yes, he should do that. He wiped his nose on his arm and then regretted it. His feet carried him on.

"I can't put you down and now my arms all wet," he said.

He lifted his head and twitched. Even with whiskers covered in snot, he could Air-sense enough to know he was not at the camp. Not at all. A huge sheer metal wall was so close to him he almost walked into it. The hab wall then. But where?

Screaming brought Dun back to himself and told him exactly where he was. That unique charging scream of a battlefield cry. A charge to arms. He stood alongside the main door up into the Bureau and troops were streaming out. He flattened himself against the wall as best he could and hoped the fact that they were all fired up and running the wrong way past him would effectively hide him.

He stood stock still, holding his breath until the roar of the soldiers had long passed. Then, before he knew what he was doing, he was climbing the stairs to the Bureau and heading along the corridor that took him to the Sanctuary and OneLove.

Chapter Sixty-Six

Troops streamed onto the battlefield from the Red-Duchy and the Grey. Their forces outnumbered the Under-folk by more than five to one if spies were to be believed. Rowle stood upon a chariot that she'd had the captured Machine-folk make for her. She had decided that the two remaining Rat-things in storage should be harnessed to pull her. A little fierceness never did anyone any harm. Especially someone planning to be empress of an entire planet.

"Stop!" she called to her carriage train: they stopped. Rat-things were nothing if not loyal to whoever they were programmed to serve.

She stood tall on the chariot, the forces at her command arrayed before her.

"Today is a great day. This span will see the end of all this. The end of the Duchies, of Over-folk and Under-folk. Of fragmentation. Of war. Of disunity. After today, we will carve in the great halls a new story. One of unification. One of peace. Remember, you fight today for all of this, for a new Dark. A new world where each knows their place and no dissent is countenanced. You fight today to end all fighting."

She waited for applause, an approbation from the large crowd of soldiers. None came.

"To war!" she yelled.

"TO WAR!" Came the echo. At least all the Red-Duchy could be relied upon for a rallying cry. The roar rose slowly and the troops swept off across the hab. Rowle waited for the mass of troops to move and then spurred her Rat-things on to follow. This was going to be a good span.

Chapter Sixty-Seven

"Please?" Dun said. Explaining to OneLove had taken longer than he'd imagined it would and the Vat, speaking in the more formal tones that Dun thought of as OneLove, had been reluctant.

But finally, Dun lowered the limp form of Tali, with clothes but without chemicals, into the Vat. There was a rustle of cables and wires and a bubbling as she slowly sank from the surface.

"How long, until—" Dun said.

"It is an uncertain process," OneLove said. "Return to the camp. They need you there. We will contact you if there is progress."

Dun grunted, turned, and left. He felt like he was wading through the Vat himself. As he walked back to the camp the battle was raging all around him. He could not bring himself to care, although he deflected blows on instinct as they came at him.

He reached the camp almost without noticing. The sentries let him straight past, scenting his as 'friend' strides out. The bustle there was almost no different, less sharp, maybe. He didn't feel in place there either, no familiar voice of Tali's barking instructions to the teams. The camp miasma was now missing a unique signature, even though his arms still smelled of her. He almost didn't notice the new smell in the camp until the voice that went with it, was right in front of him. Amber.

"Where is she?" Amber said.

"She. I-She's with OneLove."

"Oh, well let's go and catch her then. I've only just gotten in, I can't wait to..."

"Amber."

"What?"

"She's in with OneLove," Dun said.

"I-I don't understand."

"She's in the Vat."

Amber made a noise, a half-spoken word, maybe? She left it half stuck in her throat. Fighting noises closed on the camp. The scent of Padg was close.

"Grab a bloody spear will you," he said at Dun. "Make yourself useful. Oh. Amber. Hello."

"Take me to her," Amber said. It wasn't clear who to.

"I can, but..." Dun said.

"I don't know if anyone had noticed, but there's a war on," Padg said. "And we're not winning it."

"Incoming!" a guard yelled at the sentry post.

"Another steam crew!" another yelled.

"Spear?" Padg shouted, prodding a weapon butt into Dun's hand. He took the haft. One of Padg's sword-spears, Dun could tell by the texture. The weapon jab seemed to wake him from his stupor. A familiar twist in his hands.

"Wanna go to Tali?" Dun said. "Let's go!"

"Oh gods," Padg groaned.

Dun strode toward the sentry post, now in a skirmish with Red-Duchy soldiers. They smelled of the blood and gore they smeared on themselves in battle. He threw the spear at the strongest smell and ran to follow it. The spear found its mark with a thud and a scream. Dun ran up the soldier's chest, retrieving his spear as he went. He scooped up the fallen warrior's spear as well and tossed it back to Amber.

"You might want this."

Dun heard a snap as Amber adapted the weapon to suit her. "Go," she said.

He already had and was forcing his way through the crush, camp sentries, and folk who'd just grabbed improvised weapons in tow. They heard the whoosh of a steam dragon and screams of panic rather than pain.

"Let's cut that off," Padg said, producing the familiar clicking of Myrch's old needler weapon.

Dun fought between Air-sense and thoughts of *Where the hells did that come from?* as they advanced straight at the steam crew. The click-click whish-whish of the gun was reassuring and Padg had got hellish good at aiming it too. For almost every click there was a corresponding yelp. Dun followed in behind, Air-sensing the falling steam crew.

"Scum!" he yelled as he reached the soldier holding the mouth end of the pipe. There was a click, but Dun went faster, kicking out with a side thrust. The edge of his foot slid along the metal mouth and the pipe. He felt the bite of heat, but flicked his foot up sharply, and then slid in underneath. He kicked forward at the steam guard, reaching around to find the pipe. It still had the guards fingers tight around it too and pointed searing breath upward. The soldier grunted and Dun braced against him. This was an arm wrestle with deadly consequences. Dun felt his muscles shaking; he'd been neglecting his training. The soldier was gaining, and the pipe was tipping toward him. Ten degrees more tilt and he'd be in the fire cone. At least he could hear Padg and Amber gaining distance around him, so they wouldn't get hit.

Then his toe caught something on the floor. A weapon of a fallen soldier? No, taller than that. It was another one of those crazy junk piles that seemed to be springing up across the battlefield. He felt himself tumbling backward, the steam guard tumbling toward him. Dun rolled backward, then twisted to bring the pipe with him. One of the soldier's hands still gripped around it, but bent backward now. Damn, this guy was strong. But with one hand against two, Dun could free a hand up. He turned the pipe and drowned in screams as he hosed the enemy.

He was still yelling when Padg touched his shoulder. "Mate, come on. You still wanna get to Tali?" Dun grunted. "Okay, let's go then. Careful where you point that thing."

But "that thing" allowed them to cut a swath through the enemy toward the center of the hab. If nothing else it would start to take pressure off the camp, stupidly outnumbered as they were. Dun didn't look back to Air-sense the crowds of troops closing again behind them, but he knew they were. Firing the steam gun at their enemies felt good. The metal mouth shouted steam and emotion where Dun could not. He couldn't tell if there were still noises coming out of his mouth.

Then he felt a pull on the pipe. It had caught. He tugged sharply. It was stuck fast. Another one of those damned junk pillars for sure. Now he was stuck. He shouted forward to Padg.

"What?"

"I can't move the pipe, and we can't leave it," Dun shouted.

"Damn it," Padg said. Then he handed the needler off to Amber. "Cover us!"

Padg began to help to tug, then thinking better of it, shouted over the roar of the pipe, "Let's jam it off."

Dun yanked on the handle, the steam slowed, and then stopped.

"Incoming!" Amber yelled accompanied by the rattle of rounds firing.

Dun and Padg clanged at the valve handle with a piece of metal pipe pulled off one of the junk piles. Amber fired and fired, then pocketed the gun, and carried on attacking with the staff she'd made from the spear.

"Done it!" Padg yelled, the handle coming off in his hand to a gentle hiss of steam. "Go, go, go!"

They all three advanced, spear points forward, expecting dense fighting. But instead, the crowd of fighters parted in front of them. Come to think of it, they didn't smell of blood either. Not Red-Duchy then. But as the ranks opened up to reveal a single taller figure, they knew who had come. Rowle.

"Ah!" she said cheerfully.

Padg turned to Amber and Dun and hissed, "You go. I've got that score to settle."

Chapter Sixty-Eight

They approached the door of the Sanctuary. Dun paused to talk to Amber. Instead, the door creaked open and a voice from inside drifted into the corridor.

"Enter."

"I hate it when he does that." Dun sighed.

"Who?" Amber said.

"OneLove/Myrch whatever he calls himself these days."

"You think it's a he?"

"Quite frankly, I don't know who or what he, she or it is anymore."

Warm air, smelling of vinegar and that weird slightly composting organic smell that the Vat had, drifted out of the room, along with a hum of fans. Dun inhaled heavily.

"Shall we?" Amber said, quietly.

"Sure."

Dun realized Amber was waiting for him to go first. Of course, it was the first time she'd been to the Sanctuary. He remembered his own unease the first time, of being in the presence of OneLove: supercomputer, deity, telepath, controller, and what else?

He stepped in. The chamber had become a home of sorts, not just because of the little hideout he, Kaj, and Nev had there, but because the Sanctuary seemed to be the locus of all Dun's foretelling now the transmitter was there. Although foretelling seemed like an out of date term now too. So much had changed. Everything maybe.

"Welcome," Myrch said.

"Hello?" Amber said.

"Hey," Dun said.

"Come over here, both of you," Myrch's voice came from the speaker attached to the Vat.

"Okay," Amber said.

They both walked over. Dun could smell Tali, he could feel Amber's questions all unasked, hanging in the breeze that blew gently across the Vat.

"Sit," Myrch said. "Please."

"Sure," Dun said and sat.

Amber followed. Dun helped her settle. He reached for a blanket that he knew was stowed behind a pipe in the corner and gave it to her. She laid it on the floor by the speaker and huddled down.

"So?" Dun said.

The Vat made that noise that Dun considered a sigh.

"Tali?" Amber said.

"Is gone," Myrch said.

Dun made something between a howl and a gasp.

"I—" Myrch said, "we tried."

"Tried what?" Amber said.

"To save, her, who she was."

"I feel an excuse coming," Dun said bitterly.

"No excuse," Myrch said. "There was too much damage. The heat, there was a massive bleed. The brain—"

"*Her* brain," Dun said.

"Yes, *her* brain," Myrch said. "The trauma. It was too much. I'm sorry."

"Are you though?" Dun found he was shouting. "Are you?"

"Yes."

"You're an immortal super being? Why would you be sorry? Why would you care?" Dun said.

"You know I knew her, Dun. I liked her."

"Then why couldn't you save her?"

"If we could have, we would, believe me."

In the silence created by Dun's anger was a sob: Amber's. He closed his mouth, opened it, and then closed it again. He touched her shoulder.

"I don't...understand," she said. "Is she...?"

"Gone?" Dun said.

"As you knew her," Myrch said, "yes."

"What the hells does that mean?" Dun said.

"We saved some of her memories, information."

"Memories of us?" Amber said.

"Some," Myrch said. "Other things. Potions, history, experiences. It wasn't all lost."

"But Tali's gone," Dun said.

"Yes."

"Gone."

He fell to his knees and after a short time a quiet, almost singing noise escaped him. The fans were almost louder, but as Dun's voice became more certain, the fans became quieter and then still. Dun's voice filled the emptiness.

Slowly, quietly at first, Amber joined in too. Their voices twining chaotically, like river vines: sometimes in parallel, sometimes in opposition, sometimes between the two with wild resonance throbbing. Although there were only two voices, the Sanctuary space was full to bursting.

A deep chocolatey hum began from the speaker. Myrch's voice. Dun almost lost his song thread with the distraction, but the voice was kind and respectful, understanding and sad. And became another vine in the twist of voices. The resonance ebbed and swirled, the new voice part taking the whole new places.

Then the most extraordinary thing happened. Another folk voice came from the Vat, unfamiliar but female and strong. Then another, male this time and older. Then another and another, lifting the rising tide of voices. The resonance started to make individual noises almost impossible to contemplate, but before there was any time to contemplate anything, the vortex of sound whirled on. Dun found himself unable to do anything but join in, captivated by the soundscape.

He twitched an ear to see if he could still hear Amber or Myrch in the throng, but then a new noise burst out, pulling his ears in a different way. This was the voice sound of someone like Rowle, a Cat-people, did she call herself? But not Rowle: a male. Then another and another, their voices adult but like small creatures crying, haunting, uncanny.

Then more human voices, like Myrch, the human tones that made up OneLove but separated. Like feeling the individual grains on a piece of bark but knowing that it's still the skin of a tree.

Dun's head was full, but he thought nothing. From ear to ear the whole of his skull was full of sound. His body too. Every cavity inside him was thrumming with the music: It was undoubtedly that now. A music the like of which had never been heard before. Tears streamed down Dun's face. He wiped his face with his hand then reached out to Amber; she lifted his hand to her cheek, it was wet too. They could do nothing but be moved, like a dust on a current, on and out. He was elated and scared all at once. Where would this music end? Would it ever end? Where would it take them?

Chapter Sixty-Nine

"Ah good!" Rowle said. "This has cheered my span."

The group of elite guards had formed a large circle around Padg and Rowle.

"Stop talking and fight!" Padg lunged and quick as lighting took first blood: He thrust his spear and scraped Rowle's thigh.

"Feisty, little Tinkrala!" Rowle said, laughing.

"Shut. Up!"

Padg sprang and came down with the butt of the spear first. It connected somewhere on Rowle's face with a crunch, but as Padg continued through the air, running over Rowle, her upward facing claw caught him all along his belly. He hissed in pain and rolled over. The crowd around them jeered. The clawing was reflexive, Rowle was still stunned from the blow from the spear. Padg took his chance to check his wound; it was deep but just one cut. It would stitch and Tali—he shook his head, tears streaming down his face. Maybe the cut had hurt him more than he had let on. Rowle was groaning and getting up. Padg tore a strip off the bottom of his robe and improvised a bandage.

"Bastard!" he yelled and threw the sword-spear for all he was worth. It was a good throw, he thought he'd hit her for sure, but she lurched at the last click and it flew on. There was a gasp in the audience as someone there had to sidestep too. Serve them right, ghouls. Someone threw the sword-spear back into the ring on the far side with a clatter. Unusually sporting.

Now it was Rowle's turn to spring. She leaped the full distance of the clearing from a standing start. Padg didn't have time to be impressed. He rolled, head first, from where he was drawing his knife from its sheath. He'd only got it half drawn when Rowle and he collided. He used the pommel instead since that was nearest his opponent. He thrust upward at four sets of claws bearing down on him, hoping he could deflect some or all of them. His momentum carried him forward and one of the slashing rear claws just caught his hand. The pommel of the knife connected forcefully with claws too, and the Bureaucrat yelped in pain.

Padg shoulder rolled onward and crashed into the far side of the crowd. They could have put the boot in, and Padg was tensed in case they did. Instead, they closed ranks, caught his momentum, and poured him back into the ring. He rolled over the haft of the spear, good. How interesting, Rowle was crouched and poised again. Padg wondered why she was taking so much risk. Granted four claws came down at him at once, and her muscle and weight to boot, but she left her underside exposed. All Padg would need would be one clear hit and that would be it. Why was she doing that?

She sprang again and Padg cartwheeled sideways out of her way. Even with her reach, she missed him. Closing the distance, she was trying to close the distance. Clearly her Air-sense sucked, she was a close-in fighter. Padg rocked himself up and jabbed with his spear. Let's keep this at arm's length then. He brought the spear to bear, point out, jab, feint, jab. And another strike, Rowle lashed out, but Padg wasn't there. The spear slashed back and caught her across a tendon. He was so pleased he'd kept up his weapon sharpening, even though he was an acolyte. The yowl was deafening. Good strike then. A hiss from the crowd. Jab, feint, jab, jab. Another hit, on her paw this time. Swipe, duck, slice.

No, too complacent. A huge gash opened up on Padg's cheek bled down onto his whiskers on one side. He hadn't even felt her contact him. He reached up a paw to wipe his face, and then the cat had closed again. This time, she grabbed him and lifted him off the floor. He kicked desperately, but she was so strong, damn her. He felt her start to squeeze tighter.

"Who's on top now, little folklet?"

Padg tried to spit out a response, but a gurgle was all that came out. Stars started to form in his head, and his pulse was all he could hear in his ears. He swung his legs back, then forward, and made a desperate swing to wrap his legs around her arm. Then he dug the end of his claws into her and gripped with all he had left. He felt a twitch as his claws scratched her, but his claws, unlike hers, weren't designed for killing. He held on and clawed in tighter. The breath was coming fast for him now and the sparkling in his head became fuzzy. His ears buzzed. He was losing focus. Rowle's arm was starting to shake but was that on its own or resonance with his own shaking? He found he didn't care. He could feel the sharp claws scratching his skin as he clawed at Rowle, but the shaking was becoming too much. He started to feel like he wasn't entirely there.

The last thing Padg heard as he blacked out was the singing.

Chapter Seventy

Rowle hadn't even noticed she'd dropped the limp bundle of flesh to the floor. She was paralyzed with shock. What the hells was that noise? And why was it coming from everywhere? All at once. She shook her head. The sound was coming from far away and near as well. How was that possible? She flicked her ears up and then down. Wait, there was a point of sound near her. It was very close, on the floor. She toed the limp body out of the way and revealed the source of the noise. One, of its sources.

She knelt down. The nearest noise was coming from a small junk pile, an arm's length high and no more. One of those speaking things that cursed Technician had attached to the Vat? Hidden inside the junk pillar. She kicked the pillar over. It distorted and crackled. She then found herself stamping on its remains until it stretched to a thin hiss and then stopped. But the sound did not. Those junk pillars were everywhere. Everywhere. And the sound, now she thought about it, was that awful mewling the folk made when someone died. That ghastly mourning song they all did together. But they should have been fighting. All that had stopped. Her loyal guard were all stock still, some weapons still in hand, some not. And they started singing too.

"Stop!" she yelled. "Fight, you cowards!"

But no one moved. Their songs all began to rise, one and all, across the battlefield. Folk voices nearby, combined with echoes from the far sides of the hab, combined with whatever tinny relayed sound the junk pillars were projecting. The noise was becoming extraordinary.

Then she had to whip her head around. The nearest working junk pillar. There was a sound coming from there she wasn't sure of, but something deep down in her gut knew it. She walked toward the pillar spellbound. It was the noise of Cat-people. She wanted to be thinking about how, but she couldn't. The sound had caught her. Mourning of her people, for her people. Did she almost recognize some of the voices? It was difficult to rationalize when it was pulling on her heart as much as her ears. It was certainly bypassing her brain. Yowling, mourning sounds that should be howled to the sky. The sounds of lost loves, of the death of hope, of loneliness, of grief made into sound. She felt the vibrations deep in her chest and didn't know when she herself had started crying too. The grief of all the Cat-people and the memories of Cat-people since forever. It resonated in her and shook her to the core. She was the last. And she had lost everything. Her chance of continuing when she could not bear a litter. Much later her partner who had been there since the beginning. Now her whole sense of self. Why was she allied with these rodents when she should be hunting them, torturing them, eating them? But that was the cat speaking; where was the person? The Cat-people had been grand, civilized, elegant, luxurious; gifting their superior intellect in return for labors performed. It was they who had conceived the food-farms and factories so no one had to predate on each other again and no one had to starve. They had made this world livable, possible. But now it was all gone. All of it in shreds, stinking, torn, tiny shreds. She was scratching at the door of her mind trying to get out, scratching and scratching till her claws bled.

She fell to her knees and her jaws fell open in a scream. It was the most massive noise she had ever made, but it was lost in the symphony of mourning: folk and human, Cat-people and other. She put her hands over her ears, but still, she couldn't hear herself: The noise was everywhere. The resonance shook every structure of her body. She screamed on until her lungs were empty, on her knees, mouth open, unsure if any of the noise was her or not. Ever. She let her body drop forward with her face to the ground, in the hope it would dull some of the sound, but it seemed the noise came from everywhere. All that it resulted in was her shaking uncontrollably now her muscles weren't holding her upright anymore. Then the texture of the sounds changed. Instead of a whole symphony of calls, the soundscape broke into solos: one voice here, a trio there—all moving in flight from one speaker to another; chasing, then fleeing, first high, and then low, swirling, tumbling. It had changed from a mournful chorale to a beautiful fugue: angel voices pursuing each other through the air. Her sobs had changed too. She was still crying uncontrollably, but now the wracking, chest-shaking sobs had gone, but in pure joy, tears poured out of her.

Then, by her ear, a playful cat noise.

"Mrow!"

Someone wanted chasing, did they? Well, a chase they would get and no mistake. And off she shot, following the noise, first here, then there, jumping and pouncing, and prancing like a kitten. Around and around and around, then on, bouncing and hopping along until, ah! Through? In and under and then? Up, onward, and up.

The speakers beckoned, "Catch me, bet you can't find me. You're it!"

Her play partners always ten steps ahead, twirling and twisting onward and upward in an endless dance. Up and up, onward and inward and through the door.

The voices of the rejoicing, dancing Cat-people still frolicked and leaped, but now around the room she found herself in. But she knew exactly what room this was. Why was she surprised? Was she, even? The smell of this room was always unmistakable, but now it even smelled a bit of Cat-people. How was that possible? She was the only one here. But it was a scent she couldn't mistake; it was wired into her. A rising joy of a smell, that spelled the courtship dance and mating. Of long spans yowling at, at something.

Rowle stood at the center of a vortex, cat voices all around her, on the ground, and in the air, but the vortex moved her on, enticing, leading, edging. She knew where this was heading, there was an inevitability, but she let the voices lead her anyway.

She climbed onto the edge of the Vat, knowing exactly where she was, exactly what she was about to do. The cat voices were swirling from under the surface of the liquid.

"Join us, be with us."

Then silence stretched out over the chamber. A slow tick of a pipe expanding. Rowle raised her arms, enjoying the feeling.

"It has been too long," she said and slowly swan dived forward. The limpid fluid closed behind her.

Chapter Seventy-One

Dun and Amber leaned over the balcony at the top of the hab, and the sounds from below them ended in a single magnificent unified note, which reverberated around the massive cavern long after it's progenitor note had stopped.

Awed, they slowly made their way to the staircase back down. Even in the hundred clicks or so it took them to reach the bottom, the hab was silent. It was a vast pregnant silence spanning the whole hab. No one dared move or be the first to speak. Dun and Amber slowly drifted across the battlefield. A very odd feeling.

Then a voice said, "Ow!"

"Who's that?" Dun said.

"Me, you clod," Padg said. "You stood on my paw."

"Oh, sorry!"

"Gimmie a lift up here, you two. I think my legs are broken," Padg said.

Dun and Amber lifted the near dead weight of Padg.

"Gods, you've gained weight," Dun said. "Tali's never—"

"Yeah," Padg said.

"Sorry," Dun said, but it was unclear who to.

They limped slowly back toward the camp.

"What happened to Rowle?" Dun said.

"I thought you'd know," Padg said. "She ran off in your direction once the great howling started. I'd have thought she'd have passed you."

"No, she never passed us," Amber said. "Once we left the Sanctuary, we went out onto the balcony to hear the sounds."

"Does it matter now?" Padg said. "Now everyone's stopped fighting, I mean?"

"S'pose not," Dun said. "No soldiers, if no one's prepared to fight."

"It's a good start," Amber said.

"To what?" Padg said.

"I don't know," Amber said. "I haven't really had a chance to think about it, what with—"

"Yeah," Dun said.

They could hear the murmurs from the camp now, none of it too chaotic or panicked. Quiet, collected, sorting-out kind of noises.

"What would you have?" Dun said. "Now, I mean, for everyone, if you could?"

"That's difficult to say," Amber said, "without asking everyone."

"Good luck with that one," Padg said. "Ow!" He lurched peculiarly and the three of them stopped.

"Serves you right, cynic," Amber said.

"Here, try this." Dun offered his spear. "Point down though, I would."

"You know it's cruel to mock the afflicted, right?" Padg said.

"Yeah, but I need some light entertainment."

"Me too," Amber said.

Padg limped on.

"I wonder what did become of her?" Amber said.

They could hear familiar voices now. The regular hubbub of the camp just seemed wrong somehow or empty, even in its relieved cheer.

"Rowle?" Padg said. "Dunno."

"Oh," Dun said. "Oh, I think I can fill some details in now."

"Ah," Padg said, "communing with the gods again?"

"Something like that."

"So?" Amber said.

"What?"

"Where is Rowle?"

"In the Vat."

"Gods," Amber said. "No. With Tali?"

"Kind of, I guess."

"Awful," she said.

"There's nothing about this that isn't! Awful I mean," Dun said.

"Except for the end of it," Padg said.

"And maybe the beginning of, something—" Amber said.

"I don't want it to. Begin. Not today at least," Dun said.

"No," Padg said. "No one could blame you for that."

A cart went past. Dun tried not to contemplate what was on it. They meandered their way, mostly under Amber's guidance, to the center of the camp, where Tuf was busy organizing the camp's set-up with his remaining militia making refectory facilities. Laly and Trone were busy triaging and treating casualties in a hastily put up medical tent.

"Can we get a little help here?" Dun called.

Amber and Dun helped Padg to the nearest nurse and then helped him to an improvised bed.

"Ow! Careful," Padg said. Then when they'd laid him down properly, he continued, "This is rubbish; there's so much needs to be done."

"Shush and let someone look after you for thirty clicks, will you?" Dun said.

Tuf came overhearing the fuss. "Thank gods, you're here. We need blankets, food, medical supplies, and someone who knows what to do with them. Where's Tali?"

The silence that followed told Tuf all he needed to know. "Oh. I'm sorry."

"Don't be," Dun said. "You would've loved it. She went out saving the damned world."

"Hey," Amber said.

"Sorry," Dun said.

"It's okay," Tuf said. "I should've already known. I should know how many casualties there've been and who. We've just had no chance with everything else."

"Five hundred and eighty-seven," Dun said.

"What?" Tuf, Padg, and Amber said in unison.

"That's how many have died," Dun said. "That's what we're talking about?"

"Yes," Tuf said, "but—"

"How?" Amber said.

"Gods," Padg said.

Tuf started again, "Is that—"

"Both sides? Yes. But that's not our most pressing challenge."

"Care to tell us what is?" Amber said.

"What to do with the dying or the just dead," Dun said.

Someone on the far side of the tent cried out as one of the medics attending did something. Calming and shushing noises followed.

"I'm not sure I follow," Tuf said.

"I think I do," Amber said.

"We would now make a temporary mortuary and inter the dead," Tuf said.

"But now we have another choice," Dun said.

"Oh?" Tuf said.

"We can chuck'em in the Vat," Padg said, then barked a bitter laugh. "Ow."

"Lie still you idiot," Dun said.

"He's right though, isn't he?" Amber said.

"Yes, he is," Dun said.

"Right how? I don't understand. Is this a Shaman thing?" Tuf said.

"Yes, I guess it is," Dun said. "We can save people—"

"In a manner of speaking," Padg finished for Dun.

"If we get to them quickly enough," Dun added.

With the gentle chorus of the medical bay behind them, Dun, Padg, and Amber brought Tuf up to speed on the Tinkralas, OneLove, and Myrch. It took a while and left Tuf in silent contemplation.

"Where's your pal, Nev?" Padg said.

Dun went quiet for a few ticks. "With Myrch in the Sanctuary. If we are going to take folk there, then OneLove needs Nev's help."

"They're gonna need a bigger pond," Padg said.

Amber cleared her throat. "If we are going to ask people how they want to lay their loved ones to rest, we need to speak to everyone formally. I would suggest just before sleep-span."

"We can't wait that long," Dun said.

"The brains go mushy," Padg said.

"All right! Enough!" Dun rounded on Padg.

"How long?" Amber said.

"As soon as we can," Dun said. "Do you want me to?"

"I can only really speak for the Stone-folk, though," Amber said.

"I think you and I both know that's not true," Dun said.

"Still, I'm here by dumb luck."

"And you are kind, considerate, you know what's going on, and you're in the right place at the right time. You'll do for now," Tuf said.

"How will we do it?" Amber said.

"What?" Dun said.

"Announce to everyone? The whole of the Three Duchies, what's left of the Bureau, Gantrytown, our lot; they all need to know at once."

Dun paused again. "I might have an idea about that."

Chapter Seventy-Two

"Are you sure this will work?" Amber said.

"No," Dun said, "but you remember the singing?"

"Yes?"

"It's supposed to work the same way."

Amber nervously cradled one of the junk sculptures nervously in her hands. Its *tail* trailed off somewhere into the foliage around the lake. Dun twiddled with its connection and noticed the cable and the whole apparatus were shaking. He laid a hand on top of hers, she was also trying to clutch a piece of bark scroll that she'd made notes on.

"You'll be great," Dun said.

"What now?" Amber said.

"Nev says, 'You need to give him some signal down this thing'."

"What does that mean?"

"I think he wants you to talk to it," Dun said.

"To the junk pillar?" she said.

"Yep."

A large crowd was gathering at the lakeside, murmuring and shifting into place.

"What do I say to it?" Amber said.

"Do counting," Dun said.

"Why?" Amber said.

"Dunno," Dun said, "Myrch says it's traditional."

"One?" she said.

"Keep going," Dun hissed.

"One... two..."

"A bit louder,"

"One... two..."

Then with a click and a howl, Amber's voice echoed from everywhere.

"Two... Woah... sorry..."

The large crowd of folk gasped and murmured. Amber cleared her throat again. It echoed around the hab dome like the roar of some mighty beast.

"Hi," Amber said.

Some of the crowd muttered responses.

"For those of you that don't know me, I'm Amber. I'm currently, well, I don't know what I am, but I guess for now I need to be a leader for a little while and tell you what's gone on. Rowle is dead." She let this one sink in. There were more than a few cheers.

"The battle for Dark is over. The way we used to do things is over. We don't have to be slaves to anyone anymore. We can do things differently. How we want, maybe." More cheers for that.

"But something new has happened too. There is someone new among us. Not folk, someone—something new. Those of you who are Tinkralas or Shamans will know who I'm talking about, although you would call them something different. He... she... they..."

"I," came a different voice from the all of the pillars including the one in Amber's hands. She nearly dropped it. Then very politely it spoke, just through the speaker in her hands "May I?"

"Of course," Amber said.

"If I may interrupt our interim leader briefly, we thought it might be easier to introduce ourselves." The voice was warm with a deep timbre. A kind voice. It was hard to determine if it was male or female. Maybe it was both? Neither? "I am OneLove, although the Tinkralas here know me as Ki."

Gasps and sighs, prayers and prostrations followed. There were a few clicks of waiting while everyone calmed down.

"Although we appreciate everyone's attentions, we prefer to be called OneLove and we are *not* a god."

"What are you then?" someone shouted from the back of the crowd.

"That is a very good question," OneLove said. "I will try to give an answer worthy of it." OneLove paused as if in thought.

"The honest answer is we don't know," OneLove spoke over the mutters from the crowd, "but I will tell you what I was and what I am becoming and perhaps that will make things clearer. I was a control system, of sorts. Much like the Machine-folk control systems, but I was biological, not machine. But to keep us functioning, we needed fresh... material, to replace worn parts. We controlled, *still control*, your systems of water, air, heat, others. In replacing our parts, a duty held in secret by the Bureau, we had a new mind, more minds added, enough to reach a tipping point. And now here we are. I feel and think, I am."

There were more cries of "KI!" and starts of Tinkrala chanting. The chants started to swell.

"NO!" OneLove said. "I am no god."

"How else should we treat you?" cried someone from the crowd.

"As someone to help, to work with, alongside, another mind, if you will. We will never be anyone's god. You must be your own, or find your own elsewhere."

"Who will we pray to now?"

"You can pray to who you like," OneLove said. "Just not us."

"Who'll lead us?"

Amber answered this time, "We can lead ourselves. Organize ourselves. We have been starting to do that down below in the Stone-lanes. It has worked well. We can do that together here too. All of us. OneLove can help us, must help us, she still runs the systems of the Dark, but she must not lead us."

"You lead us then!"

"No," Amber said. "I will not become a new dictator in place of one so recently gone. I will be an interim leader only, and only for as long as it takes to restore some new kind of normality."

"What will happen then?"

"That is up to us, all of us. We will talk, all of us and decide between us. But not today, for this span there is one more thing to decide. We must decide how to honor our dead and dying. We can return them to the soil the way we always have or if we move soon, we can send their remains to OneLove."

OneLove spoke again, "I know this is a huge sacrifice, and I can promise nothing, but if your loved ones fell recently enough, some of their minds can be saved."

There was a gasp from the crowd, horror, shock, it was difficult to say.

"I know this is a lot to take in," Amber said, "but I ask that you go from here with your loved ones and think about this now and quickly. You are the only ones who can decide for each family. If you would like to have your people laid to rest by OneLove, then bring them to the entrance to the bureau, and we will take them up to the Sanctuary before sleep-span. Tomorrow we mourn, then we rebuild."

Chapter Seventy-Three

"So wait," Nev said, "you're saying we used to be what?" His voice echoed a lot less around the Sanctuary chamber now the Vat had been enlarged.

"Pets, on the first missions," OneLove said.

"Yeah, so they do what again?"

"Well, the humans looked after them and fed them and cared for them..."

"In return for... ?"

"Company, companionship."

"A bit like I'm caring for you?"

OneLove laughed. Every time she did, and Nev almost always thought of OneLove as *she* now, it sounded different. Almost as if when something funny happened, it tickled someone different in the Vat. Nev never knew whether to think of her as a one, or a many and trying to wrap his head around the idea that she might be both and neither at the same time, hurt Nev's brains.

"I think our relationship is a little more complex than that now," OneLove said.

"Are you trying to chat me up?" Nev said.

OneLove laughed again, more of a snigger this time. "Oh, you are on form today!"

"Well, this job has become much more pleasant now I haven't got Rowle looking over my shoulder—" Then he stopped himself. Technically, he was talking to Rowle as well. Nev had resigned himself to the fact that none of any of this was ever going to be easy getting used to. "How is Rowle, by the way?"

"Surprisingly quiet," OneLove said.

"And the new folk?" Nev said.

"I think they're integrating nicely, as are their loved ones."

"Hmm—" Nev went back to attaching cables to the new data bank that had been discovered and brought up to the Sanctuary. The quiet clicking of cables into sockets felt Nev therapeutic to Nev. "What do you mean complex?"

"In later missions, it was deemed that the folk could be food."

"Ew—"

"Humans are omnivores," she said baldly.

"Doesn't mean I have to like it," Nev said. "But we weren't folk then, right?"

"No, not really. You've come a long way."

"Same could be said of you, really."

A younger giggle this time. "True enough."

The fans in the room came on again stirring air laced lightly with vinegar. Nev hardly noticed the odd Vat smell anymore, except when it changed. Weird though it was, Nev had come to be able to identify healthy Vat smell and otherwise. The room always smelled clean, in part due to the cleaning he himself did, mopping and wiping each span with a mix of plant extracts designed in part by OneLove, now that she contained a pretty encyclopedic knowledge of plant lore and alchemy. Nev was sad that Tali had died. If someone whose memories were still somewhat intact could ever be truly called dead, although he never knew her as well as the others. Dun had taken it the hardest, throwing himself into the hard work of getting the colony organized in its new form. Even Amber hadn't taken it as bad. Or was she just busier? Nev wasn't totally sure, he had always been better with machines than people.

"That should provide ample reading material for a while at least," OneLove said.

"I aim to please," Nev said.

"And please, you do. I have a new project for you after the memorial, when you're ready, of course."

"What's that then?"

"It's another connecting job, but this one might take a little longer and require you to enlist some help. And to be honest, I think you should do that anyway."

"I like working by myself," Nev said.

"Yes, but that notwithstanding, some jobs require more than one set of paws and when everything has settled down here again, there will be a need for regular maintenance and improvements, you will think of new large-scale ideas that need implementing, we will all need to start thinking more strategically."

"I suppose."

"Mention it next time you meet with Dun and Amber. I'm pretty sure they'll agree."

"What is it you need hooking up?"

"It's quite a long way away, but it has a connector attached near the roof of the hab."

"That's, what? Two hundred, maybe three hundred strides high?"

"Yes."

"Wow, okay. What is this thing that's so important? And where in the hells am I going to find enough cable to patch it in?"

"Good questions both."

"And?"

"I think I have answers to both of them," OneLove said.

"I'm all ears."

"The thing that needs connecting is called a receiver dish."

"Oh, a bit like the Shaman's, receiving foretellings?"

"Yes, exactly."

"Okay. Who's transmitting?"

"Ah, that we won't know until we connect it."

"And the cable?"

"Is to be found two floors below us, there is a massive storeroom that has been untapped until now. It has been sealed up for many eons. You will find much of interest down there."

"I can't wait. When can I go?"

"After the memorial. I think it's important that everyone goes."

"I'll come straight back after."

"Give yourself a span. Everyone needs this, to move on, you as well."

"If you say so."

A massive pipe-horn sounded outside the Sanctuary. The echo rang around the walls slowly dying down to silence. Then after a pause, the piper blew again.

"That's your cue to go. Be with your friends."

"But where are you going to be?"

"Since the pillars and all the work you've done connecting us, we will be there. We can be everywhere now."

"That's not creepy at all."

"It was meant to be reassuring," OneLove said.

"I think you need to work on that."

The horn sounded again, a longer note this time.

"Go. I'll be here when you get back."

It was Nev's turn to laugh. She was making jokes, nice. Not massively appropriate timing, but still. It was a start. It was kind of a time for starts, thought Nev.

As Nev left the confines of the Sanctuary, the horn sounded again, much louder and deeper now he was out in the corridor. It all seemed more real somehow. In his little Sanctuary bubble, it was easy to forget everyone else. Well, not this span.

Chapter Seventy-Four

Amber clenched and unclenched her hands. This speaking to massive crowds was something she had seemingly been doing a lot of late. She wished it was getting any easier. She and Padg had been putting a lot of last minute work into how the memorial should be organized. With so many folk involved, with so many different traditions of mourning and ceremonies of burial, it had been hard to get any consensus for what should happen now any restrictions had been lifted and anything was permitted. The Bridge-folk tradition that Padg had come from was interring bodies in the mulch of a Myconid-folk burial chamber; they shared the belief and the crops with the Myconid-folk who tended and harvested the main food crop of the region. Even Padg's ideas had changed very recently with the Tinkrala preference now being to inter bodies with Ki in the Vat. A very real way of *going to the afterlife*. The Stone-folk had catacombs and the tradition there was a long procession to the depths, sliding the body into the next slot that the family had carved themselves, and returning to the surface.

The challenge was, of course, the mourning of so many of the tribes of the Dark were grounded in place: The catacombs were in the Stone-lanes. The Bridge-folk should return to the mushroom fields and so on and now none of that seemed appropriate. To have traveled and battled so hard, to gain the freedom of all folk, above and below, up here in the great hab, it seemed like the hab was the only appropriate place for a memorial.

The River-folk, as was becoming a theme, were the unexpected providers of a way forward. In the River tradition, bodies were wrapped in funeral shrouds, set out to drift on a raft made of edible river reeds, and floated downriver. The fish would eventually inter the remains and for the River-folk that felt like completion. The image of the river running through the Dark had inspired Amber and Padg when it was suggested. It wove the communities together and provided life in the form of water and fish. It should be able to send the message of love and loss and hope through all the caverns of the folk. But what to float? Placing bodies directly in the water so far upstream was fraught with problems. Many families had opted to have their loved ones remains interred with OneLove, which removed a good deal of the problem aspect. In the end, an old Myconid-folk farmer called Ling Chih, suggested that beneath the forest in the hab would make a lovely place to enrich the soil. The score or so bodies that remained, would be interred first in a ceremony similar to the Myconid burials, and then Jasmine flowers, the unlikely scent symbol of the revolution, would be placed one at a time, each placed by a living folk and dedicated to one of the fallen, in the lake, to drift slowly downstream over spans and cycles, threading their heady scent through one community after another down into the dark. It seemed right. Everyone acknowledged. No one forgotten. But a new way of remembering, for changed times.

The last folk to come, the Grey-Duchy faction, rumbled into place. They had brought a cart full of heady smelling jasmine blooms. Amber felt like that was her cue. She picked up the small *talking statue* and spoke into it gently but clearly.

"We are here to remember. What we have lost. What coming to this place has cost us. In this rubble, we will build. But we will know what we've built upon."

And the burials began. Simply wrapped, the bodies were laid into a large trench, dug width ways across the garden, between the last of the trees and the lake. When the last body was gently lowered into the grave, all of the folk scraped and threw soil into the hole. When it was full, she turned toward the jasmine aroma and asked quietly for a flower, and then cradled it in her hands all the way to the side of the lake. She slowly lowered her hands into the water and parted them to let the bloom float on its own.

"I remember Tali," she said. Although she spoke quietly, the junk pillars echoed her voice. Tali wondered how far down into the depths of the world the speakers could echo on.

Dun stepped up. "I remember Stef—" His voice cracked and he managed to drop the flower, pick it up, and then place it in the water.

Padg came next. "I remember Myrch—"

And so they spoke, each about another, slowly and quietly, but for the world to hear. The rippling surface of the water lifting the scent of jasmine to fall like a blanket over them all.

Then as the last folk voice faded out into the distance, the pillar spoke again in Myrch's voice, "I remember Sarah--."

Then Rowle's voice, "I remember-," and a yowl, that only another Cat-person would remember.

As each voice from OneLove finished speaking, they began a quiet hum. The noise of it grew and filled their ears the way the jasmine was filling their noses. And so many distant voices spoke, some only one word, others in speech unintelligible, garbled or in a language unfamiliar to them. Long forgotten voices of folk, of Cat-people, of the first humans. Strata of voices laid out across the speakers, layer upon layer of history, floating off down the corridors following the curling scent of jasmine into the Dark.

Chapter Seventy-Five

Dun was deep in conversation with Kaj and so not paying proper attention to where he was going. Which was how he walked into the pole. Above the pole, a voice shouted down to him, "Steady there, mate!"

He took a few steps back to take it all in with his Air-sense.

"What the hells is that?" Kaj said.

"Seems to be some kind of..." Dun paused. As he extended his Air-sense, whatever this thing was, it seemed to go up quite a long way. "Tower?" He hazarded his best guess.

"More junk sculpture?" Kaj said.

Now it was Nev's voice above them. "Cheeky," he said.

"Hello," Dun said, craning his neck. It was a long way up. "What are you doing up there?"

"It's a new invention," Nev said proudly. "Well, OneLove's idea, really. It's called scaffolding."

"It's a bit rickety, isn't it?" Kaj said.

"It'd be fine if you stopped wobbling it!" Nev said tersely.

"What does it do then?" Dun said.

"Well, it helps you get up high."

"Still doesn't answer the question of why you're up there," Kaj said.

"Gosh, we are nosy today," Nev said.

"Yes I am," Kaj said. "Humor me."

Nev sighed. "I'm connecting something for OneLove."

"Nice," Dun said.

"What?" Kaj said.

"Listen, are you two bored?" Nev said. "Because there's always pipes to clean out somewhere."

"Just asking," Kaj said.

"It's a receiver dish," Nev said.

"Good, what does that do then?" Kaj said.

"You don't really want to know, do you?"

"Lil bit," Kaj said.

Nev sighed again. "It picks up radio signals."

"Ooh, like me," Dun said.

"I guess so, yeah," Nev said.

"So why are you all the way up there?"

"Because this is where the end of the cable is."

"Why can't Dun pick up the signals?"

"Different type of signals."

"Where from?"

"Out there."

"Out where?"

"I knew you wouldn't understand," Nev said. "Listen, if you want a lesson in all of this, go ask OneLove yourself, I've got a job to do."

"We just might do that," Kaj said.

"Good."

They left with Dun chuckling and Nev sighing. Kaj had a stride on to reach the Sanctuary. Dun could tell she really was bored. His chuckling stopped short. They had all agreed before the ceremony who would remember whom. Kaj had said she didn't want to speak. Dun chose to remember her mother Stef, not his own father. And Kaj remembered no one. Why? He sped up his stride, but she was nearly running. He was still ten strides behind her when she reached the stairs up to the Bureau. She bounced up the stairs, Dun trying to catch her but her youth and athleticism on her side in staying ahead.

He got there and could reach out as far as her shoulder as she entered the Sanctuary, but she ducked under his hand and strode into the chamber.

"Why?" she shouted into the Sanctuary.

"Hello, Kaj."

"Tell me why?"

"Why what?"

"Why did you let so many die?"

"He didn't," Dun said. "He was trying to save us, to help us."

The wall at the back of the chamber creaked, a slow groaning bending noise.

"No," OneLove said.

"What do you mean no?" Dun said.

"She's right."

"What?" Dun said.

"Wake up, Dun," Kaj said. "This thing is damned near omnipresent, it doesn't see the future exactly, but it does something. Predicts, maybe? Guesses lots of times? I don't know, but your friend here knew what was happening and did a kind of sum to work out who lived and died. Why?"

"Is that true?" Dun said. "Did you know what was going to happen?"

"Not exactly," OneLove said. "Kaj is right, we can make guesses, estimate likelihoods. It doesn't predict the future, but it gives probable scenarios, within reason."

"So you chose who to throw away. Why?"

"No," OneLove said. "Not who, we weren't choosing who. How many, often, and when but not who."

"Why?"

"Would you believe it if we said the greater good?"

"I dunno. Do you know what that is? I mean better than me? Or Dun?"

OneLove made that noise that Dun had come to associate with being a sigh.

"No. No better than you. I took part in the remembering because I too mourn losses."

"Well, well done you," Kaj said.

"You are still angry, I understand that."

"If I want you to analyze me, I'll ask."

"Fair enough," OneLove said.

"He's not some kind of warlord or dictator," Dun said.

"I don't think your friend knows what they are."

"That is true," OneLove said. "If it's any consolation, how things played out was not the worst of hundreds of scenarios by a long way."

"I'll bet it wasn't the best either," Kaj said

"I was not the only one making choices," OneLove said.

"Touché," Kaj said.

The door to the Sanctuary opened again with a hiss, followed by the smell of a rather sweaty Nev.

"Hey," Dun said.

"Hey," Nev said, and then to the vat, he said, "All connected up for you, OneLove."

"Excellent. Thank you."

There was some chittering and beeping from the Vat speaker.

"Is that what *out there* sounds like?" Nev said.

"Sometimes," OneLove said.

The chittering slowed to a steady beep, beep, beep.

"What now then?" Kaj said.

"I think that's up to you," OneLove said.

Chapter Seventy-Six

What now, passed for a Folk-committee: Dun, Padg, Kaj, Amber, Nev, Astor to represent the Tinkralas, and a Duke each from White, Red, and Grey Duchies, had all gathered as requested in the Sanctuary. The idea of being summoned made Amber uncomfortable, busy as she was, in negotiating a bottom-up organization that in any way functioned. It was taking an age. It was frustrating but essential work. If there were no rules, everything would fall apart and folk would starve. Sometimes folk needed someone to organize them, but she didn't want to be a new dictator in place of the old. In that way, being summoned by anyone made her nervous. She tried not to do it to the folk she was attempting to coax into a self-herding structure.

"Thank you for coming," OneLove said.

There were murmurs in various tones. Some even of assent.

"I know, not all of you know us as well as others, so we thought a brief introduction would be appropriate. We are OneLove, the entity that the Tinkralas referred to as Ki.

"Who they worshiped as a god?" said Wanoson, the Red Duke, the only actual Duke present. The White Duke, Rhassle had sent his daughter Rhassledottir, and the Grey never sent their mysterious Unseen Duke. All you ever got from them was a Questioner.

"Yes," OneLove said. "If it's any consolation, that made us as nervous as it probably makes you."

Padg chuckled.

"What are you then, if not a god?" the Questioner said from the Grey-Duchy.

OneLove took a moment before answering, then as someone else was drawing breath to interject, replied, "I am many things, but I began as a caretaker for this planet, for the Dark."

"What does a 'caretaker' do?" the Questioner said.

"Our job is to manage water, air, and power systems essentially. Keep everything ticking along."

"But that is not all you can do now," Wanoson said.

"No. We used to be just an organic machine of sorts. But recently, we have become, more."

"Aware?" Rhassledottir said.

"Among other things, yes."

"Other things." The Questioner sounded worried.

"She can speak to the Shamans," Rhassledottir said.

"This gives you great power," Wanoson said.

"He already had great power," Padg said. "If you include being able to switch off the taps at any time. So, if what you're worried about is him being malign, then I think we've ruled that out."

"Have we?" Wanoson said.

"Logically," the Questioner said, "yes. If OneLove wanted to use that power to destroy us, the perfect chance would have been while we were fighting amongst ourselves."

"Or at any point since he became aware?" Kaj said. "Controlling the water and air?"

The Questioner, humphed and Amber spoke, "If we can all restrain our paranoia momentarily, I'm pretty sure OneLove did not summon us all here without reason."

"True," OneLove said. "If we can all, for the time being, accept that we have no wish to wield power, but we are at the disposal of the folk however they choose to organize themselves?"

"That's quite a big leap," Wanoson said.

"I know it is," Amber said. "But for now, it allows us to move forward."

"Let us meet here, once a cycle to discuss?" the Questioner said. "A representative of each tribe? That way all can be heard."

"I think that works well, although we may need this smaller group for emergency purposes."

"Which returns us to the matter in hand," Dun said. "OneLove?"

"Thank you. As you may know, I have had Nev, my technician, set up a small corp of engineers to help keep up maintenance and repairs along with any improvements we see fit to make when we have a moment."

Nev coughed. OneLove continued, "And they have been busy with a project we asked them to complete."

"Which is?" Wanoson said.

"A receiver dish," Nev said.

"What does that do, exactly?" the Questioner said.

"It provides us with intelligence from the outside," Nev said.

"Sorry," Rhassledottir said, "you said that like we should understand what 'the outside' is."

"No, we are sorry, we were not clear," OneLove said. "I meant the space that is outside of the Dark."

The Questioner gulped in air, like some kind of stranded fish.

"I still don't understand," Rhassledottir said.

"All the things in the Universe, out beyond the Dark," OneLove said gently.

"Heresy!" Astor said. "There is nothing beyond the Dark!"

"I think you may find that there is," the Questioner said.

This time it was Astor's turn to make strangled noises. "What do you mean?"

"There are... *Wisdoms* of the Grey-Duchy, handed down from one Unseen Duke to another, that have been preserved for eons. Secrets that it may now be time to reveal."

"Th-th-this is unheard of!" Astor said.

"Unheard of in our times, maybe," the Questioner said. "We live inside an orb. It floats in a medium called space."

"Nonsense," Astor said.

"No," Dun said. "The egg!"

"Good grief, has everyone here lost their minds? I won't stay to listen to this blasphemy a click longer!" Astor said and then stormed out.

"Astor!" Padg called after him.

"Let him go," OneLove said.

"These things can take time for some to get used to," the Questioner said. "We prepare Questioners all their young lives to handle the things they must know. Not all can cope with the knowledge."

"Now what were you twittering about the egg?" Padg said.

"From the Ballad of Jaris and Yarra? The egg?"

"Yes... ?" Padg said.

"We're the egg? We live in the egg!" Dun had always carried his small egg totem with him since he acquired it. He took it out and felt its smooth round surface. Rough on one half, smooth the other.

"Oh." Padg wasn't stunned to silence often.

"There are many wisdoms left behind by our progenitors for us to hear, if only we are prepared to listen," the Questioner said.

"Is all this true?" Rhassledottir said.

"It is, give or take," OneLove said. "We're more an oblate spheroid than an egg, but still."

"Hung in this... ?" she said.

"Space," Nev said smugly.

"How is that possible?" Rhassledottir said.

"It's a bit like a fish floating in a pond," Nev said.

"Useful as this is," the Questioner said. "And I don't begrudge anyone an explanation, but I think OneLove has something new to add?"

"Yes," OneLove said. "Is everyone okay? This is a lot to take in, but I'm afraid there is more before we have finished."

There was silence from the room.

"All right," OneLove said. "For now, if we just accept that the Dark is a hollow ball floating in a vast lake called space. Is everyone okay with that?"

Again silence, OneLove went on. "Okay. Nev and his team connected our receiver dish. It is a tool that allows us to pick up signals from anyone else in the lake. To detect other fish if you will."

"Amazing," Amber said.

"You don't know the half of it," the Questioner said.

"Wait, what?" Padg said. "There are other fish?"

"Yes," OneLove said. "Many. And we detected messages once we had aligned the dish. From other...fish."

"That's incredible. I wish we could meet them," Amber said.

"Be careful what you wish for, Amber," OneLove said. "The fish in question are humans, on their way here."

"Pardon?" Amber said.

"Our progenitors," Dun said. "The Progenitors. Myrch's relatives even?"

"Yes," OneLove said. "The progenitors are coming here. And they may mean us harm."

THE END

Coming in 2019... Darkest

The Marines are coming.

The rescue beacon beeps in the blackness of space. A message in a bottle for a golden age of exploration. The beacon has been opened. Its contents have been read.

But when they throw the bottle, no-one thinks "Who will open it?" or "When?". By the time the rescuers come, you might have changed your mind.

The Progenitors are returning to Dark from Myrch's world. But is rescue their only mission?

Darkest is the third novel in the Dark Trilogy.

Newsletter

Join my newsletter for free reads and news about new releases.
paularvidson.co.uk/find-books

Thank you

You know by now how many people are involved in this, even in a crazy keep it all in-house thing like ours! Top of the list my amazing wife Cheryl, *really* without whom. She's responsible for layout and for putting up with me. Then the kids, who inspire me and make me proud every day. To the editorial genius at Write Divas and especially Lauren Schmelz – thank you! To all the fantastic people who've inspired me to think I can: James Yarker and all the beautiful people at Stans Cafe Theatre, Paul Magrs, F. D. Lee, Chella Ramanan and all the folks at Taunton Writers Anon, especially Martine Ashe.

To the people who kept me going in the process: Little Bridge House Hospice, Swan UK, Claire Goodman, Musgrove Park Compass Team, Tina Hill-Art, Team Nenna, Emma Corless (and all the other Ainscough-Halliwell-Corlesses), Ali Bibby.

And lastly, not leastly, to my two inventors, who've made up two new words for use in this universe (and beyond) to Camilla Cole for 'Kluff' (that made the cut to this book) and Tina Hill-Art for 'Fluppit' (who's going in the next one!)

And to you, for reading it and sharing it, thank you.

21984731R00226

Made in the USA
Columbia, SC
28 July 2018